'[A] hypnotic and lyrical debut . . . Cheng's characters are finely spun, soulful creatures, and his writing is muscular, evocative and haunting . . . Cheng's talent astonishes, and the blues music that so clearly inspired him echoes through the prose.'

New York Times Book Review

'Iris Murdoch once wrote that you know almost immediately when you pick up a wonderful book. There's an ineffable magic that swims through the first dozen or so pages . . . Bill Cheng set out to write a great book, an important book. He conjures up the American South with a deliberate homage to William Faulkner's *The Sound and the Fury* . . . life for the blacks is like life for the whites, only a hundred times worse . . . It's a warning that Bill Cheng articulates all too well in his powerful debut: The best you can hope for in this encounter with life is a draw.' *Washington Post*

'Original and authentic. His sentences are memorable and often poetic . . . Nearly every individual description is truly a pleasure to read.' *Boston Globe*

'A wildly ambitious debut novel – vividly imagined, frequently poetic . . . a compelling achievement.' *Kirkus* starred review

'Bill Cheng has conjured up a rhapsodic ode to the blues and the bluesmen that move him . . . Cheng's writing is vivid and gorgeous, particularly in his descriptions of the flood . . . [*Southern Cross the Dog*] is a courageous act of literary ventriloquism.'

San Francisco Chronicle

'The rhapsodic language is so imaginative and highly charged that each word seems newly forged.' *Booklist*

'*Southern Cross the Dog* proves Cheng to be a serious talent. He confidently immerses the reader in Southern history and folklore, summoning up landscapes as powerful as those of Cormac McCarthy or Annie Proulx.' *Time Out* New York

'A vibrant world grows from the pages of *Southern Cross the Dog* and its dynamic mix of language and place. Bill Cheng conjures history with precision and style in his exceptional debut.'
Ravi Howard, author of *Like Trees Walking*

'With its evocative settings and rich McCarthyesque language, this Southern gothic packs a punch.' *Publishers Weekly* starred review

'An authentic, riveting portrait of the Mississippi Delta and its complex worlds . . . Bill Cheng embraces the region's 1927 flood, voodoo, blues, and race with breathtakingly beautiful prose.'
Bill Ferris, author of *Give My Poor Heart Ease: Voices of the Mississippi Blues*

'Think Cormac McCarthy or a 21st-century Faulkner . . . This book is a winner.' *Library Journal* starred review

SOUTHERN CROSS THE DOG

BILL CHENG

PICADOR

First published 2013 by Amistad, an imprint of HarperCollins Publishers, New York

First published in Great Britain in paperback 2013 by Picador

This edition first published 2013 by Picador
an imprint of Pan Macmillan, a division of Macmillan Publishers Limited
Pan Macmillan, 20 New Wharf Road, London N1 9RR
Basingstoke and Oxford
Associated companies throughout the world
www.panmacmillan.com

ISBN 978-1-4472-2489-1

1 3 5 7 9 8 6 4 2

A CIP catalogue record for this book is available from the British Library.

Printed and bound by CPI Group (UK) Ltd, Croydon, CR0 4YY

For Olga

SOUTHERN CROSS THE DOG

PROLOGUE

When I was a baby child, they put the jinx on me.

It was in my drink and food and milk. And when I ran, it heavied in my bones and when I sang, it stopped up my throat and when I loved, it let from me, hot and poisonous.

I saw it in my daddy, the hard lines of his face, that uneasy lope— how in his years he didn't lift his feet, but slid them, soles across this gritted earth. It settled in my mama, trembled her voice and blanked her eyes. My brother, Billy, locked it inside him and it carried him low into that deep earth, silting then into the river and dew and air, in the moths and bee catchers, borne skyward and, as will be, lowed again, into earth again again.

It's dusking.

There goes the sun.

There goes sky and cloud and light, taken into that black horizon. And I know I am bad crossed. I see its line. It reaches up, arcs. It cuts through me. It draws me on and dogs me down to that place where I am bound.

And when it is I borne down, my eyes and mouth stitched with gut, when they take my balls and brain and heart, and that deeper black claims me wholly, then let me meet that sumbitch at his eye, for I know my name's been writ—Robert Lee Chatham—in his Book.

PART ONE

THE FLOOD

(1927)

The rain kept on like a dust and it was the oldest boy G.D. who said it wasn't nothing, crossing through the woods behind Old Man Crookhand's. The wind swooped through, chattering the branches, and blew the grit against their faces. They put up their hands and trudged on, G.D. ahead of the others, cutting his switch into the bushes. *Whack, whack.* Come on, you babies, he said, and he whipped again, the vines and leaves opening around his blows.

They followed close, the boys wolfing on, whispering their jokes, trying to make the girls laugh and shiver. One at a time, they crushed across the underbrush, skimming spider vines and breaking off bits of sweetbark from the trunks to chew and spit.

The trail began to climb and G.D. bounded up the hill in wide strides. At the top, he stopped and waited for the others. He could see Crookhand Grove, a cleft of cleared land that dipped below the path. At the center was the Bone Tree. It had been dead for years, its leaves rotting in a carpet around the trunk.

One by one, the others crowded around him. They gazed out into the grove and fell quiet. There'd been stories about dead Injuns and their ghosts living inside the hollows. The wind came through and the naked branches clattered. The gang looked at one another, then up at G.D.

He spit a wad down into the grove.

Keep moving, he said.

The mule path broke out into a clearing where the lumbermen had already come through. G.D. chose the tallest tree stump and mounted it. He splayed out his arms, waving the switch like a sword before touching the edge against his cheek—a nub of twig snagging on his tooth. It was time. His eyes drooped into lazy buttonholes, looking the others over. They fidgeted under his gaze, shifting from side to side, holding up their hands, rubbing rain into their fingers.

G.D. sized them up. Their ragged clothes, the yellow mud caked to their shins. A girl unbraided a slip of hair. Her small fingers eased through the knots. A boy dug his toes into the soil, trying not to meet G.D.'s eye. Another stood with his arms folded across his chest, shifting his weight from knee to knee. He spotted her. She was tall and willowy compared to the other girls. Her hair was brushed back and she sloped her shoulders as she tried to hide her size.

G.D. pointed with the switch.

Dora, he said.

The girl furrowed her brow.

Not me!

He moved the switch to the sharp of his smile.

Yes.

That's not fair! I done it last time, G.D.!

You, Dora. Again.

It's gonna rain, she said. I don't want to get soaked.

G.D. shrugged and grinned at the others.

Best get started then.

G.D. brought the switch down against his leg. *Thwack*. They made a circle around her. He beat down again. *Thwack. Thwack*. The girl looked up but it was too late. Already the circle had tightened and they'd begun to sing.

Little Sally Water, settin' in a saucer.

Rise Sally rise, wipe your weepin' eyes.

The girl sighed, slumping. She hunched down on her knees and listened for the rhythm. Her backside bucked up, kicking out like a mule and swinging.

Shake it to the east, Sally.

Shake it to the west, Sally.

Shake it to the one you love the best, Sally.

Her frilled bloomers flashed out under her dress as she spun. The world swished inside her head. When the song ended, she righted herself and turned to see who she'd chosen. If it was a girl, they would have to start again, this time even faster as G.D. lashed out mercilessly with his switch.

Slowly the world glided back into place. She righted herself and saw him. He was big cheeked and wet eyed, and he was at least a good head shorter than her. The boy looked blankly at her through his long lashes. She'd seen him before. He was always so quiet, never laughed or cussed, floating behind the others like some tattered kite tail. He fidgeted now with his hands in his pockets, looking unsure of himself until G.D. nudged him forward.

Well, don't just stand there looking dumb.

G.D. led Dora and the boy out to Crookhand Grove where the earth was cracked and split along the roots of the Bone Tree. They were alone, the three of them, caught under the storm clouds. Thunder sounded out like split wood and they looked cautiously at the little bits of sky coming through the branches.

G.D. took both their hands and grinned.

My, my, Dora. I never knew you was such a tasteful lady.

Dora slapped his arm and his eyes sparked.

I'm gonna count to a hundred. Then you come on out.

We know how it works, G.D.

G.D. winked at the boy and headed back to the clearing, arms crossed over his head. She could hear him beginning to count.

Dora smoothed down the sides of her dress. The boy was looking at a spider threaded between two branches. It sat fat and blood-filled in its web, its legs spread like fingers.

Dora could hear the other children starting in on their singing again. They had begun another round.

Well, come on then, she said.

Come on what?

Ain't you played Sally Water before?

The boy plucked up the spider. He turned it over and watched its legs bicycle. He held it up to Dora and she made a face. Then he set it down on a trunk and watched it race up the bark.

You're Billy Chatham's brother, ain't you?

The boy shrugged.

My uncle told me your brother was wild. That he loved up a white girl and he—

Dora stopped herself. The boy sat down against the trunk and started scabbing at the bark, pulling it away in chips. He put them together in a pile, counting them out in his palm.

What's your name?, Dora asked.

Robert, he said. He seemed to think for a moment then he added, Robert Lee Chatham.

Dora looked back from where they came.

Well, let's not take too long then. Come here, she said. Stand up against the trunk there.

He dusted the bark off and pushed his sleeves up to his elbow. They drooped back down, past his knuckles. His shirt was too large. It hadn't been sized for him.

Now shut your eyes so you can't see nothing.

Everything was still for a moment. Just the slow breath of the magnolias and the sound of mosquitoes making the air goosebump and tremble. He thought he could hear the other children laughing in the distance—their small twinkling voices in the breeze. Then he felt the kiss—the damp spongy pressing against his mouth, something cold skimming the underside of his tongue, warm air brushing against the slope of his upper lip. Something small and hard pressed into his hand. When he opened his eyes, the sky had split open.

～

ROBERT RAN. THE GROUND SUCKED BACK ON HIS FEET AS HE SLID on the loose mud. The rain smashed down, ruffled the trees, and beat the trails. He could hear the children scatter—screaming, giggling. He ran faster, twigs and leaves lashing against him, the warm sting rising into his cheek. Along the farm, the pebbled road bit into his feet. He wiped the slick off his face and sped faster, kicking from his toes. The cornfield was alive with chatter, the water running down into a trough along the road, billbugs crunching under his soles.

Robert cut across the pasture. The clouds streaked white and thundered a line above the hills. He could see his house in the distance, the rain hammering the roof into a silver froth. On the porch, he caught his breath, pulling the air deep into his stinging lungs. The pour came down through the ceiling slats, and he rinsed the mud off his calves and ankles before going inside.

The air was thick and sweet with the smell of char. He hung his shirt up on a nail and warmed himself over the stove, bringing his hands over the flame and feeling the cold run out from his fingers.

His daddy came in from the other room.

Where you been, Robert?

He sat the boy down and toweled him off with the flap of his shirt.

You know your mama don't want you out in them woods.

Robert said nothing, just let his daddy's big hands comb roughly over his hair and neck and chest. His daddy sighed. He peeled off the wet clothing from Robert's body and sent him to the basket for a dry shirt. Robert checked it for beetles, snapping it over the fire before putting it on.

His daddy lifted the lid off the kettle; the steam rose up over his face. He peered in and dragged his fingers down the gray stipple of his beard.

Dinner'll be ready soon. Go on and get your mama.

ROBERT WATCHED HER FROM THE DOORWAY. SHE WAS IN HER CHAIR, her quilt drawn up over her shoulders, staring out into the rain. Outside, the mule was ducking under the shed, twitching its ears and blinking. Robert went in and touched her limp hand. She looked at him, her eyes traveling along the edge of his face—then his eyes, nose, mouth. Then she pulled Robert into her and started raking her hands across his hair, making sounds that were almost words. He could feel her strong fingers pressing into him, her body a volcano. She kissed the top of his head, his cheeks—her thumb rubbing at the ridges of his ears.

It's time to eat, Mama, he said.

He slipped his small hand inside of hers and, slowly, he helped her to her feet. He could hear the breath shift inside of her, her body clenching and then letting go.

This way, he said, walking her into the other room.

His daddy had already set out the bowls and was scooping up hominy mush with a flat stick. Robert sat his mother down and settled into the seat beside her. Then when his daddy started the grace, Robert bent his head into his hands and shut his eyes. The rain crashed above him, and he pictured a field of birds thumping their black wings. His daddy finished and Robert took a spoonful and worked the mush around in his mouth.

How is it, Robert?

It was bland and rubbery but he didn't complain.

I know it ain't nothing like your own cooking, Etta.

His mama stared into the steam. Her lips were drawn back on her round face, the edges of her eyes puckered.

His daddy shook his head and picked up his spoon.

Me and the boy, we do miss your cooking. Ain't that right, Robert?

Robert said nothing. He lifted his gaze up from his bowl, then let it drop back down.

I remember when you used to cook up those ribs. Could smell them coming a mile down the road. And Skinny, he'd be saying, Ellis, what you smiling at, and I wouldn't say nothing, just walk back here with that big grin on my face. Robert, you too small to remember but your mama used to cook them ribs so good, even that damn mule would try to get itself inside. You imagine? A mule eating ribs. If that ain't something else. He'd stay out there by the window, making a fuss like it was his day of judgment, you remember that, Etta?

His daddy reached across the table and touched her arm. She didn't move. He sighed and dug his spoon into the meal.

Ain't no mule at the window now is there?

⁓

THE FIRE HAD GONE DEAD IN THE NIGHT, BUT THE SMELL OF scorched wood stayed in the air. Robert opened his eyes. His mama was still asleep, her arms crossed over his small body. He listened to her breathing, low and ragged, as her breasts pushed into his back. Under the pillow he found the cold smooth stone Dora had put into his hand. He rolled it around in his fingers and conjured her up in the dark ceiling—her eyes, her lips, the weak taste of her mouth. There was something about her skin, damp and sticky—he could feel it spreading across his hands.

The urge to piss swelled inside him. He climbed out of bed. He could hear the rain dripping from the ceiling into the rain pots. He took his brother's coat from the wall, slung it around him. Out back, he unbuttoned his pajamas and pissed a hot stream into the darkness.

When he went back inside, the chair where his daddy slept was empty. A light crept up behind the front window and splashed out onto the floor. It burned in a circle through the fogged glass. He watched it, pulling the sag of the coat around him, thinking about his mama's ghost stories— the way the Devil can come in through a keyhole.

ELLIS STOOD ON HIS PORCH, LISTENING TO THE RAIN AGAINST THE overhang. It spilled through the slats, the floorboards, his feet. An uneasy feeling had rousted him out of his sleep and now he could see it on the road: a soft orb of lantern light coming toward him. He lifted up his rifle and trained it. Droplets splashed and beaded on the long barrel. He could hear the hollow of the chamber tinkling. The light paused at the gate, then slowly made its way up the path to the porch.

Ho there!, he called out. Come any closer and I'll pay you with lead. Easy!

Who's that?

Ellis leaned his cheek against the sight. The man slid the lantern hood and let a ray cast across his face. It was Ellis's partner, Skinny. The rain had matted his hair against his forehead. Ellis eased off his grip.

Damn it, Skinny. Haven't you any sense coming around this hour?

Give me harbor.

Ellis leaned his gun against the wall and took Skinny's hand as he came up on the porch. Skinny shivered in his oilskin coat. He hung his lantern by the window and looked at the leaks spilling through the roof.

I just come from Wilkin's farm, he said. Talking with Dave Eaton's boy. Said he saw dynamiters coming through Mayersville.

Dynamiters, Ellis said.

He scratched the rough hairs on his neck and tried take the measure of his friend.

They actually going to do it.

Skinny nodded.

Me and Eaton are going around, telling everyone what we know.

The two men stood and listened to the rain. It was filling up the countryside, and if there were dynamiters, it meant that the levee at Mayersville wouldn't hold much longer. They'd blast it to ease the pressure but the force would bust every tributary south-river of Mayersville. Issaquena County and every township along the lowlands would be buried under a swell of rain and angry river.

How long you reckon? Ellis asked.

Skinny took off his hat and squeezed the wet out. He shook his head.

Not long, I don't think. I'm off tonight. I ain't taking no chances. Going out to Winona—my boy's family is out there.

I ain't got nobody in no Winona.

Skinny sucked something out of his teeth. He fit his hat back on his head and took his lantern from its hook.

You can't stay here, Skinny said. He looked out back toward the night. I'm just telling you 'cause I known you a long ways back and I know your people's been through hard times.

Ellis looked back at the house.

Skinny, he said.

It's just a place, Ellis. Wood and nails. A house ain't like a person. You got to look after yours.

Ellis put his lips together into a knot and nodded slow.

IN THE RAIN THE MEN CROWDED THE RIVER EDGE. THEY'D WORKED through the night, sandbags at their shoulders, the numbness set heavy in their chests and arms. They sunk waist deep into the soft mud, hefting their bodies forward and up. When the lantern went, they stopped in their places and listened to each other breathe. Rain flickered white in the darkness. Somewhere beyond them was the river. It groaned and roiled, eating the banks, crisping against the rocks. After a moment, someone cut the wet from the wick and relit the lantern.

The men shifted under a cake of rain and mud and sweat. Come dawn a wound of light bellied through the clouds. In the light, they could see what they couldn't before. Piece by piece, the embankment was falling away into the current, their sandbags shooting up downriver.

There was a pop, and a jet of gray water gushed through the embankment. Shouts rose up and a wave of men raced toward the break. They shored it up with their bodies, crying more men, more men. The air cracked and the ground trembled. The water ripped through them like paper, sending them into the air, into the mud. The river burst forward and the levee crumbled under it, tearing through the camp, through forest, rising up in a great yellow wall, driving close, fast, screaming like a train, its roar sucking up the sky, a voice crowning open like the

Almighty, through Fitler and Cary and Nitta Yuma, acre by acre, through cornfields and cotton rows; through plantation houses and dog-trots, wood and brick and mortar, through the depots and churches and rail yards, through forest and valley, snapping boulders through the air. Houses rose up, bobbed, then smashed together like eggshells. Homes bled out their insides—bureaus, bathtubs, drawers, gramophones—before folding into themselves. The people scrambled up on their roofs, up trees, clinging to one another. The water blew them from their perches, swept them into the drift, smashed them against the debris. They bubbled up swollen and drowned, rag-dolling in the current, moving deeper and deeper inland, toward Issaquena.

WHEN THE FLOODWATERS CAME, ELLIS LAY SPRAWLED IN HIS CHAIR, smothered down in sleep. In his dream he could hear his boy call for him—Daddy, Daddy—up through the depths, his voice crashing, warm at first then a jolt of panic. Each call came brighter, sharper—Daddy, please Daddy—hoisting him up through miles of dreaming. His eyes opened into the bright noise of the world. The floorboards were dark and swollen at his feet. Water bubbled up through the planks. Daddy. Wake up, Daddy, he heard, and he saw Little Robert beside him tugging hard on his flannel shirt.

I'm awake, Ellis said, his voice hoarse. He rose unsteadily to his feet. They watched a rocking chair slide on its legs. The water was climbing. The boy threw himself around his father's waist and out of habit Ellis touched the back of the boy's neck.

Go get your mama, he said.

Ellis wrapped up what food he could in newspaper and crammed their clothes into carpetbags and satchels. Quick now, he called to his son. Robert was waiting with his mother, holding her hand. She was dressed in her powder-blue church dress with a straw sun hat fit over her head.

Ellis moved toward her.

Etta, he began, but then he heard the house crack under his feet. Come on, let's go.

He unlatched the front door and the water sluiced through, soaking his lower half. Ellis grunted, pushed through the doorway, and out onto the porch.

Beyond the steps, the floodwaters prickled moodily over the surrounding country. The dogwoods were stunted, their fluffed heads bowed over the water. Toward town, houses had broken free from their foundations and were bobbing in place.

Daddy.

He turned and the boy's eyes started to glass. He sent Robert inside for a rope and made a yoke around his waist, tying one end to his wife and the other to his son.

Stay close together, he told them.

Ellis went in first. He lowered himself slowly off the porch, into the rush of water. He bit down on his yell and tried to shake the ice from his head. A piano floated by and he swung to the side and let it pass. He balanced his bundle on his head and looked up at his wife and son.

Just like a bath. That's all it is, he said.

He motioned for Robert to come down next. Then Etta. Her dress flowered up around her, and she held her hat down against her head. Oh, she said. They shivered and hugged themselves, the slack of the rope floating up between them.

They waded against the current toward the telegraph poles in the distance, to Rolling Fork. Every now and then Ellis would cry out left, left, right, right and he could feel the tug against his waist, the knot biting into his hip as they dodged the flotsam. Pebbles churned in the yellow soup, hitting his legs and ribs and stomach.

Midday, the rain stopped and the sun broke through into the clean sky. The waters washed against them in thick moody rolls. Around them, people lay on their roofs, blankets spread out under them. The air buzzed with their crying. One man called out to them in a high ragged voice. Ellis watched him over his shoulder, jumping up and down and swinging his arms.

Boy! You there!

Robert looked over.

Don't pay him no attention, Ellis said.

Hey! Where you going?

There was a crack and a crown of water splashed up some feet away from Robert.

I'm talking to you!

Another crack, and Robert winced. He kept his head down and they trudged forward.

THEY'D GONE FOR HOURS THROUGH THE NUMBING WATERS, THEIR heads drooped and the space behind their eyes, deep and sonorous. Ellis felt the walls of his skull tensing. The waters stretched forever, smothering the roads and fields and district lines. Roof shingles drifted in the distance. He only dimly knew where he was, sighting out the tips of landmarks that peaked above the waterline. Robert was guiding his mama along, taking wide strides through the muck. He could hardly keep his eyes open. Ellis squeezed the bridge of his nose. The cave of his head yawned vast with air. He willed his legs forward but they refused.

Ellis shut his eyes. He did not know how much longer they could go on. He could make out a noise in the distance. It was a song, coming through warm and brown. He opened his eyes and across the water he saw a boat skimming between the rooftops, and the man in it, pulling his oars back and singing toward the sky.

I'm only going over Jordan, I'm only going over home, the man sang. I'm going there to see my Father, going there no more to roam.

Hello, Ellis called out.

The man let the oars hang loose in the water.

Hello!, the man answered.

The man paddled toward them, pulling up the water in white lashes. He was youngish—handsome with a thin sprinkling of hair on his sharp chin. How do you do? the man said. He extended out his hand. Name of Stuckey.

Ellis lifted his own hand up from the water, wiped it on his shirt, and shook it. I'm Ellis Chatham and here's my family. We been crossing over from Issaquena County.

Looks like you Chathams are wet in a bad way.

Was wondering if you could carry us some, Ellis said.

You don't say.

The man's tongue worked something over between his teeth. He leaned against the gunwale and flicked something away from his hair.

What you got in them satchels?

The muzzle of his pistol rested over the lip of the boat. Come on now, let's see them.

Just some food, Ellis said. Clothes. What little we got. We'd be happy to trade some—

The man gestured with his gun. Get in, he said.

We ain't looking for no kind of trouble, Mr. Stuckey.

The boat, the man said.

Ellis wedged his hands under Robert's arms and lifted him up. He set the boy down on the boat floor. Etta was next. Stuckey pulled her up by her arm, the heel of his boot anchored to the transom to keep from falling. Her dress clung to her thighs and she plucked the sticky cloth from around her legs. Her hat flipped off her head and went into the water. On board, her legs gave under her and she crawled to Robert, gathering him into her arms and cooing into his ear.

Well, well, Stuckey said. He reached for Ellis and heaved him in.

Looks like I caught me some duckies.

The rowboat was wide and long. The Chathams set themselves up at the stern-side bench. Stuckey went through their sacks, throwing their clothes and keepsakes carelessly on the puddled floor. He found the loaf of bread and tore into it, his breath squeaking through his nostrils. He snorted, swallowed, and tossed the rest to the Chathams.

Stale, he said, wiping his mouth.

Ellis stared at him.

Go on. Eat, Stuckey said, opening up another satchel. Son of man, eat thy bread with quaking and drink thy water with trembling and carefulness.

Ellis broke the loaf into pieces and handed a piece to the boy. Robert ate slowly and quietly, nestled in between his mama's arms.

What you going to do with us?, Ellis asked.

The man stood up. Etta tightened around the boy.

Row, the man said.

Stuckey hung his hand off the side of the boat, letting his fingers slice into the water. They were in the basin, where the water had gone high-deep. Beneath, dogtrots and lean-tos hung in the water—neither floating nor sinking. Now and again, something would bubble up to the surface. A chair. A table. A blouse. He skimmed up the blue wad of cloth, then spread it open. It was small. A girl's. He looked at it amused, then set it back in the water.

You know, friend, if there's a heaven, I hope it's a dry one.

Ellis had stripped off his shirt—a thin skin of sweat greased his body. With each stroke, he let out a breath. Behind him, Etta was still clutching the boy, shivering, staring back at the man.

Stuckey sat up.

You a man of God, friend?

Ellis kept on with his paddling.

That's all right. You don't have to tell me. Me, my daddy was a pastor outside of Tunica. Tiny little place. A flock that wasn't more than a sheep and a half. He made me say verses and passages every night at supper. It got so's I'd turn hungry every time someone read from Corinthians. That man used to go on and on, about the angry God and the loving God.

Stuckey leaned forward.

Now which one of those you believe in?

Ellis lifted the paddles up and let the boat drift. He stared hard at the man. The sun had started setting and was bruising pink overhead. Mosquitoes skimmed along the surface of the water, and he could hear the creaking of bust-up houses shifting beneath them.

Stuckey shook his head.

You said you from Issaquena County? You hear about that boy they hanged two months ago? Fourteen. Was off fooling with some plantation owner's daughter. A real beauty. A real lily as they say. Well, right before they strung him up, they got the rope round his neck, they ask him why he'd done it. You know what he said?

Ellis clenched his face together. The tendons in his shoulders tightened.

Love! You believe that?

Stuckey laughed.

Now, I done a lot in my time. Don't even start me to talking. But go near a white woman? Never. I'd never be that reckless. Shoot.

Stuckey opened his arms and swept them over the boat. In the distance, a train lay on its side, figures huddled on top of the boxcar. Telegraph poles had collapsed together in a nest of crucifixions, their cables willowing into the dark water.

I mean, will you look at this mess?

It could've been the ocean for all Robert knew—the water going on and on forever in every direction save for the small stitch of telegraph line in the distance. They rowed over a switching station, and he looked over the side to see the trains underneath.

There's nothing to see, Stuckey said. He was lying across the length of the boat, his hat tipped over his eyes. He crossed his legs and Robert could see the soles of his boots, worked and muddy.

Robert's mama had fallen asleep holding him. Her head was slumped against his shoulder, her chin hooking down from behind. She breathed slow and deep.

He could feel himself slipping off as well, watching the rhythms of his father's rowing—the muscles in his back crimping on every stroke, the greased sheen of his body with the sun on his neck. There had not been any crying or wailing for hours. There was not another soul. Only the oars patting the water.

Robert stood up suddenly, tearing free from his mama's hold. He stared out toward the horizon, shading his eyes against the light. He had heard it. Like a piece of wire humming. Ellis held the oars midpaddle. Stuckey lifted the hat from his face. They looked out together. The clouds were spread thin over the horizon, the underbelly gone red and raw. The others had heard it too. Muffled and small, but it was there all the same. A voice. A human voice traveling out across the water.

He rolled his head back and set his arm over his eyes.

Well, Stuckey said. Go on then.

They spotted a slice of high ground where the sun dissolved into the water. They rowed toward it, watching it grow by degrees into a grass jetty—a narrow arm of land, slanting up into the hill country. A man on the banks hollered out across the water, Lord Lord Lord! Show mercy for us the poor and the sinful.

The man's shirt was unbuttoned, his preacher's collar splayed open. Around him were piles of white cloth. It wasn't till the boat had almost touched land that Robert saw that they were men and women done up in baptismal robes. Their heads were pressed into the grass as they moaned and twitched. Men in tan uniforms were stepping carefully among them, touching their wrists or feeling their foreheads, then scratching their notes out on their clipboards.

The boat floated into the shallows and Stuckey stood up.

You get off here, he said. He pointed to their bundles. These you won't be needing anymore.

Robert climbed out of the boat and waded toward the shore, his mama and his daddy following behind him. His legs were stiff and he was so tired he felt like he would fall through the earth.

He looked behind him. Stuckey was already at the oars. He smiled back at Robert, lifting up one hand to wave. Then he took up the paddles and worked them back, sliding out toward the dark water.

Wash the devilment from your souls!, the preacher cried. From gambling halls and cathouses! He has seen our wickedness!

Robert felt his daddy's warm hand graze the back of his neck.

He has seen our wretchedness! Let us be clean! Take the Devil from our souls!

Over here!, a voice called out. Three men in uniforms came running toward them. They pulled the Chathams up from the bank, one by one, and wrapped them in blankets. Robert's mama sat down on the grass. The men tried to lift her up, but she closed her eyes and shook her head.

The men looked at each other. Then they took out their clipboards and started in on their questions. Ma'am, what's your name? Do you know your address?

His mama only stared, holding the blanket tightly around her front. His daddy tried to say something, but a man in uniform stood in front of him.

Sir, sir. I need your attention a moment.

Robert listened to the way they talked, those cramped, pinched voices. They were young and extraordinarily white, whiter than most white men he'd seen. There wasn't any kind of burn on their noses or faces or necks, just pale apple flesh.

Son, you need to tell me your name, son. Before we can help you, we need to know your name. For the chart.

Robert, his daddy said. Answer the man.

The man wrote something down on his sheet.

Sir, I need this young man to speak for himself.

That's my boy Robert, his daddy said. He's only eight.

Sir. Please.

Tell him, Robert. It's all right.

Sir, another man said. I need you to pay attention to me. You can talk with your family later but for right now, you need to talk to me.

Now hold on there, his daddy said, standing.

Sir.

Now hold on.

Sir. Sir, please, sir, they said.

The men circled around his daddy. Their hands were up in front of them, as if they were afraid he might pounce.

Robert watched the scene. More men in uniform charged down the hill past them toward the water. People were still coming in—some on boats, or pieces of wood yoked together with twine. They called out for help and the white men would splash down after them.

When he turned back, his mama was gone, the print of her wet body still on the grass. He looked around. The white men were moving swiftly from one person to another. They went around carrying blankets and urns of coffee. A woman was crying, cradling a bundle in her arms, and one of the men was trying to take it away. Robert kept looking. He saw his mama walking past the preacher, toward the water's edge. No one else noticed her as she moved among them, stepping over their prostrate bodies, her blanket dragging in a tail behind her. Robert's daddy and the men were still arguing. Robert got up and ran after her.

He caught up with his mama at the flood bank and slipped his hand quietly into hers. She looked at him as if trying to place who he was, then she shifted her shoulders and cinched up the blanket tightly around them both.

Farther down the bank, a man was howling, beating his head with his fists. He rushed out into the water and it took four men to pull him back. A terrible wail escaped his body and he struggled in their arms before finally going slack.

Robert's mama squeezed his small palm.

Serves them right, she said.

Robert put his hand in his pocket. Dora's stone was still there. The preacher's voice gathered in some far-off part of his mind like silt. Years later, he would think back to this moment, holding the stone—its smooth black surface digging into the meat of his palm, the water still sticky on his skin. Love, the man had said. Will you look at this mess?

PART TWO

HOTEL BEAU-MIEL

(1932)

Augustus Duke wiped the pollen from his goggles and cranked hard on the gearbox. The A-Model kicked forward, churning yellow air under the tires. There were flowers on the roadside—whole bouquets of roses, irises, carnations—dried into fists. The smell followed him all the way to the Big Farm. It was in the air, in the hollows of his nose and mouth, puddled up in the jaw of spit. He watched the Farm rise up from beneath the road, the acres of plowed earth and wood houses behind a six-mile stretch of chicken wire and guard towers. Up at the gate, he turned off the engine. A guard came out from the guardhouse and met the car. His uniform was unbuttoned and his undershirt was matted with sweat.

Help you?

Duke unstrapped the goggles, massaging the red circles around his eyes. He showed him the envelope from his pocket. The guard turned it over, read the name, then frowned.

Have to telephone the warden.

The man went back into the guardhouse. Duke climbed out of the car and spat into the dust. The sun made the air slow and prickly, and he ran his tongue along the sticky sucking walls of his mouth. Beyond the wire, he could see the Negroes lined along their furrows, their spades cutting into the dark earth—hear their soft grunts, their exhales.

The guard returned. His uniform had been loosened.

Warden said to stay here, the guard said. He handed back the envelope. You can wait inside, out of the sun, if you like.

Duke followed the man inside. It was small and cramped like a garden shed. Shelves cluttered with papers and boxes of ammunition lined the inside wall. A small glass window looked out into the camp. Duke bumped the telephone from the wall, and the guard reached over and placed the speaker back on the carriage.

The guard sat down on a stool and wedged off his boot.

Can't stand that smell, the guard said. He burst a blister under his big toe and rubbed his fingers on his trousers.

They say you get used to it but ask me, seems like it gets worse every day.

Duke didn't answer him.

The flowers, I mean. The Overnight runs right through here.

Duke had seen it driving up, first the tracks chasing alongside the road, then the train racing up, spitting gravel against his car. He remembered the hobo eyes that stared out at him from the half-open freights.

That's how come you got this smell, the guard went on. They got these nigger girls come in with their hair all done up. All up and down the state. Lined up for hours sometimes. We tell them every time. No flowers. So they trash them right on the roadside there.

The guard tugged the top button of his shirt and aired out the pits of his arms.

They hide things, you know? You'd be surprised. The women are sneaky. Sneakier even than the men. One selling her cunny from Aberdeen come up to see one of our lifers. Says he was her sweet boy. She was hauling this whole bloom of lilacs and daisies and whatever else. Draped up over her shoulder, sticking up in her face, practically falling out of her arms, there were so many flowers. A sight to see. Didn't no one seem to notice that those flowers were tied off with a foot of piano wire.

The guard clucked his tongue and cut his hand across his throat.

No flowers after that.

The guard worked a finger under his heel and horned his foot back into his boot. The boot kicked forward and Duke stepped back to dodge the arc. He took out his pocket watch and hooded his eyes into slits.

The guard looked at him.

They're animals, plain and simple. Take that boy you're waiting on. Eli Cutter. Now that one is a piece of work. You heard about what he done?

Yes, Duke said.

The guard clicked his tongue.

That poor girl. Her insides all rotted out.

Duke watched the guard take full measure of him. He chewed down on his bottom lip and nodded slowly.

And now here you are with that fancy piece of paper of yours. Well, don't that beat all?

Duke looked steadily at the guard. He worked his tongue against the roof of his mouth. He slipped two fingers past his teeth and drew out a flap of dead skin.

Well, piece of advice. You just watch yourself around that one. Everybody here knows to keep clear of Eli.

The guard motioned toward the sky.

He ain't clean.

A gunshot cracked in the distance and the guard's jaw turned taut and fierce. He leaned against his rifle butt and stared hard at the fields. Nothing had changed. The prisoners kept up their work as the sergeants drove their horses steady down the lines. There came another report, echoing into quiet.

I wouldn't worry. Chances are, that wasn't your old boy, Eli. You got a cigarette? It'll cut the smell.

Duke reached into his jacket.

The guard eyed the pack and let a smile tighten on his face.

He fit a cigarette between his lips. Duke struck a match, lit the guard's and then his own. The cigarette crackled like radio air.

~

ELI BROKE TWO EGGS IN A LITTLE CUP AND WITH HIS LONG THIN fingers, he scooped out the yolks. The strands shivered and dripped and he rubbed the yellow between his hands, then back through his hair. A prison trusty stood in the doorway of the bunkhouse, tugging on the straps of his dungarees with one hand, balancing his rifle with the other. Eli watched the trusty in the piece of mirror, his fat lips working into an angry bud.

Eli patted down the rest of his hair and wiped his hands on a rag. He slipped on his jacket, straightened out the lapels, then set his hat neat on his head. He gave himself one more look—narrow face, clear almond eyes, a spray of silver on his mustache. Eli sucked back on his teeth.

Outside, he could hear the inmates plucking their spades dully at the earth as a skin of red dust settled outside the bunkhouse.

The trusty cleared his throat. You ready?

Eli grinned, turning from the mirror.

Show on.

They walked through the prison farm, Eli in front and the trusty behind. Outside, the sky was wide and full, doming above the wire fencing. The cotton fields lay spread in dark tracts while the inmates stooped over in their rows, cutting the soil with their hoes, their leg chains twinkling.

They crossed to the laundry lines outside the administration building. The prisoners looked up from their washboards, cheeks flecked with soap, hands bleached and sudsy over the blue-black water. They pressed their cracked rutted faces against the glass. No one made a noise, only the crackle of soap sounding as they waited for Eli to pass.

At the gate the warden stood with his suit stiff and freshly pressed. Beside him was a man. He looked like an egg, round and pale and smooth except his nose, which was blistered and full of blood. The man was staring hard at Eli, the small muscle in his throat going up and down.

The warden sent the trusty away.

This the one you wanted?

The man unfolded a square of paper from his pocket.

You're Eli Cutter?

He was surprised the man knew his name. Yessir, he said. That's me.

Out of Natchez?

And happy to be here.

The man read aloud from his paper:

Cutter, Elijah Paul. Age, thirty-eight years; height, five feet eight inches; weight, 129 pounds; nativity, Adams County; complexion, mulatto; hair, black; eyes, brown; mole behind left ear; scar on the right thigh. Sentenced from Wayne County, October 29, 1929, for the crime of manslaughter; term, fifteen years.

The man looked up from the slip of paper.

The warden smirked. Well, not quite fifteen is it, Mr. Duke?

The man ignored him. Let me see your hands.

Eli rolled up his sleeves. His palms were dusty and cracked, but his fingers spanned out wide like a cellar spider, knobby at the knuckles but smooth and womanly down to the tips. He touched his thumbs together lightly.

That's him, the man said. He reached into his jacket and handed the warden a thick envelope.

I trust this settles everything.

The warden smiled. He patted the envelope across his palm before tucking it under his arm.

He's all yours, Mr. Duke, he said.

They drove for hours, neither of them talking. Eli fought down the excitement in his gut. He gazed out at the surrounding country. The hills rolled past and in the distance there were clusters of houses—towns he'd spent years in. They flashed in some dark part of his brain—barrelhouses, hotels, barbershops, his arm around some young smiling thing, the two of them stealing out to the potter's field, their naked bodies on the cold wet grass.

The man named Duke stopped the car at a clearing along the road. Out beyond the tall grass was the old colored church, burned-out and gutted. The walls were charred black and had fallen through in places, strands of wild millet growing through cracks in the floor.

We're here, Mr. Duke said. He hefted up a small leather suitcase and carried it out with him.

Flies flicked around their eyes and nostrils, buzzing drunk and angry. They stepped over the smashed pews and collapsed roof, the wood groaning underneath them. There were chalk lines scratched into a piece of wall, and empty bean tins on the floor. The stink of shit hung humid in the air.

They climbed up to what had been the pulpit and the man pulled the cloth from off the organ. With the heel of his hand, he wiped down the bench.

Have a seat, he said.

Eli sat down and Mr. Duke lifted up the fall board. The keys were clean and white.

Been a long time, Eli said.

Mr. Duke opened the case. He lifted up what looked like a phonograph and pointed the horn at Eli. He flicked a switch and there was a grinding noise. He flicked it again and the noise evened out.

Play something for me, he said.

Boss?

I want you to play a blues for me.

Eli set a finger on a key. It was cold and foreign.

Go ahead, Mr. Duke said.

Eli rolled up his sleeves and knuckled his fingers, trying to rub the buzz out of his joints. He floated his big hands above the ivory, the cords tightening into a claw. The pads of his fingers touched lightly over the keys; they were cold and smooth and sent a shiver through him like a sword.

The pedal clunked into its place. Eli touched the first note. Soft. Then he touched it again, letting it ring out. His mind burned. He closed his eyes and struck. A chord boomed beneath his hands. His heart was beating. He let the sound flare then cool. Something in his throat unhitched. Another chord. Then another. Beneath him, the organ trilled. He felt its air against his face. His heart fired in his chest.

When Eli had finished, Mr. Duke switched off the machine and folded the horn back into its case.

Marvelous, Duke said. Simply marvelous. You're as good as they say.

Mr. Duke placed the fall board down and sat beside Eli on the bench. His large belly strained against the buttons of his shirt.

He rubbed his thick palms against the knees of his pants. Eli could smell him from where he sat, the stink of mold in his clothes.

Mr. Duke placed his hand on Eli's shoulder and the man's grip tightened.

I am starting a traveling musical act and I've been looking for a Negro to play the piano for me. Thirty dollars a week. Thirty dollars and your freedom.

Eli sat there stunned. His head was swimming and he had to brace himself against the bench to keep from falling over. Eli began to laugh, shaking his head and cupping his palms over his face.

Mr. Duke handed Eli a sheet of paper and showed him where he could put his mark. They shook hands and Mr. Duke counted out a hundred dollars in crisp new bills.

There's a town in Calhoun County by the Skuna River called Bruce. A colored woman by the name of Lucy Quinn runs a hotel out there. The Hotel Beau-Miel. You take this money, get yourself a nice suit and a meal, and meet me there in two weeks.

Eli folded the bills together and tucked them into his pants pocket.

In two weeks? What're you going to do till then?

He watched Mr. Duke slip the paper with Eli's name into his case, then secure the two brass latches over the lid. He hefted it up with one arm and started for the door.

With his free hand, he gestured to the burned-out walls of the church.

Why, Mr. Cutter, someone's got to find something for you to bang those magnificent hands on.

THE JOSTLING ON THE BUS KEPT THE SLEEP FROM SETTLING. HIS eyes stung and his groin itched. The other passengers were asleep. Eli could hear them snoring, making low wet sounds, dreamy half words. The country spread black against the windows. Here and there he could make out the reddish glow of tramp fires through the pines. He closed his eyes and half expected to open them up again to his bunk back at the Farm and smell the stale sweat and manure hanging in the air.

But instead, he smelled perfume.

It drifted faint from the front of the bus. A fire lit up in his head, his nerves going hot and bright at the tips. She climbed on board, a gloved hand steadying herself on the back of a seat. The silhouette of a pillbox hat floated into the aisle. She took slow careful steps toward the back of the bus, arms feeling the dark space ahead of her. Her hips bobbed—*Swish! Swish!*—stopping in front of Eli.

Evening, she said.

Eli slid over and cleared a space for her to sit. The scent of calla lily grew thick and heavy. He could feel its weight in his mouth, like a lump of sugar on his tongue.

You a pretty little thing to go riding around this hour, he said.

Couldn't find no one to carry me, she said.

Now I don't believe that. You weighed five hundred pounds, I'd carry you. On my back if I had to.

The woman snickered. Maybe, but you can't take me any place I need to go.

Don't you worry. I know all the right places.

Oh, I bet you do.

I know all the right spots, he said again.

Eli couldn't see her face. He wasn't sure if she was ignoring him.

You going to see your man?

You're awful lippy, mister.

You didn't answer my question.

The woman was quiet for a while. I'm going to see my husband.

If I had a wife like you, I wouldn't never let her out of my sight.

Don't get fresh with me, she said. You don't even know me.

I don't mean offense. All I mean is lots of things out in these roads at night. Not all of them safe.

Like you.

Eli laughed.

Me? Sure. But there's plenty worse than me. When I was a little boy, my grandma told me about a gypsy woman live out in the country. If a little boy or little girl was in devilment, she'd come at night and take them away. Boil them up and eat their bones, then she'd spit them out and put them in her little conjure bag.

The woman laughed. He could make out the swell of her breasts, the smooth slope of her neck. The whites of her eyes glowed a dull blue even in the dark.

You ever been in devilment, little girl?

Bad boy, she teased.

'Cause I can devil you right.

He touched his fingers lightly to her skirt. The warm of her thighs came up through the cotton.

The woman laughed. I'm a full-grown woman.

Very grown, Eli said.

A grown woman ain't got no need for tall tales.

Maybe you ain't never had a tale tall enough.

Don't matter how tall if it don't do nothing.

Eli smiled. You don't believe me.

He could feel the bus rolling over the uneven country, a deep tremble plucking at his groin.

Let me show you something.

Eli unbuckled his belt and slid his hand down his waistband.

What're you doing?

He brought out his hand and in his palm was a small flannel bag. The woman let out a surprised laugh, then clapped her hand over her mouth. He untied the drawstring and took out a round dark pit.

This here is my little devil.

Oh, a *little* devil? Is that it?, she said, pouting.

Eli ignored her.

It's got powers on it. He held it out in front of her, rolling it gently in his fingers.

Go on now.

It's true.

Snuck it right from under that gypsy woman.

What's it do?

What's it look like to you?

It was dark and round and shriveled.

It looks like a man's . . . well, a man's part.

That's right, he said. He danced the pit dreamily in front of her, first in front of her eyes, then under her nose, grazing her upper lip.

His other hand settled lightly on her knee. He drew swirls gently on her skin.

All I got to do is give it a little rub right here, he whispered.

He passed his thumb over the ridges of the pit. A warm musk flowed from his fingertips and he glided his hand up her thigh.

Can I hold it? she asked softly.

He brushed the pit gently around the underside of her palm, then up the curve of her wrist, away from her stretching fingers. He could smell her honeyed sweat now, through her perfume. His frenzied blood ached under his skin.

Just a little rub right here.

He was born Elijah Philip Cutter outside of Natchez in Adams County—gray and small and out of breath—a caul across his brow. When he was two, his mama cut out to California with a man that might've been his daddy, leaving Eli to his grandma to raise up. He was a sickly boy. At night he could not breathe and would instead sit up in his bunk, his lungs filling with panic, and he'd listen, the rusty harp inside his throat, the ringing of the bottle tree.

When he was five, his grandma took him down to the small one-room shack out beyond the rail yard water station. All around he could hear the great breaths of steam let out from the chimneys. The house sat out beyond the weeds, its walls soot stained and ivied. His grandma unlatched the door and guided Eli in. There was hardly any light. He could barely make out the shelves that lined the walls, the dark dusty jars of powder and bone. There was a great shifting breath. He almost did not see him, sitting there on the bed. He was old, his eyes two milky orbs inside his skull.

The Devil's in your throat, his grandma said. It got to come out.

The man laid his frail hand upon the boy's body and undid the buttons one by one. The fabric fell quietly away. On his open chest, the man pressed his ear. He listened for the rattle of his soul.

When he was done, the man had him lie down on a sheet of wax paper. Eli looked at his grandma, who only nodded approvingly, and he obeyed. He spread himself out on top of the thin paper, and the man knelt down and lit a candle at his feet.

Shut your eyes, his grandma said.

Above him, the man moved, shifting his weight, the floor straining against the balls of his feet. Eli could hear his hands, hear the wet slick of oil between the man's palms as he rubbed them together. A band of warmth stretched across his chest.

Don't move.

The heat was unbearable. It lay heavy like a second skin. He could feel the sweat between his shoulder blades, gathering along the ridge of his spine. It traveled down and down, a cold pearl at the base of his back.

And inside, he could feel the small thing fighting in his chest, struggling against the root man's ministrations. The Devil rustled. His lungs filled with feathers. There were hands upon him now, kneading hard against his breast. His heart raced. The air was shrinking. He could not breathe.

And there was the thumping in his breast, and God's hand in his throat. And there was his soul against his ribs. Outside, the trains let out their bellows, and in one sick lurch, he spit the evil yolk out onto the butcher paper. Eli hacked and wheezed and felt air crack deep into his core. The man stood him up and wrapped up the paper around the yolk, tucking the yellow mass into one of his dusty jars.

FOR YEARS, ELI WENT TO SEE THE ROOT MAN, DRINKING HIS POTIONS and huffing powders from his mason jars. In the afternoons, he helped him hunt through the thatches of johnsongrass outside the rail yard. The old man squatted down among the weeds, his desiccated hands searching through the loose soft soil. He plucked mushrooms from the cold black ground and tucked their caps inside his cheek. He'd hold them there for hours before spitting the runny mash across an Indian head penny. All the plants he could name by touch, the grittiness of the leaves, the firmness of the stalks against his fingers. Sorghum and boneset and chase-devil. He'd take a spade and dig down, prying up long tangles of blood root, and John the conqueror and the musky dripping vines called devil's shoestrings.

Folks would come from miles around—as far away as Prichard and Mobile and Tillmans Corner. The line would stretch out the door and Eli would watch them, their slack and tired faces, the nervous hands. Eli listened as the root man dispensed his advice: mashed-up snake root and grooveburr in a sachet under your bed. A strip of yellow cloth and powdered anise seed inside a flannel pouch. There were tricks for money and tricks for love and tricks to turn the Devil from your door. There were mojo hands and evil eyes and black cat bones. And all around was the invisible world, Eli realized, each of us caught in its strange currents. If he shut his eyes, he could almost hear it—the thump of blood. The driving noise. The deep and ancient undertows.

The first trick he ever laid, Eli made a wish and rubbed a piece of lodestone to a purple kerchief. He buried the rock underneath a linden tree and burned the kerchief, setting the ashes into the wind. In time the universe would answer. When he was thirteen, a man came to his grandma's house. He was tall and dark and slim with a mouth full of gold and he told the boy that he was his father. With him, he'd brought an old pine-top upright piano. The man said he had a job selling them all over the country. When Eli's grandma found that man inside her house, she ran him off with a meat cleaver. She chased him clear out of town before he could recover his piano.

For hours every night Eli would sit at the box, studying the keys. He'd pry open the top panel and watch the wooden hammers rise and fall across the long raking cables. He taught himself, and in time the piano became almost second nature. He liked the way his arms spread its length, the way the sound gave underneath his fingers. It became a conduit of his will. Anger and joy and sadness swooping out of his soul and into the air.

And yet when he sat himself at the bench, when the fall board lifted away to reveal the peninsula of glowing keys, he could not say he was entirely himself. The hands were not his hands. They moved without his moving them, tensing into claws, doing their jitter jump. The chords rose like a heat above the keys and the thought occurred to him that maybe it was not his will that drove his hands, that spanned his arms, that struck and stroked and stomped his feet against the ground.

ELI LEFT HOME WITH HIS MOJO BAG, A DECK OF CARDS, AND A HEAD full of humming. He spent years on the chitlin circuit—playing at the Queen City Hotel, Po' Monkey's Lounge, Doke's Barbershop, and in the tiny jukes up and down Chrisman Street. He earned himself a name as a demon on an upright. For hours he'd play, his face stern and his clothes sweat-heavy. Folks would jam into the tiny halls, their bodies full of heat, and Eli would shut his eyes and feel their swell in the back of his mouth, their beating feet in his throat.

Rumor had spread about the devil bag he kept at his waist, and after a set, there'd always be some desperate woman waiting for him outside. She'd tell him her troubles, and he'd listen—his face a blank, lost in the hiss of the gas lamps.

When she finished speaking, he'd look her square in the eye.

You got to be sure, he'd say, his hand laying warm across the back of hers. 'Cause once it gets doing, can't get undone.

Then he'd take her money and walk her back to someplace dark and quiet where they would not be disturbed.

~

IN THE DAYS AFTER THE FLOOD, IT WAS SO CALM YOU COULD SEE clear through the water like it was a sheet of glass—torn-up roofs, stove-pipes, drowned livestock made stiff and waxen. The D.C. men had come down on special order and they went around in their standard-issue tan, speaking in clean soft voices, sketching their plans on rolls of yellow paper. At night they went into the refugee camps, their lanterns flashing and disappearing through the weeds. They went to the coloreds first, rousting them from their beds with promises of work and food and a chance to help their country. And then there was Eli who was already up, who never slept much to begin with—Eli with his mouth on the mouth of a bottle of corn whiskey. He was by the fire, shooting craps—the dice heavy with mercury and firing sevens.

He didn't see the D.C. men, didn't see them come up till one of them put a hand on his shoulder.

You serving your country now.

In the morning, they lined him up with the others and gave them each a ration ticket. They fed them on stores of stiff bread and a thin soup before driving them up-country to the levee camp. It was a wide and grassless clearing set along the water break, where rows of pup tents crowded into one another. The latrines were a network of shallow trenches running through the camp and out into the water. The mosquitoes raged thick and black, flitting on their eyes and skin and shit.

They gathered the men to the water's edge and one of the D.C. men stood himself up on a supply truck and sketched out what needed doing: a berm, ten feet high, six feet across, running two miles downriver. The work would be hard and long, but their work would live on in the state for years to come, he said.

Then someone asked, How long we got to live here?

And the man said, Long as it takes.

Then they were given shovels.

THE MAN IN CHARGE WAS A FORMER OVERSEER NAMED HOMER Teague. He wasn't from D.C., but he'd run a plantation somewhere roundabout Indianola, and the D.C. men had figured that running coloreds is running coloreds. Teague was a fierce drinker. When he was angry, his face would turn wine red, and he'd uncoil that long bullwhip he kept at his belt and snap it in the air. If you didn't shovel or haul fast enough, he'd pull you out of your line, and stretch you out under a tree and tear you through with a piece of splintered hickory.

He lived out with his sister, Emaline, in a plantation house outside of town, a creaking place where the walls looked like bone and the stink of sulfur came up through the mud. It was always on his boots, kissing yolky daggers into the earth.

Maybe it was the difference in their ages, but where her brother was mean and quick to anger, Emaline was gentle and easily moved to emotion. She was sixteen years old, a bird of a child. Some days, she'd come down to the camp done up in her gingham homespun, toting a basket of apples for the men.

Eli would greet her as she came down the line. Unlike the others, Eli wasn't afraid of smiling at white women, big and toothy, full of nothing behind it. He'd bow, tipping some invisible hat, before righting himself and accepting her apple.

But the biggest, reddest apples she'd save for her brother, who looked forward to her visits. Teague would crunch them between his teeth, gold-colored juices soaking up in his red beard. He'd lick the sticky off his fingers and Emaline would dab her kerchief on his lips and his hands, shaking her head, saying, Oh, Homer.

For months, Eli worked out in the levee camp under Teague, digging ditches, driving mules, and hauling cement. Breakfast bell comes at five, and if you ain't got your card, you ain't eating—then it's down to the riverside till the quit bell rings. In those long hours the men would wait on those bells, hearing them when there wasn't nothing to hear at all—just a magpie screaming or some faraway train going, tearing through the world like it was made of butcher paper.

The work was hard and grueling but on Saturdays, they'd clear out the equipment shed and him and a few of the boys would get a special dispensation into town. They'd come back with barrels of white whiskey and a hog to slaughter and roast over the fire pit. Once they stole a piano—took four goddamn men to lift—and Eli would drink that white whiskey and beat those keys and make them forget. The crooked card games, the lying women—one more song, just one more song. They'd rise to their feet, and shut their eyes, feel the wash of sound against them, pulling back like sand on the tide. And those D.C. white boys would just look the other way, down at their rolls of paper, at their pencil sketchings, and let those sorry niggers alone.

ONE MORNING HE SAW HER, EMALINE, STUMBLE UP THE GRASSLESS path. The sun was on her shoulders, moving through her hair. Eli had been working at the wall, reinforcing the berm with cement when she stopped and greeted him, her high laugh speckling above the rill of moving water.

You're a performer, she said to him. That's what one of the men told me anyways.

Eli let his shovel rest.

Yes, miss, he said. He stood the shovel against the wall and wiped his brow with a kerchief.

I knew it! How come you never told me that before?

Eli shrugged and glanced down the line to where her brother was busying himself with a mule driver and his team. He seemed irate, pushing that small man about and violently unhitching the beasts from the wagon.

Nothing to tell, I suppose, Miss Teague.

Well, what're you doing out here?

Even performers got to eat, he said.

She thought for a second, then crinkled her nose, laughing.

What do you perform at?

I play the piano, Miss Teague.

She clapped her hands together.

The piano! Can you teach me to play?

Eli smirked. I can teach you to shovel.

She laughed again, touching the back of her wrist to her mouth.

You're too much, Mr. Cutter, she said before she continued down with her morning greetings. She was an attractive girl, he recognized. He watched the other men get mealymouthed around Emaline Teague, hemming and hawing and striking the ground with their heels. She flustered them with her jokes and that was her right, he supposed. But in his gut he could feel the danger there—her brother's hot eyes on those around her.

There were rumors about Emaline and her brother and the things that went on in that plantation house on the outskirts of town, but near as Eli knew it was only idle talk.

Then one day Emaline stopped coming down to the levee camp with her basket of apples, and it seemed like that foul angry weather would never lift from Homer Teague. He'd come down to the banks, red and mean, his eyes puffy and his cheeks swollen, looking for any chance to take his meanness out of some nigger's hide.

He'd work his strop hard, taking whole teams sometimes out under the shady oaks. Each of them would off with their trousers and wrap their arms around a tree trunk. Real hard now, he'd hiss. Like hugging your sorry sag-ass mamas, and Teague would snap the whip in the air, rubbing his wrists and elbows. Real tight now.

The men would close their eyes and feel the breeze move over their naked parts. The lash came down hot and sudden. They'd jerk against the pain, digging their bodies into the bark. Those who cried out, Teague would whup harder, lashing his shoulder down, and when the D.C. boys checked in on the camp's progress, they'd nod to each other. They'd picked the right man for the job.

THERE'D BEEN RAIN THAT SATURDAY NIGHT AND THE MEN CAME in, shaking off their clothes and hair, cramming into the makeshift barrelhouse. The whiskey stores were running low and their mood with it. Eli took the bench and began to play. He hadn't had anything in mind particularly, just noodling to pass the time. He played something slow and blue and wearied and the men slouched down in their seats. They looked up at the ceiling, at one another, at the long lashes of smoke that ghosted the air. No one stood. No one danced. Eli shut his eyes, listened to the rain. The world was filling up.

When he opened his eyes again, he was surprised to see Emaline there in their barrelhouse, the one white face in a sea of black ones. The others watched her in shock as she moved through the drifting smoke and took a seat near the piano.

What was that you were just playing?

Oh—nothing, Eli managed to say. Just a blues.

A blues?

He could feel the others watching them. Hear their low voices.

Your brother know you out here with us?

Don't talk to me about Homer. Not now.

Well, all right, he said.

It's pretty, she said. Whatever it is.

Thank you, Miss Teague.

She touched his hand and he took it away.

I need to see you, she said.

She rose and he followed her out, well aware of how it would look. They passed out into the rain and ran across to shelter underneath the equipment shed.

They tell me that you can do things, she said. With powders and such.

Eli was silent for a moment. Something was happening. What it was exactly, he could not say. There was something. A change in the air. A hardening in his gut. Yes, he said after a while.

I need help. Her voice was weak and small.

It was dark around them and he could not see her face.

I don't lay tricks for your kind. White folks, I mean. It's not something that's done, Miss Teague.

They were silent for what felt like a long time. Eli could feel the liquor working through him, the warm ache inside his skull. She was crying, he realized. He let himself put his hand across her back.

What's wrong?, he asked.

Oh, Eli, she cried. I don't know how to begin to tell you. The pain is unbearable, you must understand. I've not been able to eat or sleep in weeks.

She seized his hand and laid it across her stomach. There's this pain in me, spreading like a fire.

Eli looked at her and swallowed hard.

You been to see the doctor?

He can't help me, she said.

Eli nodded. Okay, he said. Come back here tomorrow night. I'll have something for you.

That night he hunted through his pouches for birthwort and penny-royal. By candlelight, he ground them down with the edge of a lucky nickel and knit up the powder in a worsted sachet. He cut a slice of co-hosh root and blessed it twice with St. Jude oil. He tucked it under his tongue, let the bitterness seep into his jaw.

There was a devil in everything. In the good and the bad, in the water rising into his mouth. In every outstretched finger of his hands. In the secret inside her belly. Eli turned to his shaving mirror. The hardening in his gut had not gone away and he felt anxious. For what, he could not say. He looked at his reflection, as if for the last time. He asked for pro-tection. For Emaline. For himself. Would it work? Had it ever? He blew out the candle. He was not sure.

The next night, she was where he'd told her to be. The moon hung above the river, blighted and bad and full. A sightless eye. And beneath he could see its twin, smeared and milky on the water's surface.

He handed her the sachet in a yellow kerchief.

Brew it up, he told her. And when the water gets a kind of clear yel-low, drink it down. Every drop.

She tucked the bundle into her pocket and started to go.

He took her arm.

I never done this before, he said. I don't know what's going to happen.

She squeezed his hand and went on.

FOR WEEKS, HE'D CRANE HIS NECK OUT INTO THE LANE AND LOOK for the red checkcloth homespun and the basket of apples. But Emaline was nowhere to be found. Eli just kept on at his work and on payday, he'd beat the pine-top box, beat the sound from its cables, throw back his head and roar out for the world. He'd roll and sway and feel his troubles lift and lift until, like air, they weren't hardly nothing at all. Nothing like the furious sound beneath his fingers.

It'd been a wild payday. A few whores had come down into the camps that night, perfumed and big thighed. They fit easy into the crook of men's arms, across their laps. The camp had gone through three barrels of whiskey that night, and there was some talk about a fourth, but everybody was already walking lopsided, with their words wet and running together. Eli stooped over the piano and the men would scoop their girls around the floor, testing their warm hands on those warmer bodies, the coins jangling in their pockets.

But soon night passed into early morning, and one by one the crowd trickled out. There were only a few stragglers left, half asleep in their seats and Eli at the bench, numb except for his fingertips, which were bright and eager.

Suddenly the door swung open and he turned to see Homer Teague filling the frame.

The man looked different somehow. Brittle. Pale. From his color, Eli could tell the man had been drinking. He'd been done up proper in a waistcoat and hat as if he'd just come from a party. Quietly, he crossed the floor and took a seat by the piano, the same seat that his sister had taken.

Eli became unnerved and stopped playing.

Go on, Teague said. His voice was soft. Almost childlike.

Eli didn't move. It took only a moment for the room to empty. Soon they were alone—Teague and him. From the open door blew a bad wind. He could see the shadows twisting on the floor as the oil lamp squeaked on its hook.

What's the matter?

Eli swallowed hard. He set his hands down on the keys, unsure of himself. His hands were two dead slabs on his arms.

Play a blues, Teague said. That is what you do, isn't it? Go ahead. Play.

Eli turned back to his keys—his throat suddenly dry. The liquor was a weight behind his face. He knuckled his fingers and tried to rub the buzz out of the joints. His big hands floated up and rested over the ivory. The pedal clunked into its place.

And then at once, his fingers fell through the keys. A chord exploded from the pinewood piano. Then another. A rush of sounds and rhythm. His hands jumped and scurried and bit. Black keys, white keys. Pounding hard and soft, in unison and apart. Eli could feel the wood cracking around him. The walls were shaking.

A splinter burst from the body of the piano. Eli winced and grabbed his stinging cheek. He could feel the blood burning in his face. There was a blemish on the piano, a small dark patch he had not noticed before. Slowly, his eyes adjusted. It was a hole in the panel, small and clean where the bullet had just embedded itself. Eli turned. Teague's hand was full of smoke.

His eyes were red and pocketed, staring at the floor. More than anything, he looked exhausted. He slumped in his chair, breathing heavy. Teague let the weight drop from his hands. Slowly, Eli rose from the bench. He began to run.

The sheriff found him holed up in an old farmhouse two miles from the camp. He was curled up inside the chicken coop, among the feathers and the shit, his hands bleeding from climbing wire. He turned his head away from the sheriff's light and moaned softly. The sheriff stood over him, calm and sad.

Come on, son, he said as he helped him up. You got a few things to answer for.

He felt the man's touch on his shoulders, and a wave of grief rose into his throat. He stepped out into the field. It was low flat tract, without grass or trees or shrubs. A place where nothing grows and the earth has no memory, and the thought came to him that all that is borrowed must one day be repaid.

The boy let in the just-rained air, cool and dewed, and stuck his head out the window. Overhead, the sky was swollen. The cottonwoods were in full bloom, their catkins fat and set to bust. From the third-story window he could make out the road that led out to Bruce proper, toward the Skuna River, and beyond it the railway station. He raised the window higher to give himself room, then he climbed backward out onto the ledge. He'd grown four inches in the last year and now he felt the pinch behind his knees as he anchored his large hands against the wall and slipped his weight outward. The roof edge was slick with rain. His fingers hooked and locked into the grooves. He let his body dip out, his full weight pulling against his fingers hard and sudden. For a moment he hung, groundless, outside the Hotel Beau-Miel, before hoisting himself onto the roof.

Farther into Bruce, he could see rows of houses, the movie theater, the restaurant, the market. A car cornered onto the main stretch. From where he stood, it looked like a large beetle smashing through the puddles.

He went low onto his belly, watching it from over the shingles. The car skidded and came to a halt in front of the hotel. He waited, watching it idle.

A door opened.

At first all Robert could see of the new girl was her green slicker. It floated beside the car, climbing out beneath Miss Lucy's waiting umbrella. The car started up suddenly, and the girl slipped into a mud puddle.

Miss Lucy picked the girl up and hurried her into the house.

When he was sure they'd gone in, Robert made his way back to the edge of the roof. He peered down at the three-story drop and lowered himself down, feeling for the sill with his toes. He went inside, closing the window behind him. He tidied the room, tucking the sheet firm under the mattress and fluffing the pillows. This was to be the new girl's room, and Miss Lucy had instructed him to be thorough. He gave the place a once-over, then entered into the hall.

Robert!

Miss Lucy was still in her traveling clothes. A powder-blue floral-print dress and a string of pearls. She had let her hair down and the gray had started to show, striping faint over her left ear. She held out the green slicker and a yellow dress splattered with mud.

Put this in with the day's wash.

Yes'm.

Robert took the bundle from her. He turned to go but Miss Lucy stopped him. She looked him up and down, and he realized then that the front of his coveralls was wet.

What I tell you about staying off my roof?

Sorry, Miss Lucy.

People don't come here to get spied on.

No, Miss Lucy.

You'll break your fool neck one day.

Yes, Miss Lucy. Sorry, Miss Lucy.

Miss Lucy shook her head.

You're dripping on my floor, she said, waving him away.

• • •

The Hotel Beau-Miel was Miss Lucy's baby. She scrounged and saved for thirteen years selling her fish, secreting a dime on every dollar of her earnings for the place. There were rooms, and beds, and a desk out front, and a book for folks to put their names. John Smith. John Doe. John Jones. And the women took the men's coats and their hats and their hands and showed them up to their room, their mattress, their spread and pillow. They'd show them how the curtains slid shut on the rollers, show them how to lock the door, how to lay their shirts and pants, so neat so clean, on the chair backs to keep from wrinkling. They'd show them and then they'd show them—fifteen for an hour, twenty-five for three—anything they'd want to see.

On a good day, the house groaned with customers—a man to every room and to every room a bed and to every bed a girl, sometimes two if your pockets could keep. And in the front hall, and in the kitchen, and in the parlor, you could hear them lowing. Even in the jam cellar, where Robert slept and kept his quiet hours, dark save for the single cast of sunlight on the wall, the dust would roll from the wood slats, shook loose from all their thumping. He watched the motes spangle and gust and fall in drifts, and once, from through the pane, he saw float down a woman's stocking.

Men would come for miles, their hair slicked back and pomade sweet. Miss Lucy would show them in one at a time and they'd smile and sign her big book and open their wallets. And it was Robert who broomed the floors and beat the dust and mopped the stoop. It was Robert who changed the sheets, boiling them with the gowns, the kimonos, the blouses, the dresses and skirts and underthings.

Out in the yard, Robert stocked the pit with firewood and lined it with coals and old newspaper. The sun climbed overhead, baking the late morning. He spoiled six matches trying to get a fire lit, dropping their crooked heads in the grass. His daddy had showed him once, old newspaper lined with hog fat to bait the flames. When a match caught, he cupped it with his hands and brought it careful to the pilings. He moved the tub over the flame and set it on its moorings. When the water started to boil, he cut a brick of soap into three pieces, then stirred it into the tub. After some time, the water started to grease and foam. He dropped the load in and stirred it with a long paddle. After the soap had lathered and the water had worked into a boil, he heaved the tub off its moorings, fished out the clothes, and let them cool on the grass. Then he dumped the remaining water over the coals and went inside.

There was a book of maps in Miss Lucy's parlor, and there in its pages he could see the stretch of the Mississippi River, a jagged blue vein from Minnesota to New Orleans, opening south, spilling into the ocean. And off the blue snaking line lay the postage-stamp-sized borders of Is-saquena County. On the page, it was only inches inland from Bruce, and not the hundred-some-odd miles of ravaged country he'd traveled. With his thumb, he traced the roads to the hatched lines where his home may have been. It was no use. He couldn't match the map to the country in his head, the anonymous roads, the bending land.

In Miss Lucy's book, there was no mark for Crookhand Farm or the twisting mule paths that striated the wilderness, or the dusty straight where he and his brother used to race. Nowhere was the grove of tupe-los, and the heady perfume that, in the summer, would wash out from its depths.

They were gone. There was nothing.

The door creaked, and he dropped the book. The new girl stood in the doorway.

She was beautiful. Smooth tawny skin. Large daring eyes.

You the wash boy?, she asked him.

Her dressing gown wasn't sized near enough for her. Her collar plunged and when she swallowed, Robert could see the cords of her neck tighten. She came into the room, barefoot, and he realized she'd just washed. Her hair was matted down and tied back. The gown was wet and clung to her body in places.

Miss Lucy told me you had my dress.

Robert stared at her. Her voice was sticky and had the dull ring of tin in it.

Well, do you or don't you? That's a very important dress. It was from the king of Spain. What you do with it?

Robert looked around him.

Speak up, now!

I—

You didn't use soap, did you?

That—

The girl let out a groan.

You can't wash my dress like it was just some beat-up pillowcase. Don't they teach you nothing 'round here?

The—

Well, where is it?

In the yard, Robert managed to say.

She groaned again and grabbed his arm. Come on then. Show me.

She near jerked his arm from the socket, dragging him through the halls. The girl was as tall as Robert, her long legs taking the floor in wide strides. Robert found himself stumbling behind to keep pace. He watched her shoulders flex underneath her blouse, the line of her back and neck diving into her gown. He directed her into the kitchen, and they burst out into the yard.

She found her dress laid out on the grass.

Of all places!, she cried.

I wasn't going to just leave it like that . . .

Oh, so the boy can talk can he?

She shook the dress open.

Look at this!

She held it up. There were brown spots all down the front.

Let me see, Robert said.

He took the dress and began rubbing at the blob of rust. It wouldn't come off.

My favorite dress! I swear, you people got your head screwed on wrong!

Robert started to speak, but she snatched the dress from his hands and flung it across the yard. Robert watched after her, her fists tight to her side, stamping back to the house. Robert picked up the dress, looked again at the stain. He touched it gently at the hip. Then the back. He spread the dress neatly and laid it out under the sun. Then he took his rinse bucket to the pump and went on with the day's wash.

After he finished with the wash, Robert did the ironing, watered the garden, swept out the stoop. At lunch, he took a little bread, then went straight to dusting out the parlor. All day the women jawed on about the new girl, Hermalie—how Miss Lucy had put her up in the good room on the top floor, how she gave her a Chinese fan and her Portuguese chest— how Lucy was grooming her. They told stories. She was Miss Lucy's daughter, sent east then come back to run the hotel, that she loved up the governor and now she had to wear her apron high. That she smoked and drank and raised hell, that she was run out of Florida for her deviling, that even the state militia couldn't keep her knees shut.

The whole day, the women would stop outside Miss Lucy's room and put their ear up to the door. Then they'd scuttle off with some new gossip burning a hole in their mouths.

Come full dark, Robert locked up the house, went into the kitchen, then down into the jam cellar. He lay on his cot and pulled his blanket over his head. His ears rang, and with his eyes closed, the room felt like a bell—shimmering, sonorous.

He slept uneasily, waking up in a sweat. His jaw was numb and he realized the smooth black stone was in his mouth. He spit it into his palm and dried it on his pajama leg. Then he roused himself out of bed and lit a candle.

The girl's dress was sitting on his shelf. He took it upstairs into the kitchen and spread it flat on the table. The stain had gotten worse—little brown islands stretched across the middle. He rinsed it again in a basin of cold water, plunging it and replunging it. It didn't do any good. He went into the larder for a lemon, peeled the rind and squeezed the juices over the stain, something he'd seen his mother do, before the flood—before Billy.

He massaged it into the cloth, grinding his knuckles into the fabric. He held it up to the candle. The stain seemed lighter somehow, but he was too tired to be sure. He dunked the dress again, squeezing in another lemon. His hand began to sting and he ignored it, working on, kneading his flesh against the cloth, his fingers bright with pain, on and on into the still-dark morning.

t was Miss Lucy who taught him his letters—how to read and write—and every week he'd send letters all through the state, to courthouses and newspapers and homeless shelters and police stations. He'd write page after page, sending for information on Ellis or Etta Chatham. He remembered that night as his father led him out across the field, Miss Lucy waiting beside the open carriage. She took his hand. Why don't you come riding with me, Robert?, she'd said and it struck him as odd that she knew his name. He turned and already his daddy was starting back across the field, clutching his head, speeding across the dewy grass.

He was not sure when he decided, but at some point he knew that Ellis and Etta were dead. Five years had already passed, and he sprouted like a weed, tall and awkward, while the features of his face smoothed into a serious and sullen mask. When he passed by a mirror, it shocked him sometimes, how much he looked like his brother. The nose was flatter and the mouth a little less wide, but it was there in the eyes and cheeks and the small flare in the nostrils.

In the beginning it had been difficult. Miss Lucy had tried her best to explain—how his daddy thought he'd be better off here, with a roof over his head and a hot meal every day with plenty of people to look after him. For weeks, Robert cried himself to sleep. Miss Lucy would sit beside him stroking his back, and his muscles tensed against this woman's touch. This woman who was not his mother, who was not anyone he had ever seen before.

But with time and work, the hot burning in the pit of his gut passed into a dull throb. He buried himself in the duties of the house—sweeping and cleaning and running errands for Miss Lucy's girls. He came to like Miss Lucy and even some of the other girls at Beau-Miel. He liked seeing them day in and day out, listening to their idle talk and dirty jokes, smoking their fancy cigarettes, chewing their food with their mouths open; the bickering and fussing and making up. It gave a rhythm to the days, the months, the years, smoothing out the rougher edges.

If he let his mind wander, he could almost feel at ease. He would be in Miss Lucy's parlor, nestled in that big red armchair of hers with the fire going, bone tired and head buzzing, and he'd coast along the gray moonless space between wake and sleep. He'd hear Miss Lucy at her desk with her ledger books and her fountain pen, the warm hum in her throat. It was not home but it was something.

It wouldn't take much for this feeling to disappear.

A crass word. The pained and animal hollers of drunken rutting coming from one of the guest rooms. One night, one of the girls had burst into the kitchen screaming. She was clutching her breast, holding the blood in from where she'd been bit. The police were sent for, but the man had already left. That night, after Robert had mopped up the blood and bleached out the sheets, he could not get to sleep. He sat up in his cot, his arms across his chest, trying to keep from trembling.

In the first week that he'd been at Beau-Miel he'd overheard one of the girls call him "abandoned." When Miss Lucy found out, she docked her two weeks' pay, but the damage had been done. He knew the word already, had read it in one of Miss Lucy's books. Now the word stained deep into his meat, its edges ringing in the hollows of his body. *Abandoned.*

Thirteen years old and already broken.

The heat was stifling, and Miss Lucy and the new girl had gone out on the porch to cool. The new girl moved to the railing. She wiped the slick from her neck, sighing into the still air. Standing there, she could seem almost graceful, her long limbs swishing slowly in the heat.

She turned and watched as Miss Lucy rolled back her head, the tips of her two gold teeth peeking over her ripe lip. Bees, fat and honeyed, went drunk through the azaleas. One of them buzzed the flower of Miss Lucy's ear and Miss Lucy swatted it away. The girl leaned over the railing and tried to catch a breeze. There was nothing.

It's too hot for rutting, she said.

Miss Lucy offered her the ice bowl. She pressed a chip against her forehead and let the melt run through her eyebrows, the swell of her cheeks, down onto her neck.

Can't we go over to the creek?

You just keep your eye on the street.

It's too hot. Nobody's going to come out.

Wouldn't be so hot if you stopped your jawing, Hermalie.

The road had been empty all morning. Two blocks over was the end of the Negro quarter and not a soul stirred in the heat. Across the road, a yellow dog had lain itself down under a leak of shade coming off Percy's Pharmacy.

Miss Lucy offered the girl another shard of ice and she tongued it for a moment before spitting a clear lozenge into her palms.

Hermalie! That's disgusting.

My hands are hot.

Throw that away. Where's your manners?

Hermalie hucked the ice across the railing and beaned the yellow bitch on its snout. It snapped up and started barking, straining against the chain around its neck.

Lord, girl!

I just wanted to see what it do.

Eat up your pretty little face. Tear you right to pieces.

Lucy slid her hand across her cheek.

Right there. You understand? I don't want you troubling that animal.

The Widow Percy hollered through the pharmacy screen. Quiet! Shut up out there!

She came out onto the walk in a dingy housecoat. What was left of her hair lay wisped like a question mark.

I told you quiet!

She stamped down her slippered foot, and the dog pushed back its ears and turned toward her.

The Widow Percy looked back at the hotel.

You leave my dog alone now, she cried. You leave her alone, you hear, or God help me I'll set her loose.

Miss Lucy stood up out of her chair.

You go on in, Mrs. Percy. No one is fooling with your dog.

You think I don't know what goes on over there.

We're just sitting, we're not doing nothing.

You ought to be ashamed.

Don't go getting yourself agitated, Mrs. Percy. Just go on in.

The woman patted the dog down its back, mumbled something, then went in. For a moment, the street quieted again. Hermalie picked up another rock of ice and polished it on her neck.

The windows were open in the house and she could hear the other girls upstairs. Someone cleared her throat, and there was the soft snap of cards hitting a table. From the pharmacy, the slow static breath of a wireless twisted into a whine before settling to a signal. The afternoon seemed to stretch out every which way. Hermalie touched her smooth cheek and tried to imagine a line of divots tracing from her ear to her mouth. She shook the idea away. She thought some more about the creek—wading out to where the water rose to her knees, settling down onto her back. When she was younger, she'd cup her hands and bring them down along the flat stones and feel the crayfish tickling her palms.

Miss Lucy, can we please? Just for a few hours?

Hush! Look!

Miss Lucy gestured with her chin. Out on the sidewalk, a tall figure in an olive suit strode down the walk, snapping his legs.

His hands were in his pockets, and his loafers kicked out from under him. He looked up and down the road, crossed over, looked up at the houses, then crossed over again. Then he walked over to Percy's Pharmacy. The dog looked at him and growled. The man stooped slightly and put his hand on the dog's nose. He began rubbing it, then up to the crown of its head, scratching behind its ear. Slowly the dog's head lowered onto the concrete. It rocked onto its back and curled its paws in the air. The man grinned. He bent down and stroked its gray belly. Then he stood, straightened his suit, and went into the pharmacy. The man came out again a few minutes later with a bag of cooking salt. He looked across the street and waved his hat at Miss Lucy and Hermalie.

Miss Lucy squeezed Hermalie's arm.

Well, go on, she hissed. What you waiting on?

Hermalie climbed down from the porch. She cocked her hips and rolled her walk, and the man touched his hat again. Well, hello, he said and she touched his arm and Hermalie said something to him, and the man laughed. She giggled along with him, swishing her head from side to side. Soon, they both came back from across the street, her arm looped underneath his.

This is Miss Lucy, she said. Miss Lucy smiled and held out her hand. The man bent low and kissed it.

You can call me Eli, he said.

At breakfast the next morning Hermalie turned up late to the table and Robert had to bring a folding chair in from the yard. He watched her as she ate, forking up her waffles, pushing a jigsaw piece across the syrup. She liked to cram her food into her cheeks so that they swelled, and when she chewed, she puckered her lips, trying to hold it in.

After everyone had left for church, he went into his room to pack: a jam sandwich wrapped in paper, a brick of soap, and Hermalie's dress crushed down in a gunnysack. On his way to town, he watched the families coming and going in their church clothes, suits pressed sharp, little girls in their pleated skirts. A father came out of the house, and the mother hurried after him. She turned him to face her and undid the knot of his tie, then did it up again.

Robert passed through the Negro quarter, then turned down Calhoun Street, following it to the main stretch and into the town proper. Inside the barbershops, men lined by the mirrors, lifting their chins and patting their fresh necks. Children crowded the candy carts, their small hands tight with pennies. In a side alley, a gang of young boys congregated around a game of dice, hooting and smacking each other's backs.

Robert came at last to the Sunday grocer's. He smoothed down the front of his shirt and went in. The shop was empty save for the grocer himself, asleep behind the counter. His face was red and pocked, and a few strands of gray hair fell down past his cap. His pink mouth was partly open, his tongue clucking softly. His hands twitched as his body rose and fell. Robert touched the bell and the man sat up, startled.

What, what is it!

He yawned and rubbed his leathery face.

Dr. Sloan's Wash Powder, Robert said. He placed a quarter on the counter. The one they got in the newspaper.

Boy, can't you read?

The man pointed to the WHITES ONLY sign in the window.

I just need one box, mister.

You got some nerve, boy. I ain't even supposed to let you in here. Now, why don't you be a good fellow and go on over to the colored grocer. I'm sure he'll sell you some wash powder.

They don't got that kind. I need Dr. Sloan's specific.

Robert pushed the quarter toward him.

See? I got money.

Son, you ain't got coin enough to get me to sell to you.

I see it right there. On that shelf there. If you—

Not for you it ain't. As far as you're concerned, that shelf is empty.

Please, I—

Don't you raise your voice to me, boy! Now when I say I don't sell to coloreds, I don't sell to coloreds. Now scoot out of here before anyone catches you!

Robert's hands were damp with sweat. Something hot was building under his eyes. He put his palm down on the counter and felt for his quarter. His lip trembled. He stood there for a moment, not moving.

What are you doing now?

I need that wash powder, he said.

The man stared at him, astonished. He stood up from his chair and took down the box of wash powder. He slammed it down on the counter.

There. Dr. Sloan's. You happy? Maybe it'll wash the muleheadedness out of you.

Robert blinked. He reached for the box.

Thirty-five cents, the man said.

Robert looked at the box. On the side, he could see where someone had written in dark pencil, 17¢. He placed another dime on the counter and went out.

Robert walked south along the edge of town, toward the river. He could hear it beyond the lawns of sweetgrass and reed beds, rilling over the rocks. The sun was high overhead, and his clothes had started to stick to him. Flies buzzed his eyes and ears and mouth. He swatted but they circled and darted back. Finally, he made it out to the landing beneath Pontotoc Crossing where the river drifted calm, flecked with cottonwood dander.

Robert swung the flour sack from off his shoulder. He stripped off his clothes and ran out beyond the shallows. The river rose up to his hip, then took him completely. He dove down, the sun spangling at the surface. He came up and sucked down the air hungrily, passing his hand through his hair. It was calm, save for the crappie splashing against the river's skin, their ringlets widening toward him. He dove again, toward the river bottom where it was cooler. Something caught the light.

He thought of the grocer and let himself dare that it was a half dollar. At each pass, he tried to kick toward it, but the water brought him up again. He found a hold on a rock shelf, and he let the air bubble out of him. He shot his hand toward the thing, a brown cloud blooming from his fingers.

When he came up again, he brought the fist of mud into the sun. He pressed through it, feeling for the thing. It was small and hard, like a shell or a bead. He rinsed off the mud, and then held the thing up between two fingers. A single gold tooth.

After his swim, Robert found a place to warm himself on the bank. He unpacked the dress and spread it out in front of him. The stains were dark as blood. He soaked the dress and sprinkled Dr. Sloan's over the blotches. Then he worked the small yellow flakes with his fingers, building the lather into a dull head. His hands began to sting. He plunged the dress into the streambed and raked it against the bottom stones. Then up, again, then down, washing the yellow, odored soap downstream. He twisted the dress into a rope and slapped it against the flat stones before he unrolled it and started again.

Robert hadn't river-washed in years, but that old tightness came back into his arms. He squared his shoulders, the muscles lining up, his elbows primed like pistons. Scuttle bugs flitted across the surface of the water, and he felt their wings shy against his ankles.

Dr. Sloan's left a stink in the water like weak tea, but by the second hour, the stain started to give. Robert stretched out the fabric, and the brown runneled over his forearms. He dunked it into the water. The water plopped near him and at first he thought it was a fish but then there came another and another, cracking on the bank. He looked downstream and there were a gang of five white boys, throwing rocks.

Hey!, one of them called out. He ain't got no clothes!

Robert hurried on his trousers, but the boys raced up to the landing before he could light out. They were each of them carrying fishing canes.

You the sumbitch soaping up the crick!, one of them said.

Robert muttered something. He could feel his voice cracking and he covered it with a quick cough. The boys circled around him, fussing through his things. They upended his pack and picked through his food.

Fellas, look at this!

One of the boys poked the dress with the tip of his cane. He lifted it.

Your daddy give this to you? You do something sweet for him?

Before he knew what he had done, a dull sick feeling went up his arm as the boy wheeled backward, gripping his nose. For a moment all was quiet. Then the boys dropped their poles and let out a cry. They piled on top of him, kicking and punching and butting with their broad thick heads. Robert wriggled free. He found his footing and managed to get to the box of wash powder. It flew from his hands in a fine cloud. There was a terrible scream and everyone turned toward the noise. One of the boys stood there, stunned, his eyes clenched tight and rimmed with red, his mouth twisted open.

Oh my God, you blinded him! You blinded him!

His friends tried to dunk his face into the water, but it was too shallow and he ended up beating his forehead against the stones, blubbering with each thrust. Finally, someone managed to spill enough over his face to clear out most of the soap. They picked up the boy and hurried him away.

Robert stood where he was, his chest rising and falling. After they'd gone, he washed his hands in the water. His mind would not settle. He saw the sun on the water. The trees moving. The air moving across his back. His fingers were burning. Robert saw the dress. The stain was hardly noticeable now. The tooth, he realized, was gone. Either stolen or knocked into the water. Somewhere, a church bell was ringing. The afternoon service was being let out. He put on the rest of his clothes and started on his way back.

On the road through Bruce, folks trudged slow in their church clothes. They walked stoop backed with the sun above them. Robert could hear the shop bells twinkling, doors banging lightly against the jambs. The windows were thrown open and the curtains tied back, and he could see inside the shops, and the people inside could see him, Hermalie's dress slung about his shoulder. In one window, it was dark enough to catch his reflection—his face swollen and cut, his trousers speckled with mud. He wondered what part of him looked like his brother. A car honked behind him, then swerved to avoid him. He began to cry.

When he got back to the house, he rushed behind Miss Lucy's azaleas and fell to his knees. He felt the roar of acid in his throat. In one swift spasm it spilled out of him. He lurched again. A door opened and shut. He wiped his eyes and saw the Widow Percy watching him from across the street, her dog steadied in a chain around her fist.

That night Robert slept in fits and starts. When he woke, his head was fuzzed with dreaming. He couldn't remember what he dreamed but it was still there, down in the meat of him, buzzing uneasy. He pulled his covers over his head in spite of the heat and let the sleep take him under again. Sometime after, he awoke to the noise of someone coming into his room. He opened his eyes, and there was Hermalie, framed in the doorway. She was still in her church clothes—a cotton blue dress and white stockings. He hid his face with his spread.

Miss Lucy wants to know where the gooseberry jam is, she said.

He pointed to the shelf by the wall. She picked it up and balanced it in her hand.

You going to lunch with us?

No, he said. He didn't recognize his own voice.

You eat already?

No, he said. Haven't eaten.

She went to the cot and shoved his feet to the side. He could hear the crepe of her skirt rustling as she sat down.

I can bring some food down here and eat with you, she said.

Robert closed his eyes and wished for her to leave.

Why, what's— Oh! What happened to your face!

She peeled back the blanket.

Nothing, he said.

Your eye is all swole up.

She made to touch him but he flinched.

I'm fine, he said. I just want to sleep.

For a moment she didn't move. He waited for her to leave and when she did, he fell back asleep.

When he woke again, the swelling had gone down. He touched his cheek gingerly. It didn't sting as bad as it had, but the skin was still raw. He sat up, staring at the ceiling. There was no light from the window. The room was all dark, save for the small bar of light underneath the door.

His right arm felt cold and strange, and he realized that he'd been lying on it. He lifted the deadweight and set it on his lap. The hand, he noticed, was made into a loose fist. He uncoiled the cold bloodless fingers, rubbing the life back into each of them.

They were coming. There wasn't time. He worked his fingers against each other, every nerve prickling. He swung his legs off the cot and when he stood, a weight fell from his dead hand. It clattered somewhere in the anonymous dark. How long had he been holding it? Dora's stone.

He felt around in the darkness for the dress and found it where he had left it, folded neatly beneath the cot. He packed it. He climbed up the stairs and threw open the door, the sudden light knifing into his eyes. The words were a jumble in his mouth, but he could feel it in his chest, his heart thrumming, its sharp edges cutting into tissue. He was running now, out the kitchen and into the hall. Then up the stairs, two, three, four steps at a time, his whole body vaulting forward. And as he came to the third floor, his eyes refocused, he marched down the long hall, every bedroom door shut, and did not stop till he came to Hermalie's room.

He knocked. Hermalie, he said.

There was no answer.

He started to say it again but stopped.

There was a noise coming from inside. He was barely able to make it out. Quietly, he knelt down to the keyhole, lowering his eyes toward the brass plate. He put his hand on the floor for balance and touched on something gritty. He brought his hand up. Small white grains pressed into the flesh of his palm. He stood up slowly and looked around him, at the ring of salt circling the door.

Augustus Duke drove through the night and into the morning where dawn fire spilled out above the Luxapalila Valley. Through the saplings, he could make out the canal—a shimmering serpent of silver-black water. For days he'd been on the road, hunting throughout the state for the right instrument for his new investment—Eli—and in that time he had not slept, nor had a decent meal. The road had taken a toll physically. His back ached from the hours of driving, and his bowels were packed hard in his gut. A skin of grease lay in a sheen across his face.

And yet still his mind itched with excitement.

He had found him. He had finally found him.

There was a fortune to be made. First, here, in these hick backwaters—then up north, to the Roxy Theater, the Paramount, Carnegie Hall. He imagined the crowds they would draw—the hundred-count bodies going down the block and around the corner. From miles around they'd flock to hear him. Eli Cutter. The Singing Con. The Murdering Musico.

He'd first heard his name in a music hall in Bronzeville in Chicago. Duke was a younger man then, fresh from college. His father, Hiram, a medical doctor, had died the month before. Duke had been feeling depressed and on a whim he wandered in to hear the darkies play. The room was hot and smoke filled, the sticky residue of stale liquor underneath his soles. It was a shock when the band started up—the thrumming noise, the savage howls. He watched the Negroes as they danced, palms smacking, their eyes rolled back into their skulls. Duke sat in his chair, his hands wet with sweat.

Later that night he overheard the performers reminisce about a piano player named Elijah Cutter. They said he was a black jinx, that when you shook his hand, you could feel a bad wind move through you. Chill you to the core.

Cutter was unclean, one of the men said. Kept goofer dust in his shoes and a bag full of devils. It wasn't natural, how good he could play, frenzying from chord to chord, from note to note.

Duke spoke up.

And where is this man now?

The performers looked at him then fell quiet.

Duke stepped out of the hall and wrote the name on the back of a matchbook. After he sold off what was left of his inheritance, he traveled for years up and down the country, the slip of cardboard in his left breast pocket. He went into the dance halls and juke joints, to the corner musicians and the traveling medicine shows, and he'd ask about the mysterious piano player, Eli Cutter.

Some said he'd been killed in a bar fight in Laredo, or that he was working on a shrimp trawler out on the Gulf, or that he had gone mad from syphilis and was locked away in some New Orleans crazy house. He chased these leads across the country, ending where he started—with a head full of tall tales and nowhere closer to finding Eli Cutter.

In the idle hours of the night, exhausted from the road, Duke would lie in bed with a bottle of rye and read through his notes. He had an age. An approximate height. Nothing firm. He would shut his eyes and feel the pressures shifting in his skull. In his mind's eye Elijah Cutter was long and tall with fingers that stretched like spokes on a combine harvester. There was no face, no voice—just a shade without shape or form.

If he was quiet, he could almost hear the music in his blood.

Duke would pull hard from the bottle, feel its heat in his chest and his face. He could fail. He recognized this. Life on the road had not been easy. He'd already spent the bulk of what his father left him on gas and hotel rooms and booze. And with every cent that passed from his purse there was Hiram's ghost throwing reproachful glares. Five years had passed and nothing had come from this fool venture. He might never find Eli.

And even if he did, what then?

On the road, he would turn over their meeting in his mind. The more he thought on it, the less confident he became. He could not quite understand what it was that drew him toward Eli, toward a man he never met, toward a music he'd never heard.

For Duke, Eli was an empty space, a hole that needed filling, and every story Duke had ever heard only helped in widening that hole. Elijah Cutter was a man defined by his own mystery. Everywhere Duke went, he would hear the nonsense accounts of backwater magic and hoo-doo curses. He did not believe in a secret world of rewards and punishments. Only the competition of men's wills.

One day, he drove his car out to a camp meeting. He listened to the preacher give his sermon and at the end of the services, Duke walked out of the tent and into the evening full of disquiet. There was a soup line set up out in the field, and a fight had broken out between two men.

He moved through the mob, pushing his way to the center. He saw the two battered bodies, one on top of the other. One of the men's shirt was off and his lips were flecked with foamy spittle. He was beating the other's head against the ground.

Duke saw the man and he realized what it was he was after. Proof. Evidence that all a man was allotted in this world was what he could steal or scam or hard-bully.

He would carve out his piece of this life, leave a mark that ran harsh and deep and jagged. He would loose this Elijah Cutter out into the world, have him sing and dance and fool. He would be rich, yes, but that was not his main concern.

He wanted what was his.

He learned in time that there was an Elijah P. Cutter doing time in Wayne County. Duke tracked him down to the prison farm, where he found a scarecrow of a man in a secondhand suit. Eli was shy, Duke remembered, as he drove him out into the field. Quiet and unsure of himself.

But he set him down in front of the organ. He watched the man roll up his sleeves and unbutton his jacket. Eli rested his hands against the keys, his body bending forward as if magnetized. Duke heard the roaring chord and all at once, the man had become transformed. He watched the hands move, the sound erupting fast and full and driving.

Duke smiled.

He had done it at last.

DUKE REACHED BENEATH HIS SEAT AND NIPPED FROM THE FLASK. He followed the canal, the engine humming in his ears. The shantytown spread across an acre of raw black earth along the water's banks. He made his way down toward the sheet-iron houses and canvas canopies. The fire pits were still smoldering from the night before, and all through the camp, he could see braids of smoke washing skyward. Duke cut his engine and a group of hoboes swarmed around the car. They crushed against him as he climbed out, tugging on his sleeves and the hem of his coat. They were lice-ridden and filthy and he pushed past their open palms.

When they saw he had no money to give, they dispersed back to their business.

A small black boy was squatting in the dirt, busying himself with digging up the earth with his hands. The boy glanced up and Duke reached into his pocket. The boy's face shifted. Duke made his way over and squatted down beside him. He showed the boy the crumpled bill.

I'm looking for salvage, he said.

The boy pointed down the lane and Duke slipped the dollar into the boy's small dirty hands.

Good boy, he said.

Toward the water, he could hear the nag of pelicans as they hunted along the garbaged shore. Along the shanties, shadows shifted behind the sheets of corrugated iron. They were watching him, nervous and cagey from hunger.

He came to a patchwork of canvas canopies bound and staked into the ground. The salvage man, a filthy-looking Negro, was sitting on his prize, a dirty old settee. The man was old, his hair gone from his head and a grizzled beard knotted into hard mash-flecked kinks. He was smoking a pipe and resting his right foot on top of a soap crate. There were sores on his shins and ankles, and the toes of his left foot had gnarled together into a palsied club.

Behind him were the junk piles, a crumbling structure of pillaged miscellany stolen and trawled from the surrounding country. Taken as a whole, the heap was a junkman's trove—gray and black and rust-colored treasures. Duke let his eyes narrow, saw the individual pieces caught under the weight of the rest. There were jewelry, picture frames, old books and clothes—the strange intimate effects of people he would never know. A woman's comb. A rusty shaving razor. The spiral of a watch chain.

I'm looking for something, Duke said to the man.

That so?

There was disdain in the man's voice. The man eased forward in his seat. From behind one of the piles came two small children—a boy and a girl. They were barefoot and poorly dressed in their sackcloth clothes. The girl was chasing after the boy, swerving around the furniture piles. There was a crash and the noise of crying. The boy had knocked over one of the piles and was now sitting in the dirt whimpering while the girl looked on.

Eunice!, the man barked.

At the sound of his voice, a woman materialized from within the tent. She was tall and slim with small firm breasts and hips that belled out like a tulip. Duke stared at her. Her inky hair lay heaped in a wet mop atop her head. She let her eyes fall on Duke and then to the man.

Yes, Pa?

She spoke slow, calm, watching Duke as he watched her, her large doe eyes opening and closing. A heat rose in his throat. He let his gaze travel across her skin, young, nubile, vital, the sun trapped under the small hairs of her arms, the thin band of dewy sweat on her lip. Duke coughed to hide his excitement.

Control those young'uns, the man said.

Yes, Pa.

She walked off and gathered up the boy.

Is that your family?, Duke asked.

The man leaned forward and narrowed his eyes.

What's your business here, stranger?

Duke told him what he was looking for—a piano or some such instrument. He was ready to pay, he assured the man. The man listened and nodded.

This way, he said.

He hefted himself up, supporting himself on the crook of Duke's elbow. One leg was shorter than the other and he swung it as he walked, rolling out his hips and shoulders. They walked out among the heaps to where the furniture had been freshly salvaged, still stinking from the mud beds it'd been trawled from. From across the lot, he could see the woman Eunice cradling the boy in her arms, whispering into his ear.

The man guided him through the stacks. He was talking, going on and on about the history of each piece, how it'd belonged to someone way far back in his family, but Duke had not been listening. He wished he had brought his flask along with him. His throat was dry and he was finding it hard to concentrate.

They came at last to a large cabinet underneath a canvas sheet. The man pulled off the sheet.

It looked like a piano but smaller, with a skeleton of reeds set across its back. He ran his finger along the edge of the body, tracing the warp of the wood. Duke lifted up the fall board and pressed a key. Sure enough, a note thunked inside the thin wood body. Duke looked at the man and the man shrugged, wiping his nose across the back of his arm. Duke bent down and studied the row of reeds, picking at the small brass teeth along its spokes.

They settled on a price and the man helped him rope the beast across the top of his car. When they finished, he shook the man's hand, and he reached underneath his seat for his flask. You have a cup?, he asked the man. The man went off and returned with a small tin cup. Duke poured the rye and he toasted to the man's health. The man said nothing, swallowing, then returning to his tent. Duke sat in his car, watching him limp up the lane. He tried to catch a glimpse of the woman Eunice, but he did not see her.

As he drove he could feel the new weight—the strain on the axles, the strange friction on his tires. On his way to Bruce, he managed to turn off the wrong road and got himself lost. It took forever to reorient himself. He managed to find the canal again and continued along its straight.

A few miles outside of Bruce, Duke finished off the rye and he pulled off the road. His head was buzzing and a warm feeling came over him. He trudged across to the canal edge and unzipped his trousers. It was evening, and he felt triumphant. The air was cooling and the stars were starting to make their show. His penis was in his hand, raw and sticky. He thought of Eunice. He thought of Eli. The rest came easy.

obert told no one about that afternoon at the creek. He woke every morning with a hole punched through his chest. He could almost feel it, right there, the air escaping across the nickel-shaped opening beneath his collar. He was excitable and jumpy and he could not set his mind to any one task. Loud noises startled him. A knock on the door. A car on the street. Everywhere he went he felt he was being watched. In town, running errands for Miss Lucy. At the grocer's or the dressmaker's or a quick run across the street to Percy's Pharmacy for polish or wax or tablets. That uneasiness followed him inside, into the halls and parlors and guest rooms of the hotel. Even alone in his room, he'd wake up in the middle of the night, his sheets twisted around his legs. He would stare out into the dark, certain that someone was there.

All day and all night there were strange men coming and going from the guest rooms. Sometimes, when he could work up the nerve, he'd sit at the foot of the stairs and watch them as they passed. He'd study their faces and he'd wonder which, if any, had come for him. More than once, Miss Lucy had asked him what was wrong, but he would not tell her. He could not risk her finding out.

So he soldiered on with his weekly duties. On the first of the month, it was his job to go into town with an envelope of money and settle Miss Lucy's accounts. It took hours sometimes. He was of a mind to rise early and get in before the rest of Bruce had even had their morning coffee. But Robert hadn't slept well the night before and he didn't leave the hotel until well into the afternoon. He walked down the lane, along the tall stalks of johnsongrass, his head crowded with buzzing. It was the first cool day in a long time, and the river air swept in from the south and with it, the warm heady musk of linden trees. The light was clean and clear, like after a storm, with the clouds swept off into the shoulders, leaving above him soft blue sky.

He arrived in Bruce and began with his rounds, first to the butcher, then the wigmaker, the dress shop, the locksmith—settling all Miss Lucy's accounts for the previous month. The moonshiner he saved for last. He walked off the main drag toward the small brick building off Pontotoc Road where the air was harsh and chemical.

Robert always disliked visiting the shiner. There'd been a fire last year when one of the stills exploded and the man's face had been burned into a smooth pink plaster. Robert paid the shiner for the previous month, then ordered six more cases of corn whiskey and rye on top of Miss Lucy's usual. After the accident, the man had lost his vision to rotgut and bad jake so Robert counted his money out in singles, guiding the blind man's trembling hands to the stack of bills. They were cold with flesh as smooth and slippery as an oyster. It took time for the man to thumb through each bill, murmuring the tally in his hoarse slow breath. Robert looked out the window. The sun would be setting soon.

ROBERT STARTED DOWN THE ROAD AND IT WASN'T TILL THE DUSK had passed into a deep black pitch that he realized it was not the road he'd come in on. Somewhere, along the way, the paths had forked and forked again, and now he was lost, tucked in the nook of anonymous country, where the tall loping forms of wisteria passed into the sky, and only the deep chatter of crickets marked the time. One foot in front of the other, he told himself. Just like that. All the way home. And at *home* the word caught and broke in his mouth, and he could not fight anymore against the wrenching in his gut. He doubled and he spasmed, and the sick rushed out in acid chokes.

For a moment he wanted nothing more than to be still.

There was the beat of blood in his face, the ragged breath, the whirl of insect wings passing in the dark. He braced himself by his knees. The sweat lay like a sheet on his body. He brought his head up to where he thought the road should be. Beyond he could see light birth out from the rise—a warm red halo that danced and stretched across the width of the road.

Robert straightened. There was drumming. A staccato rumble, and he knew that it came from the marching of horses. That the light was torch fire.

He began to run.

Something whizzed by his face and he sped faster. He heard the stones crashing in the dark—smashing through the hedge, beating into the dark road, spinning off trees. Somehow one of his shoes had slipped off. He could already feel the slick of blood pool around his toes. He bounded down to the bottom of the hill and threw himself into the bushes. Something cut him. The skin above his eye and his cheek throbbed. He tried to still his breath. Their light drew closer. He buried his breath into the dirt, puffing the loose soil from his nostrils. He could smell the sour of piss and it took a moment for him to realize it was his own. He shivered and pressed his mouth harder into the dirt as he waited for the riders to pass.

~

HE WAS EXHAUSTED BY THE TIME HE FOUND HIS WAY BACK TO Beau-Miel. He could barely feel his limbs as he went out back and washed himself down under the hand pump. The water was cold but he scooped it over his face, let it run down his body. The cut on his foot throbbed dully. His mind was blank, empty. There was little it would hold on to. He scrubbed off the bits of dirt and grass that clung around his shins, dried off, and walked naked into the house. Inside the small jam cellar, he lay down on his cot and shut his eyes.

He dreamed of his brother—whole again, alive, without his rope-scarred neck and catgut eyes. They were on a shore together, and up the beach was his daddy and his mama calling out to them. They waved their arms, and when he woke, he felt the word again in his mouth. *Home.*

He got up and put on a fresh pair of trousers and a clean shirt. He stepped out into the empty kitchen. There was no one there. He looked out the window into the backyard and he realized he had slept through most of the day. Lunch had been served and the plates already washed down and put away.

He walked out into the main hall, then up the stairs until he found himself outside Hermalie's room. He knocked twice and when she opened, he pushed past her into the room. She asked him what he wanted.

Nothing, he said.

He went to the window and pulled down on the gutters like a bar, raising himself up, one leg over, then the other. He half expected her to scream, but she didn't.

Once he was over, he stood on the roof, straight and tall like a weathervane. No one would see him. There was a lump in his throat and he felt it catch. He sat down on the sloped shingles and looked out toward the town.

He stayed like that for hours. Come sunset, the dogwoods blazed and the sun set moody below the western hills. Out toward Bruce, rows and rows of gabled roofs held the last of the greasy sunlight. He was alone. No mother. No father. He was alone. At the eastern edge of town, he could see the flamekeepers already starting work, moving from lamp to lamp, their torches like bright pinpricks. He shut his eyes and tried to picture the lamp cases, the gas catching and brightening. His face was warm. And above the lamps, in his mind's eye, there were cables arcing, black and dead, hanging slack from their telegraph poles—untapped, alone. Soon they would go miles, hissing along roadways and cornfields, over riverbanks and rail lines, chasing and chasing, through flat swaths of open country, carrying in their coils heat and light. There! Lines flying over kudzu and magnolia and lantana, over houses and churchyards and markets. Up they go in Mayersville, Jug's Corner, Crookhand Farm, all through the state, wood struts thrust like crucifixes, high above the river swell and levee walls and flood camps—he felt himself shaking, the slick running down his eyes and nose and cheeks—the tract of dirt where he was born, where his brother lay, bone and ash and worms, the cables crossing and recrossing, a giant hex in the sky, bearing down like a net on the souls beneath it, him and his daddy and his mama and his brother, on Dora and Hermalie and Miss Lucy, down and down. He felt himself standing. His lungs were full of fire, heaving for air. Something snapped under him and he felt himself turning backward. Did he mean to jump? He was not sure. The shingles moved under his feet and all at once there was air.

HE CAME TO AND THE PAIN CAME SLOW, SLEEP LIFTING LIKE THE tide going out. It prickled at the edges somewhere under skin and meat. Already Robert forgot his dream—like it'd fallen out of his head, and in that skull-space something was hot and pulsing. Piece by piece, the world returned, first his body, skin and eyes, mouth, hands. Then his name. He opened his eyes, and his brain turned over. He let out a moan and shut his eyes again. He tried to lift the blanket over his face, but his arms were too weak.

How you feeling?

Robert tried to turn but his ribs sent up a flare of pain.

He wanted to ask where he was but already his eyes were adjusting. The mildewed ceiling. A vein of daylight played against the wall. He could hear the curtain fluttering on the other side of the parlor.

I fell. I remember I fell.

The voice laughed.

Robert lifted his head up and he saw the man named Eli sitting on Miss Lucy's desk. He was in his shirtsleeves, the front of his shirt drenched in sweat. Next to him was a pitcher.

The man filled up a glass and brought it to him. He sat down on the arm of the couch.

My arms hurt, Robert said.

All right, the man said.

Robert felt the damp sheet lift off his body. His shirt was gone and his chest was wrapped in gauze. Sitting above his heart was a small flannel pouch. He tried to bring his hand up to it, but it still hurt too much.

What's this?

The man tilted the glass into Robert's mouth. Robert swallowed the cool water.

I want to tell you two stories. Just sit quiet and listen.

Once upon a time, God told the Devil, Devil, you been fooling around this place too long. I'm tired of you going all over Creation, causing trouble, making men drink and tell lies and chase women. So I made you this place, what they call Hell, and that's going to be your place and you do what you want there and leave my stuff alone. And the Devil said, Well, I don't know. Why don't you take me around and we'll have a look. So God took the Devil down to that place, and he showed him where he'd be staying. And it was all dark and full of fire and there wasn't nobody around except the most wicked of folks. But the Devil, he's no fool, he says, That don't look too good to me. I reckon I'll keep doing what I been doing. Then God said, Too bad, and wrassled him down, and he got him by his tail and he says into his ears, There's only one boss around here. This is my show so out you go! And that's how come the Devil come to live where he lives, and God lives where he lives. And they've been splitting souls between them ever since, like playing cards, and there is and ever will be but one boss, forever and ever amen.

Now the other story goes like this. It goes that there ain't no God and there ain't no Devil, just a lot of Bad blowing through this world. Sometimes that Bad will come up on people, find them out like a length of lightning. It fix its eye on you and dog you worse than God or the Devil or just about anybody. It rides around with you, hanging from your neck there, all through your days. It tell you lies to make you mad, or tie up your feet and make you fall. A kind of Bad that don't ever come off. You understand?

Near everybody's got a devil. Some folks got two or three. That one in that bag? That one is yours.

The man was silent for a time.

You don't understand.

No, Robert managed to say. The boy was wheezing. Little beads of sweat had formed on the faint hairs above his lip.

You are bad crossed.

Crossed?

Crossed worse than the blackest jinx. Bad and trouble is set to follow you through this earth, you understand me?

He patted the pouch with two fingers.

And this'll keep you safe.

He produced an Indian head penny from between his fingers.

Open your mouth, he said.

Eli placed the penny on his tongue, and Robert could taste the warm metal. Eli untied the pouch. He widened the opening large enough for Robert to peer down. There was salt in the bottom and what looked like a small walnut.

Spit, he said.

Robert spat out the penny, sending with it a glob of saliva, and Eli cinched up the pouch.

You see this little string here? You put it around your neck like this, and you don't let anyone ever take it away from you. Don't ever take your devil out, because he might not let you put him back in. Don't lose it, don't show it to nobody, and don't you play around with it. This is your devil, see. You're tied to it and it's tied to you. And it don't make too much sense now, but trust me, Robert, you gonna need each other.

After some silence, the man went out the door, closing it gently behind him. Robert closed his eyes again and let his head settle into the pillow. He worked his arms through the pain and brought his hand over the pouch. He ran his thumb along the stitching. He squeezed the soft flannel and felt the contours of its insides rise to his fingers.

During his stay in Bruce, Eli burned his money on drink and women—fifteen for a girl and three for a handle of gin. All night, he barrelhoused at the jukes, scamming cards and doing the Texas Tommy Swing. He came to be a mainstay at the hotel. There were times he'd get drunk and hire out two big-boned girls and have one on each side when it came time to help him up those stairs and into bed. He liked it at Beau-Miel. The sheets were soft and the girls were warm, and when he woke up, two or three in the afternoon with the weight of God stomping on his head, there was always a little cold breakfast set aside for him by the hotel's proprietress.

Miss Lucy was a sexy woman—plump and heavy bosomed with a voice that rang deep and sooty. In her eyes he could still see the traces of her younger self—the rude arrogance sparking in those warm honeyed halos. Eli would lose days in her establishment. He'd drink from her stores of bootleg liquor and watch the world dissolve into a blur of sheets and sweat and grabbing limbs.

There were mornings he'd wake up still submerged in a cloud of whiskey and sex and the day would pass easy like a nail traveling a groove. He was outside of himself, looking down. He could see the strings. He could see the hammers as they struck, every man and woman and child a note waiting to be sounded.

In the evenings he'd go out onto the porch and have a cigarette in the open air.

It was good here. Sitting alone on the stoop, the sun going down. He'd let the ember crawl to his fingers as he watched the light die above the horizon. Some evenings, he'd stay and witness the stars gathering in the wide black sea. He'd look up at their mute light and at times, he'd feel nothing. Just cool air, the sear of smoke in his lungs. He could almost feel free.

A low and lonesome mood would descend upon him and inevitably, his mind would track back through the years to the levee camp, to Homer Teague, and his sister, Emaline. In the past, he would touch these thoughts and his gorge would rise and an all-consuming rage would overtake him. But now he felt nothing. No regret nor longing nor sadness. It was something that had happened and that was all.

How capricious this place, this world. She'd been alive and now she was dead and no flannel pouch could change that. He recognized that at any given moment, the world could turn itself on its head—all could be taken, all could be returned. One moment we are free, and alive and full of blood, and in the next we are cold. Inert. Passing into history.

What were the rules?

He wasn't sure anymore. He could not be certain that he ever knew.

He looked up. A bad moon. An evil wind. Down the road were two headlights slicing apart the dark air.

Soon there would be a reckoning.

uke had not been back to Beau-Miel in years. The hotel stood in his memory as a place of pause and peace—a temple where he could seek respite in between the long months of crossing and recrossing this country. He would arrive on Lucy's porch, his head full of dust and road, the ends of his fingers tingling. Everyone needed something to go back to. A hot meal. A bed for the night. It was like coming home.

His first stay at the hotel, he'd gotten lost somewhere in the maze of roads outside of Bruce. His head was splitting and his memories of his father had sunk him into a low black mood. He remembered the sky that evening, full amber, the air aquiver in the heat. In the burgeoning dusk, the building looked almost violet, its gas lamps all aglow.

He went in and had a drink in the hotel parlor with an attractive black woman. He could not remember what they talked about, only that he felt an ease and comfort he had not felt in a long time. She was in her large red chair and he was on the stool beside her, turning the glass of strong gold liquor in his hands.

Are you staying here?, he'd asked her.

You could say that, she said. I own this place. This is my hotel.

He felt the rush in his blood. She was young and exotic, and she locked her eyes against his. They drank together into the early morning, one glass after another. He could feel himself losing himself. The world spun away from his feet. He hung all his memories of Beau-Miel around this moment. Lucy propping her head on her palms, her eyes looking lazily back at him as if there was nothing left for him to understand.

Here, all things were possible.

IT WAS DARK WHEN DUKE CAME AT LAST TO THE HOTEL. HIS HEAD was thrumming and he was aching for a drink. On the front stoop, he could barely make out the figure of a man. He called out to him, thinking it was Eli, but the man stood up and went inside. Inside, one of Lucy's girls was at the front desk, asleep in her chair. There was no sign of the man.

He rang the bell and the girl startled awake.

Is there an Eli Cutter staying here?, he asked the girl.

She flipped through the registry.

Yes, she said.

And is there a room vacant next to his?

The girl looked in the book and said that there was.

I'll take that one, Duke said.

Duke signed the registry, and the girl came around and took him by the elbow. She walked him down the carpeted hall and up the staircase, her small warm body against his. He swallowed and his throat was dry and clacking and painful. When they came to the room, she stopped at the door. She held his key in her hand.

Was there anything else you wanted?, she asked him. She smiled and he could see the small gap between her teeth.

Duke felt a shiver.

There anything you need?

Her voice trailed off.

He could not help but grin.

Yes, he said. He was aware of his size, towering and bearlike over this creature.

My throat is a little dry.

～

THEY SAT TOGETHER ALONE IN HIS ROOM, HE IN HIS CHAIR AND she on the bed, stripped down to her underwear. He lit a candle and watched her as she poured from a jug into a clay cup. With the cup she crossed the narrow space between the bed and the chair and sat herself across his lap. Her fingers raked against his smooth hairless head. She tipped the cup into her mouth, letting it run out into his.

More, he said. Do that again.

She pincered her knees around his sides and hoisted herself up. She guided his hands up her body. He was surprised at the heat—her volcanic body. He could feel her moving through his clothes.

You want more?

She reached for the jug and tilted back his chin, parting his lips. She poured. It was warm and messy and he gulped hungrily. His throat bucked against the sting, but still she poured.

No more, she said, laughing. You'll get it all over me.

More, he said.

Nuh-uh. Don't you think it's time for something else?

She climbed off and knelt beneath him. He adjusted himself as she slid down his trousers. He could feel her begin to work. His breath was pounding. His breath became short and clipped. He could feel his muscles uncoupling.

Oh my, she purred. Aren't you something?

He could feel her nails raking against his thighs. His skin felt bright and alive. He rolled his eyes back into his head. His head began to swim. He hummed with pleasure.

Do you know who I am?, he whispered. His voice was full of wind.

Mmm . . .

She moved slowly. He felt himself engorging. He clenched.

Do you know the things I can do?

⁓

DUKE WOKE THE NEXT MORNING, HIS THROAT RAW, HIS SKULL THROB-
bing. He sat up. The room was a mess and the girl was gone. The floor
was littered with empty jugs of rye. He swung his legs from the mattress
and hawked a wad of bright red phlegm into a kerchief. He made a half-
hearted noise of disgust and rousted himself out of bed. He struggled out
to the basin and splashed his face with cold water before finally putting
on his clothes.

He went out and knocked on the door of the adjacent room.

There was no answer, only a knot of sheets torn from the mattress
and heaped in a nest on the floor. The air was rank with booze and sex.
On the sill, he noticed candles melted down into stumps and a row of
small unmarked jars. He had heard about Eli's superstitious inclinations
but had yet to have the opportunity to see it firsthand. He crossed into
the room and picked up one of the candles.

It was smooth and slick in his hands. He set it down and wiped his
fingers on his shirt before going back out. He hunted through the halls
and in the kitchen and the parlor until at last he found him outside in the
backyard with Lucy. Duke's head was aching and the bright morning
light was a knife in his already battered brain.

The two were sitting on a splintered picnic bench, talking in low
hushed voices. Eli's eyes were bloodshot and his clothes were crumpled.
It did not appear he had gone to bed the night before. His face had a tell-
tale sheen of grease, and his hair was matted still from where he'd been
wearing his hat.

For a moment, Duke stood at the door and watched her. It was her. He would recognize her anywhere. She had gotten older, certainly, but if anything, her age had made her more desirable—the shock of silver across her temples, her full doughy breasts. She was strong. Powerful. Eli said something and Duke heard her laugh. That same laugh, he remembered. Full mouthed, full bodied—heavy and sticky and golden with sex.

Duke cleared his throat.

'Morning, he said.

He crossed over and they both fell quiet. Duke clapped Eli on the shoulder, perhaps too roughly.

I see you've found the place, all right.

This is Miss Lucy, Eli said, standing.

Yes, we've met before, Duke said.

Lucy cocked her lovely head to the side. A curl of hair swung down in front of her face and she passed it back behind her ear.

Have we?

Some time ago, yes.

Oh! Well, excuse me, she said. A lot of folks come through here.

She held out her hand and Duke was suddenly aware of how sweaty his palms had become. He bent and kissed the back of her supple hand.

Yes, Duke said, I can imagine.

An uncomfortable look passed across the woman's face and he realized he'd been staring at her a little too intensely. Duke averted his gaze.

I hope Mr. Cutter here has not been giving you too much trouble, miss.

Lucy laughed. No, no trouble at all.

Mr. Cutter here is a person under my employ. A musician.

Oh, she said and looked to Eli. He never said anything to me.

I'm sure the old boy is just being humble. I'll have you know that you've been acquainting with a genuine star. You see, he's been waiting for me here these last few weeks, and it seems that we are finally re-united, isn't that right, Eli?

Yes, boss, Eli said. His voice was dumb, flat.

Duke ran his hand across his nose to hide his anger.

I'm impressed, Lucy said. I look forward to hearing him play one day, Mister—

Augustus Duke, he said. He watched her face but if she recognized his name, she did not show it. He bowed to hide his disappointment, then straightened himself, the smile forced hard against his face.

If you would indulge me for a moment, miss, I believe there's something I'd like both of you to see.

He walked them to the front of the house to where he'd left the car. The A-Model was well worn from hard travel. A skin of dust coated the walls, and the wheel wells were caked with mud. Across the top, the cabinet was covered in a canvas sheet and tied down with ropes. Duke could not hide his excitement. He and Eli unstrapped the thing, and together they lowered it down on the ground. Duke worked the slack of the canvas into his palms. With one hard yank, a cloud of dust kicked into the air. Lucy turned her head, covering her eyes and mouth.

There it was. A small organ with large flat pedals at the base and what looked like knobs spaced above two rows of keys.

That some kind of piano?, Lucy asked.

It's called a harmonium, miss, Duke said. It uses air and reeds instead of steel cables. The principles are essentially the same.

Oh, she said.

It looked to have been from before the flood. There was water damage to the body and the valves were still caked with river mud. Eli gingerly lifted up the fall board and a cluster of weevils frightened into the keys.

Duke narrowed his eyes.

Is there a problem, Mr. Cutter?

Eli set the fall board back down and said nothing.

Looks like it has seen better days, Mr. Duke, Lucy said.

Some repairs will have to be made, of course, Duke said. But I'm sure if anyone can do it, me and Eli can. Well, come along, Eli, help me get this thing inside.

Inside? That thing is not going inside my place, Lucy said. I keep a clean establishment, Mr. Duke. You'll have to take it someplace else.

Duke could feel the rush of heat in his cheeks.

Eli cleared his throat. He looked at Lucy, his eyes still and staring, his mouth made into a firm hard line.

Please, he said softly.

Lucy shut her eyes and took a small breath.

You can keep it in the yard, she said. Then she turned around and went inside.

THE HOTEL KEPT ITS LIQUOR IN A SMALL STORAGE ROOM OFF THE second-floor hall. That afternoon he'd seen Eli sneaking out with one of Lucy's girls, their hands all over each other, full of laughs and whispers. Duke hid himself behind a wall and waited for the two to leave. When they were gone, he walked to the door and saw that it was locked. The thought occurred to him to tell Lucy what he had seen—that her precious Eli had been pilfering from the hotel's wares.

In the end he decided against it. He wouldn't want to seem petty.

It did not take long to find the key. It sat on top of the jamb, under a skin of dust. He fit it against the lock and let himself in. He took a jug from off the shelf, then closed the door behind him, replacing the key where he had found it.

That night he did not ask any of the girls to join him in his room. He was far too worked up. Instead he tucked alone into the rye. The liquor was strong and chemical. Every pull came hot and searing. He reeled like a boxer, his eyes filling with water. The world would go alternatingly dim and bright as the corners of the room rearranged themselves. His mind was on fire, and all he could think to do was to throw himself back and forth across the room. He crashed against the furniture and the bed and the wall. In a rage, he hefted the mattress from its frame and flipped it onto the floor. His hand was warm and buzzing. There was blood. He took a kerchief and wrapped it tight against his palm.

All night he passed in and out of consciousness. His words were a slurring of his angry and animal thoughts. Suddenly the idea came to him. It was clear and bright. A sapphire.

He saw the guests gathered in the small downstairs parlor. There, at the front, would be Eli—his hair swept and coiffured, his smile a bright shine of teeth. He saw him, saw him take his place at the bench, his eyes seeking Duke out. And there on the edge of the heat and smoke and stink, he saw himself and Lucy, her eager eyes bent toward the vortex of anxious noise, her hand squeezing tightly against his own. And with a nod or a look, he would loose his creation—the years of hunting and searching—and Eli would fire down on those keys with his perfect hands, and croon out in that perfect voice.

There would be no doubt then.

She would know what Augustus Duke was capable of.

THE NEXT MORNING, HE HURRIED DOWN INTO THE PARLOR. LUCY was at her desk with her ledger book. He explained his idea and she listened patiently. Her face was a mask, her eyes peering out through the small lenses of her glasses. They would split the proceeds, he told her, sixty-forty. She would provide the guests and he would provide the entertainment. He was aware of how he was sounding, manic and deranged, the words tumbling out without reserve. He gripped the edge of the desk, smacking his hands against the top as he spoke.

When at last he had finished, out of breath, Lucy paused and looked at him. He could feel her eyes take him in. In his haste that morning, he had forgotten to tidy himself up. His clothes were wrinkled and out of place.

Have you slept?, she asked.

Duke laughed.

Who has time for sleep? There's too much to do! Do you know what we could get done together, Lucy? You and me?

Lucy thought for a moment. She seemed disquieted but in the end she relented.

How long until that thing of yours is fixed?, she asked.

He leaned across the desk, toward her.

Not long. A few weeks, he assured her.

He offered her his bandaged hand. She took it reluctantly and with that the deal was struck.

⁓

DUKE WORKED FOR WEEKS REPAIRING THE HARMONIUM. ELI WOULD rise in the afternoon to find the man already in the yard, his jacket slung on the bench, his shirtsleeves rolled, sprawled beside the carnage of rotten boards and brass reeds. Day by day, more and more of the monstrosity was stripped down to its parts. He'd sit cross-legged on the grass like a buddha, motes of dust casting through the sunlight. He'd contemplate each piece, picking up a reed pipe and staring through its hollow, blowing across its rims, tracing a pink finger along its length. He would hold up brackets to the light, watch the sun catch on their edges.

Every piece had a purpose. A function. On good days, those functions would streak like a bolt of lightning across his mind and his hands would move hurriedly, fixing various pieces together. But by and large, the process was a struggle. Sometimes he would have headaches and after some hours, his mind would stagger and stall before grinding to a halt.

He would heave a deep breath and shut his eyes, and he would reach for his flask and suck hard and deep and wait for the fog to clear.

Eli was useless to him. He did not know how the pieces fit together any more than Duke did. Duke would make him clean the pieces or else go into town to search for a suitable replacement. More often than not, Eli was tasked with taking Duke's empty flask and having it refilled in Miss Lucy's liquor room.

Duke was alone the evening he finished the repairs. He nailed the panels shut and leaned his foot on each the pedal. A warm and brassy hum sounded through the wood. He looked at it. He had not done a half-bad job. The thing had been fixed by patchwork. What could be salvaged had been cleaned and fixed and what couldn't was replaced. He levered his foot back and pressed again. It was almost human, its noise like a choral breath—he let his hands fall cleanly through the keys and shut his eyes, listening to his box full of souls.

ELI HAD BEEN ASLEEP FOR ONLY A FEW HOURS BEFORE HE WAS awoken by a sharp pain in his chest. He opened his eyes and there was Duke hovering above him. Under the candlelight, he looked red and bloated, the flesh around his eyelids swollen so that the eyes had narrowed into two black beads.

Duke brought the candle closer. He held it at its soft shaft and tilted it down. A glob of hot wax escaped from the base of the wick.

Shush . . .

Eli cringed and Duke clapped his hand over Eli's mouth. He could smell the liquor in his sweat.

I was dreaming of you, Eli, Duke whispered.

How'd you get in here?, Eli mumbled.

Shhh . . . Through the keyhole. Now pay attention. I was dreaming of you. And in this dream, I saved your life. I had saved your life, Mr. Cutter. Eli Cutter. I rescued you and you were indebted to me.

He let another droplet of wax fall. Eli winced.

You were in a dark place and I used my powers to bring you into the light. This is what I dreamed.

He removed his hand, sealing a finger to Eli's lips. He set the candle on the table and brought himself to a mirror. He undid his bow tie and then reknotted it. Then he started smoothing out the ruffles in his suit and combing back his hair with his fingers. When he was satisfied, Duke blew out the candle and staggered out of the room.

For the first few nights after the accident, Robert had run a fever and Miss Lucy cooked him up chicken broth with garlic hearts and hunks of cheese to build his strength. It did no good—his head kept burning. One afternoon, he was found wandering through the front yard, hobbling toward Percy's Pharmacy. Hermalie watched him from the stoop. She called his name and he made no answer. He paused at the curb as Percy's dog appeared from behind the store. Its ears were back and it was growling. Robert kept advancing.

The dog started toward him. She scooped up a rock from Miss Lucy's garden and rushed out across the road. She hucked it hard and caught the dog across the crown. It turned on her, snarling and oozing blood. Hermalie menaced her fist above her head.

The dog raised its hackles and bared its teeth. She turned and saw that Robert had collapsed. She stamped her foot twice and the dog backed slowly away, disappearing beneath the pharmacy.

When it was safe, she sat the boy up and tried to get him out of his daze.

Wake up, Robert, Hermalie said.

She shook him and pinched his cheeks.

Open your eyes.

Robert moaned.

You all right, Hermalie said. Come on now. Let's go inside.

She stood him on his feet, and together, they went back into the house.

⁓

FROM THE CELLAR, HE COULD HEAR THE GOINGS-ON ABOUT THE house. He mapped the footsteps of the guests—the hard clean tap of their leather shoes, the fast patter of heels across the hall, from one room into the next. He lay on his cot, listening as the world drummed above him. He could hear voices through the wood. Joy. Sadness. Longing. Excitement. Anger. He listened and listened, till all the voices stretched above and around like the walls of some deep cave, leaving him, alone, in its center.

For days he waited for the knock on the front door. The groan of the wood as it swung open and the clean tight voices that would ask for him.

But weeks passed and the riders never came. No knock on the door. No stamping of hooves. No torches by night. And still Robert could not get his mind to settle. He startled still at the slightest noise. He could not eat and barely slept. Sometimes the thoughts would run together, one after another, for hours on end. It was exhausting. It left him frayed and tenuous and unable to concentrate.

He shut his eyes.

Hermalie's gait he knew now by heart—her weight against the floor, the quick tattoo of her feet as she ran from point to point. He heard her move through the room, down the hall, then the stairs, then finally to the kitchen outside the cellar door so that when she knocked three times, he knew right away who it would be.

She came in with a tray of juice, hard toast, and eggs and set it roughly on the shelf.

Eat your breakfast, she said.

Not hungry. Thanks.

She glared at him, pursing her lips and sighing sharply.

Robert looked at her.

Well?, she said.

What?

Ain't you going to say nothing about my dress?

She was wearing the yellow dress he'd first seen her in. The stains had lifted, leaving only a pale egg-colored blotch that in the dim light of the cellar was hardly noticeable.

It's the one that got ruined. I decided to put it on for you.

Robert tried to force a smile.

It's nice, he said.

I was thinking about wearing it tomorrow night. Eli's going to play something for us. He's got a piano all set up in the parlor and all the girls are going to go. You want to come?

I don't think I'm up to it, Robert said.

Hermalie shrugged and looked down at her shoes. For a moment no one spoke. Hermalie reached into her pocket and brought out a pack of cards.

Before I forget, I found this in one of the rooms. Figured it'd give you something to do while you're laid up.

He took the pack and laid it on the sheet in front of him.

I don't know any games, he said.

Not any? Didn't no one teach you?

Robert shook his head.

Here, I'll teach you how to play casino. That's easy.

She slid the cards from the pack and boxed them even against her leg. She arched her palm and sent the cards cascading into one another. She dealt out the cards and Robert gingerly lifted up his hand. Hermalie explained how to capture and trail and build. They played a few rounds and she corrected him when he set down a bad card or played out of turn.

You're good at this, Robert said.

She shrugged.

I learned from my sister.

You have a sister?

Oh yes. Five of them. We were six girls, me being the last of them. Daddy used to joke that every girl that popped out of our mama was another patch of hair gone from his head. Figure on my account, Daddy must be smooth as a melon now for sure. Joanna, she's the oldest. She's the one that taught me casino. She taught it to me and so now I'm teaching it to you.

Robert leaned his head back against his pillow, his eyes pointed toward the ceiling, someplace far away. Suddenly he drew in a long breath and dragged his arm across his eyes. Hermalie rested her hand on his leg, the hot rising from the blanket. Robert buried his head into his hands and started to convulse silently.

I'm sorry, Hermalie said. She tried to gather him up into her arms, but he wouldn't let her touch him. Sorry sorry sorry I didn't mean . . .

She wanted to do something for him. What, she didn't know. She lifted up the blanket and touched his bare knee. He didn't seem to mind. Slowly, she drew her fingers against his skin, against the fine loops of his hair, then slowly, her touch journeyed up into the swampy regions inside his thigh. She brushed her fingers against something and his body tightened.

Hermalie looked into his stunned face. She repositioned herself on the bed and stretched her arm farther, where she found him, waiting. It was hot to the touch. She drew it from its sheath and his stomach flexed. She looked at him. Close your eyes, she said and he did, turning his face away. She squeezed him gently, the outer flesh damp and soft, the blood pulsing. She worked slowly, her arm chafing against the rough blanket, the constrictive fabric tightening around her knuckles. She could hear him mumbling to himself, small noises uncoupling in his throat. Finally, the hot erupted, dribbling down her fingers. Everything in him went soft. With his eyes still closed and his face buried in the pillow, she lifted up the blanket and scooped up the strands with the side of her palm, wiping her hands on the fringe of the bedsheet.

The cards lay in a mess on the floor. She bent down and gathered them up, tapping the corners square. She looked at Robert. His face was turned away. She bent down and kissed him on the cheek.

We can play a different game next time, she said.

Okay, he managed to say.

She put the deck back into its pack and set it on the shelf.

As she left, Robert tugged the devil free, hanging it outside his shirt. He held the flannel pouch lightly in his palm; he didn't know if he could hurt it or make it mad if he squeezed too hard. He rubbed his thumb against the puckered mouth where the twine tightened. He was not sure what had happened. He balanced the devil in his hand, heard the salt ring against the coin. She'd touched him. He had made this happen. But rather than lift his dark and oily mood, it had made him feel empty and alone.

He could hear the dog pace anxiously outside Percy's Pharmacy, the chain dragging across the hot concrete. It was no doubt barking at some passerby, but through the walls, it sounded far away and haunting, calling out from the world's end. Robert sat himself up and directed his ear to the window. It started up again, a series of five hacking barks building into a flutelike keen. Robert shut his eyes. Felt a brother to the mad wind.

From his cot, Robert could hear thunder in the distance, the hungry murmur of cloud and sky. Then came rain—*pock, pock, pock*ing— over the roofs and trees and windows. His fever had long since broken, and though he still felt weak, Robert had grown tired of lying in bed, tired of being still. The world was not forever, he told himself. He threw off his sheets and stood himself up. The ground was cold and he felt it through his soles. At first he was uneasy being on his feet, unaccustomed to the weight of his own body. He climbed up the steps and threw open the door.

There was no one in the kitchen. No one in the front room or out in the back. He thought for a moment that the hotel had emptied, that once again he'd been abandoned. Then he remembered that tonight was the night of the show. From the hall, he saw the crowd out on the porch. He ignored them, moving past to the staircase and climbing up to the third floor. He knocked on the door and it gave way under his hand.

Hermalie was sitting at the mirror.

Robert, she said.

He walked across to the window and opened it, letting in cool sweet air. He sat at the sill.

I like you, he said.

I like you too.

She looked at him, her face furrowed.

So why are you so sad?

He looked below into the yard. Something moved through the bushes. At first he thought it was the mutt from across the street, the one that belonged to that Percy woman, but it was sleek and black, almost oily in the way it passed through Miss Lucy's roses. The dog sat down beneath the window and looked up at him.

I don't think there's much time left, he said.

Robert turned. Hermalie had sat down beside him.

He looked at her and felt something collapse. He leaned toward her and they kissed. Her tongue slid inside his mouth. They made their way over to the bed and he laid her down. He suspended himself above her. His hand moved across her small breast and settled on the hard nub between his fingers.

She unbuttoned his trousers and he felt between her legs. Robert, she said. He didn't answer. The blood stood in his chest. He slipped his hands down the soft cotton of her underwear and massaged the dark mound of her hair, then down still to the moist folds between her legs. She made a small noise in her throat. The little devil tapped lightly at his chest. He found the hem of her skirt and lifted it over her head. She hummed lightly and guided his hands down her waist into her warmth. A cold wind blew in from the window, and he could feel her skin prickling.

Above them, thunder rolled, and stitch by stitch, he could feel the sky unravel.

IN THE HOURS BEFORE THE SHOW, DUKE LOCKED HIMSELF IN HIS room and began his final preparations. He laid his suit out on the bed, then went to the shaving mirror. He passed a razor through the errant hairs of his chin and cheeks, scraping along the soft supple flesh until the skin filled with an itchy bloom. His nails he filed down into perfect half-moons.

He let himself have a nip from his flask to even out his nerves, then proceeded to dress himself. He put on his shirt and his pants and his jacket, and with his large thick hands, he worked out the knot of his violet bow tie. He reached into his breast pocket and found the small silver ring, his father's. He took another pull from his flask. He heard a knocking. He opened the door and on the other side was one of Miss Lucy's girls.

Elijah Cutter?

Duke narrowed his eyes.

No, he said. Wrong room.

Oh, the girl said. Sorry about that.

Wait, he said.

He noticed the case of liquor behind her and the envelope in her hand.

What do you have there?

It's from Miss Lucy, sir. She wanted it sent up to Mr. Cutter.

Mr. Cutter is resting before the performance tonight, he said. You may leave these things with me.

The girl shrugged. She handed him the envelope and brought the case into the bedroom. When she left, Duke tore open the envelope and read Lucy's note. *Best of luck tonight.* He felt suddenly weak. He reached for his flask, having forgotten that he had already emptied it. In a rage, he launched it across the room.

He tore the ribbon from the case of liquor. He uncorked a jug with his teeth and emptied it in one manic pull down his throat.

He found Lucy downstairs with who else but Eli in the parlor. They were alone in the empty room, a row of chairs already arranged to face the harmonium as per his suggestion. They were at the bench, their bodies side by side. Eli moved his hands over hers, guiding her hands above the keys.

It's gorgeous, he heard her say.

This, madam, is just a box, Duke found himself saying, startling them. They turned quickly on the bench. Duke strode confidently across the room, his unlit cigar pinched between his thumb and index finger.

What is truly gorgeous is the smooth and thrilling mind that sits before it.

Duke clapped Eli hard on the shoulder.

Without this magnificent man, the box is mute, incoherent, worthless—knowing no grace, nor beauty, nor soul.

Duke dug his fingers hard into the flesh. Eli winced but held his tongue.

Oh . . . yes, Lucy said, unnerved. Of course.

I was hoping to speak with you, Duke said. He struck a match on the back of his thumb and lit his cigar. Privately, if you don't mind, miss.

Very well, she said.

Duke grinned. He bowed and swept his arms to the side.

After you.

She stood up from the bench. Then she bent and kissed Eli on the cheek.

For luck, she said. A look flickered across Duke's face and he made a show of puffing on his cigar.

Duke led Lucy back into his room. The shades were down and the afternoon sun spread across the room in bars of amber light. He shut the door and slung off his jacket. Already his shirt was soaked, dark gray halos blooming underneath his arms and neck.

Can I pour you something?

He gestured to the case of liquor on the floor by the bed and watched her, trying to read her face.

No, thank you, Lucy said.

He hunted for his flask. He went around the room, violently jostling the furniture. Finally, he found it hidden between the wall and the dresser. He smiled at it, clucking his tongue, and uncapped it. He uncorked another jug and began to pour messily into the spout.

Mr. Duke, I believe you've asked me here for a reason.

He took a deep tug, then wiped his lips on his sleeve.

Matter of fact, I did, he said. He fought down a belch and sat down on the edge of the bed. He motioned for Lucy to sit next to him but she remained standing.

I've thought it over, he said, and I've decided that I am unhappy with our current arrangement.

He kept watching Lucy's face.

After all, it is *my* man, *my* instrument, *my* show. This very night I can go out on the road and earn twice what I'll take in here.

You're joking, Lucy said.

I can part with thirty percent. Thirty percent, you'll agree, is an act of generosity.

Lucy rolled her eyes and folded her arms.

I'm not running a dance hall, Mr. Duke. People don't come here to listen to music. Time they spend with your box is time they're not upstairs with my girls. So you tell me, who's taking the real loss? Sixty-forty as agreed.

Duke nodded slowly. They could hear the music coming from downstairs. It was both eerie and soulful, coming up through the floorboards, charging the air. Eli must have started practicing. Duke looked at Lucy, her face turned toward the door, her look faraway.

That old boy can play, can't he?

Yes, Lucy said. She closed her eyes. Yes, he can certainly do that.

He was in prison when I found him. Doing fifteen years for killing a girl. Did you know that?

I didn't, Lucy said. Why are you telling me this?

Duke set the flask down on the bed. The two soft orbs inside his skull peered out at her, red and glassy, the right lid twitching.

All right. As you say. Sixty-forty. What can I say, you've called my bluff.

Duke stood up from the bed and shrugged deeply.

I'm sure there's another way for us to settle this. After all, he said, you are a beautiful woman. And I am a man.

He was surprisingly fast, given his bulk. Before Lucy could react, he had grabbed her and pinned her body against the door. She struggled against him and he forced his tongue into her mouth and tasted the rush of iron.

She pushed him away.

Mr. Duke! What's the matter with you!

She sneered, wiping her mouth.

He could not help but laugh. His tongue was bright and stinging.

Come on, Lucy. Just a little luck for tonight?

Lucy spat. Her jaws tensed.

You will not speak like that to me, she said.

Oh, does the whore have pretenses?

Duke came at her again. There was a flash of dull light and Duke seized her wrist, twisting it until the stiletto dropped from her grip. She let out a cry and raked her hand across his face. The shock sent Duke stumbling backward. There was a crash, and then a thud as he tripped on the empty jug. A horrible sucking noise escaped from his chest. He rolled over onto his knees and started hacking for air.

Lucy readjusted her clothes.

Don't you forget yourself, Mr. Duke.

She bent down and picked up her knife. Fifty-fifty. If that don't suit you, you can find your own way out.

Duke gripped his face. His hands were shaking.

He called out after her.

So that's your choice, is it?

She ignored him and walked out to the hall.

~

BEFORE SHOWTIME, ELI DREW HIMSELF A BATH AND SCRUBBED HIS body down. When he'd finished, he went to the mirror, swept back his hair with a fine-tooth comb. He put on the cleanest shirt he could find and took an early supper of chitlins and rice alone in his room. All around him, the house was humming. He could hear the girls, running back and forth, stealing each other's makeup and powdering up their parts.

When it was time, he went downstairs to find the parlor had already filled up. They made way for him as he entered.

He passed by Lucy, who had staked a position near the door. She looked distracted. He winked at her, hoping to get her attention, but her arms were folded and if she saw him, she did not show it.

Duke was waiting by the harmonium. He did not look well. There was a series of gashes across his face, and his skin had turned an angry plum. He puckered at his cigar. Eli took his place at the bench and Duke leaned into his ear.

You're late, he said.

Sorry, boss.

Never mind that. Just get ready.

Duke cleared his throat and rapped twice on the wood top.

Ladies and gentlemen, your attention please.

Duke scooped off his hat.

My name is Augustus Duke. Thank you for joining us for this evening's entertainment. Before we begin, perhaps a small token to show your appreciation of God's work on this earth.

He handed his hat to one of the guests.

Don't be shy. Just a coin or two to wind up our precious music box.

When the hat came back around, Duke bowed deeply before the crowd and shoved the money into his pockets.

Ladies and gentlemen, the man who sits before you tonight is an interesting specimen—a native to your parts. He has walked amongst you, eaten what you have eaten. Drunken what you have drunk. And yet, who of you truly knows Eli Cutter? Oh, his is a long and varied story, and I have traveled far and wide to make record of it.

Who would guess that this gentle, simple man, is—point of fact—a beast among lambs! He stands here before you accused of idolatry and devil worship! A murderer and rapist of children!

Duke turned to Eli.

Mr. Cutter, are there laws yet, either of man or of God, that you have not broken? Ah! And here you are, gifted with a talent of such grace, of such stupefying beauty—it boggles the mind.

But enough of that—I believe I have done you justice. If you would, pleasure us with one of your tunes.

Eli gaped at Duke.

We . . . we didn't talk about . . . I'm not sure—

Duke hissed at him.

You do what you're told, Eli. The rest you leave to me.

He looked out into the crowd. The guests seemed unsure of themselves. They murmured nervously to one another.

Now, Mr. Cutter. A song.

Eli started playing "My Creole Sue." It was slow and pretty, but he was only a few bars in before Duke cuffed him hard across the neck.

No, goddamn it. None of that.

He leaned in close and held the burning tip of his cigar above Eli's knuckles.

You'll play what I goddamn tell you.

Duke smoothed out the front of his shirt. He cleared his throat and smiled at the crowd.

As I was saying, Mr. Cutter is going to play us a blues.

Eli looked out at the room.

Go on, Duke said.

Nervous laughter rippled across the room.

Eli adjusted himself on his seat and he took a deep breath. The air stretched out in his lungs and pressed against the ache. The keys started to blur. Eli shut his eyes. He stretched out his fingers and tensed the cords of his neck and hands. From behind, he looked like a buzzard, arms spanned wide and high above his shoulders, his head bent forward. For a moment he hung, coasting along some invisible thermal. Then *Boom!* He beat against the keys. *Boom!*

Eli threw his head back, and the hands surged down again. *Boom! Boom!*

He stood up and punched hard at the notes. The box hummed beneath his fingers. He could feel the audience behind him, their hearts rattling in their throats, the piss swelling in their groins. They wanted a blues. So he let them have it. *Boom. Boom.* Like a hammer at their skulls. *Boom. Boom. Boom.*

He opened his mouth and powered violently through the noise.

My baby's gone, my baby's gone.

DUKE SNUCK OUT OF THE PARLOR AND MADE HIS WAY TO THE SUPPLY room. The key was missing so he forced the door open, tearing the bolt from the jamb. It seemed the stores had been replenished for the evening's performances. There were jugs upon jugs laid out before him and he gathered what he could into his arms. He uncorked one with his teeth and began there first, spilling the contents in long chemical trails. Then he went out into the hallway and, traveling up and down its length, drenched the curtains and the furniture. When he'd emptied one jug, he returned to the supply room for another and started again, staggering from room to room.

The gall of that whore, Duke fumed. And after he had laid so bare his feelings! His face was burning. She had played upon his weaknesses. Duke laughed sadly at how he had allowed himself to be fooled. Schemes and lies were a part of Lucy's trade and she'd had years to hone her craft. She'd made this place a trap for men.

He felt the liquor spill through his fingers.

He would've shared his life with her. He would've offered her greatness. He heaved a sigh.

Now, instead, he would have to teach her humility.

He ended his trail at the kitchen, spilling out the final jug on the tiles and mopping it with his shoes. He took the matchbook with Eli's name from his breast pocket and lit the cover. The Negro's name burned quickly in a fang of heat and light. He bent the cardboard down toward the greasy pool. All at once his arm erupted in a hot white sleeve, spreading across his shirt. Duke dashed out into the rain and smashed his burning body against the grass.

The fire spilled in eager sheets across the floor, up the stairs. Bright liquid white, massing and suffusing through the wood. Piece by piece, the hotel would come apart. The glass would burst and the pipes would buckle. Smoke and flame would suck down into the air-filled rooms.

But now in Hermalie's room, Robert lay in the cool dark. Hermalie's head rested on his chest, and he moved his hand gently across her crown. Between his legs he was sore and throbbing. His heart pulsed strong and small inside his chest, electric with some unnamed anticipation.

He held the pouch absently between his fingers.

I did this, he found himself saying.

Yes, you did, Hermalie said.

She drew a shape above his breast.

I like it here, she said.

He put his arm around her, placing his warm hand on her bare shoulder.

He liked it too, he thought but would not tell her, suspicious that his words would somehow break this spell.

She burrowed into his side.

Don't you love when it rains? Makes me think of home.

He did not say anything.

For the time being, he did not see the flames spike and stretch outside her door. Soon the house would fill with smoke and screaming. The eaves would crash, puffing cinders into the rain-filled night. And Lucy and her guests would stand under the storm to watch the smoke rear through the wood-bone frame, oozing through the bursting windows.

But here, in this moment, he could still feel the life inside Hermalie. The blood moving warm beneath her skin, into her bird heart. Breath filling then emptying.

Do you hear that?, he asked.

And she moved her head slightly. Hear what?

Robert sat himself up, leaned toward the strange pull in the air.

And behind the crunch and pop of cracking timber, the druggist's wife would stand on her stoop and laugh and hoot and smash her palms, and her dog would howl and drag its chain—as the whorehouse of Bruce was damned to ash.

But he sat up now, and he listened. There it was, inside the walls. Somewhere someone was singing—my baby's gone, my baby's gone.

PART THREE
SALVAGE

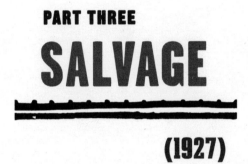

(1927)

During those first days when the water was up to the roof, Uncle Reb slept on his deering rifle to keep the wet from the powder. He wrapped it up in our only quilt while me and Nan Peoria shivered and cried, bedded down with nothing but dew and prayer and flood spray. He told Nan Peoria, This here rifle is keeping us from the mercy of God. Then he sighted a bird far upstream and dropped it from the sky. When it floated down to our eaves, there was hardly any meat on it at all.

About a week in, Nan Peoria got the pneumonia and when she died, Uncle Reb just rolled her off her spot, didn't say no good words or nothing, and that's how come I remember what he said about that rifle. She rolled away kind of stiff, then the current took her, and that was all there was to Nan Peoria.

After Nan died, I huddled up with Uncle Reb at night, which was all right because he had that quilt, excepting that that old rifle was lumpy and sticking at me in places, and some nights Uncle Reb would press into me and whisper Dora, Dora, and when morning come, he'd tell me it was just my fool dreaming.

THE FIRST MORNING I'D SEEN THE BOAT, THE FOG WAS STILL HIGH. Something was out in the water, sliding slow toward the eaves of the Waller farm. I shook at Uncle Reb but he swatted me away. There was a low thump, and that's when I knew it was a boat hitting up against drift-wood. I heard a man's voice. He was singing.

Uncle Reb, I whispered. Wake up. There's somebody out there.

He wouldn't rise till I pinched him. He stood up and flung the quilt off his rifle. He leaned it toward where I was pointing, swinging the mouth of the thing left and right. The water steamed a little, and a breeze swirled the fog around. There was nothing.

God almighty, he groaned.

We should've said Amen Jesus. We should've said good words over her.

Uncle Reb stretched up, scratched himself with one hand, then went to the edge of the roof to make water. Turn your head, he told me. When it was okay to look, there were bubbles already running downstream. He knelt down and checked the waterline.

Dropped an inch overnight, he said.

There was something, I told him. It was here then it was gone. I heard singing.

Go back to sleep, he said. Then he spit over the side and stretched out on the quilt. He wrapped the gun up and draped his arm over the stock. Then like nothing, he started snoring.

⁓

THERE WASN'T MUCH TO DO DURING THE DAY EXCEPT BE HUNGRY and be sad. We hadn't saved much—just some clothes, Nan Peoria's Bible, and my Sally doll, which Uncle Reb threw into the water and ru-ined on account of his having a temper. What food we had, we couldn't mete out more than a week. So I read Nan Peoria's Bible and I pretended it was Bible times and we was on what they call an ark, and every bird I seen I pretended they was doves till Uncle Reb sighted one up and felled her. And so I didn't play Bible after that.

SOMETIMES, WHEN UNCLE REB WENT OUT ON ONE OF HIS SWIMS, I'd put my ear up against the roof tiles, and the house would shift and mumble and groan on like some big belly. I tried to imagine maybe there was fish in there, swimming around my things, little silver ones flapping, going in and out of the cabinets with those tiny yellow eyes, always looking at everything but never got nothing to say. And I thought maybe when the water went down, Nan Peoria could fry them up with a skillet, and Uncle Reb would eat the heads like he showed me one time, eyes and brains and everything.

I ASKED UNCLE REB WHAT HAPPENED TO NAN PEORIA AND UNCLE Reb said she died.

And I said how come she died.

And he said because the pneumonia got her.

And I said well, where the pneumonia getting her to?

And Uncle Reb laughed and said, Down the Gulf of Mexico.

But that ain't what Nan told me.

SOMETIMES WHEN I GET MY DREAMS, NAN PEORIA IS PUTTING HER hands on my shoulder. They're warm and I can smell that sweet oil she wears before she goes to bed. And I try to turn over and get a look but only she don't let me. She says to me, You can't wake up yet.

IT WAS EVENING THE SECOND TIME I HEARD THE BOAT. WE'D BOTH of us heard it, moving across the water, a man's voice humming. Uncle

Reb was already up. A mist rolled thickly across the water plain. He stared out toward the neighbor's house, his rifle against his leg, his fingers kind of loose in his grip, like it was a hand he was holding. Flies buzzed all around his ears and his eyes, but he didn't swat them. He was just watching.

There were rings in the water widening out toward us, and I could hear the spilling coming off a pair of oars. It slapped soft, and bumped the boat and spilled again, moving closer and closer. Uncle Reb put the rifle up against his shoulder.

Ho there, he called out.

His shoulder jumped and there was smoke.

Ho, he said again.

Whoa, a voice answered.

Who's that?

The man drifted out from the mist, his hands up so his long coat came down almost like a pair of wings.

Easy, brother. I bring peace.

The man turned a little sideways, and there were little canvas bundles on the other end of the boat.

You come on easy there, Captain, Uncle Reb said with his rifle still up. That your salvage?

It's salvation, brother.

Uncle Reb let the rifle down an inch so he could look over the man's goods.

Bring it over here, Uncle Reb said.

The man paddled over till the boat bumped up against our roof. Uncle Reb put one foot down on the boat floor, anchoring it.

All right now, I'm the one with this here rifle. Just you remember that.

From your mouth to God's ear, the man said.

Now get on over to that far end there.

The man moved to the back of the boat, his arms still raised. Uncle Reb went on board, aiming his rifle to the man's chest. Balancing the gun with one arm, Uncle Reb started untying the bundles with one hand and emptying them on the boat floor. There were cans mostly, but also some bread and what was maybe jugs of clean water. The man looked at me and winked.

When Uncle Reb was bent down low, reaching one arm deep into a gunnysack, the man kicked the side of the hull, rocking it. Uncle Reb near fell over excepting that he put one hand down on the boat edge. And quick as anything, there was a pistol in Uncle Reb's face.

The man said, Easy, brother, easy.

The rifle passed out of Uncle Reb's hand and lay flat on the boat floor. Uncle Reb righted himself.

The man said, Now let say you invite me aboard your lovely home.

He moored to our roof with a length of rope, and when he crossed, he bowed deep and said his name was Pat Stuckey. He went through our things, but there wasn't much to begin with. Uncle Reb's box of shells and a tin of rolling tobacco. He flipped through Nan Peoria's Bible, holding the cover open and rattling the pages. Uncle Reb sat down beside me, his arms crossed over his knees, not looking at neither Stuckey nor me.

Roll it, he said to Uncle Reb, handing him the tobacco.

Paper?

Use the book.

Uncle Reb tore a page cleanly from Nan's Bible and started to roll. I bit my tongue.

Stuckey took a match from his breast pocket and lit the hand-rolled. He drew on it, then passed it over to Uncle Reb.

What're you going to do with us?, Uncle Reb said.

They sat together cross-legged on the quilt.

Haven't puzzled that out yet.

Come sundown, it didn't look like Stuckey was going to quit us. He took a coffee can from inside his jacket and set it down on our quilt. He matted the bottom with a fist of dry peat. Then he took Nan Peoria's Bible and started tearing up pages, crushing them down into the can bottom.

You can't do that, I said.

Uncle Reb hushed me.

Now how do you figure on that, miss?

You can't use those. Those are the Good Words.

Uncle Reb ripped up a few more pages, then took a match to them. Stuckey took a small gunnysack from his boat and drew up two skinned rabbits. He cut a slice with his knife, then laid a strip out on the flat of the blade.

He held the flat over the can.

Meat commendeth us not to God. For neither, if we eat, are we the better; neither are we the worse.

The can smoked and a tongue of flame licked up and out toward the blade. The fat started dripping down the edge. We hadn't eaten in days except maybe the heel of some stale bread. I couldn't remember the last time I had meat. It sizzled on the knife blade, sweetening the air. Something pinched at my stomach. Uncle Reb stared at it, his eyes wide, his mouth pooling up with his spit.

When it was all cooked up, Stuckey held the knife out to me.

Careful, it's hot, he said.

No, thank you, I said.

Stuckey smiled. He held the blade to Uncle Reb. Uncle Reb didn't waste no time; he plucked up the meat and put it in his mouth. It steamed out of his mouth, it was so hot. He sucked his fingers and his eyes watered and Stuckey laughed. Stuckey cut up another strip and started cooking, and Uncle Reb and Stuckey went on like that all night, feeding my uncle on little bits of rabbit, so's that my stomach was fussing me all night and come morning, there wasn't nothing left but a pile of bones and two little rabbit heads.

⁓

NAN SAID, WAKE UP, AND I DID.

Then Uncle Reb said, How much?

And Stuckey said, How much for what?

You take a man's livelihood, you're taking the whole man.

I pretended I was still asleep. There was a long quiet, just the water babbling all around, and there was a hawk screaming about something. The dew was cold on my skin.

Then Uncle Reb said, The girl. How much you give for the girl?

And that's how Uncle Reb got his rifle back.

⁓

STUCKEY ROWED I DON'T KNOW FOR HOW LONG, OVER PLACES HE told me what used to be Hollandale and Rolling Fork and Silver City. There wasn't nothing left but a sheet of water. Little crosses stuck out where the churches were, and little roof islands, empty except for maybe a blanket here or bits of straw there. There was something under the water by the penny cinema in Silver City, all cloudy and covered in what looked like little yellow hairs, I couldn't make out what.

Where are we going? I asked.

Your new home.

We went on and on, till there wasn't no town at all, no houses or building or nothing—just bits of treetop sticking out with the leaves all stripped. By dusk, we were drifting toward a forest of blackgum. Weeds and roots scraped the boat bottom as we came into the shallows. We found ourselves in a great swamp. The gums came up like bars over the mossy water. Stuckey brought the oars in and steered us through by hand, managing us forward through the marsh grass.

There were bits of mirror nailed to the trees.

What're those for?

Keeps away the ghosts, he said. Ghosts don't like mirrors. Can't stand the sight of them.

And I didn't say anything more after that.

We stopped where the ground was soft and flooded. Up above, branches blocked out the sky. The air was hot and still. Nothing moved. Stuckey dragged the boat up a mud bank and tied it off.

Rest of the way we go by foot, he said.

The water came up to my ankles. Stuckey made me carry one of the smaller satchels and he shouldered up the rest.

Don't dawdle, he said. We don't want to get stuck here come nightfall.

He marched ahead. The long tail of his coat floated behind him as he pushed across the swamp, a cloud of mud rising around his boots.

We'd gone some time before it began to darken. My toes were numb in the water. There was screaming coming from the trees. We looked up and saw a line of crows flying away from where we were heading. Stuckey started singing: Old black crow, old black crow, did the farmer pluck where your feathers don't grow.

The cabin was set out on a small clearing, the earth pocked from where the trees used to be. The boards looked blue-black and rotted. Stuckey took me around back where I could make water. He turned his back as I crouched out in the grass, next to a small pump, staring out into the woods. There was a small path that led out behind the scrub to what looked like a henhouse. He waited for me to finish, then he took me into the cabin.

Inside, the junk had come together into piles with only a narrow strip of floor to move around on. There were chairs stacked on top of chairs. An old bureau had been stripped of its doors and heaped up with brass pots, sketches, bundles of old newspapers.

Stuckey set his bag down by the door and made his way to the stove. He lit it, then he picked up an old steel poker with a little hooked head and pushed around the coals, sending up a breath of sparks.

Come here, he said.

I didn't move.

Don't make me come to you.

When I wouldn't move, he grabbed me and yanked me toward him.

He thrashed the poker into the embers and little sparks licked out of the stove. When he took the poker out, the head was all red. He took my leg with his hand and twisted it toward him.

I shut my eyes.

There was the smell of something burning. After a minute, he let go of my leg.

When I opened my eyes, little fat leeches were squirming on the floor.

He put the poker back in its place. He stamped on their fat bodies.

We're going to have to get you some proper boots, he said.

STUCKEY PUT ME UP IN A CRAMPED ROOM WITH A MATTRESS AND A little bureau pushed against the wall. He changed me out of my clothes and gave me a cotton dress that itched all over and didn't fit right in parts. He looked me up and down, made me turn for him, and he clicked his teeth and pinched the scrub of hair on his chin.

Pretty as the morning, he said.

He looked me up and down a little bit, then without a word, he left room.

The window was boarded up, but there was space enough between the boards to see through to the outside. On top of the bureau, there were cane poles and little fishhooks. After a while, Stuckey came in again with a plate of biscuits and some cold beans.

Eat and then go to bed, he said. We'll talk tomorrow.

When he closed the door, I heard it lock behind him.

I ate up the beans and scooped up all the juice with the biscuits. I filled up my mouth faster than I could chew, pushing the food through with my fingers. When I was through, I had licked the plate clean and my stomach was starting to feel a little funny. I left the plate on the floor and tried to sleep.

Before the flood, there was only one bed and it was Uncle Reb's—a beat-up old thing he traded a Guernsey heifer for. It was all cut up and the stuffing was coming out but Uncle Reb got in a terrible fit if anyone went near it. Me and Nan Peoria had to sleep down on a pallet of crushed hay and dry grass. At night, I could hear it crackle softly under me, and come morning, there'd be little bites all up and down my arm.

Here, there was a mattress and it was strange the way the bed went up against my shoulders and my back. It pressed at you the way nothing else did, rising up to fill the spaces you couldn't fill yourself. I turned and beat on it for a while, but there wasn't any way I could get any sleep. Instead, I pulled the sheets down into a pile at the foot of the bureau and curled up against it.

I slept I don't know how long. The room was all dark and I couldn't see nothing. There was somebody in there with me.

Nan Peoria put her hand across my mouth.

Don't breathe, she said.

It took a while for my eyes to get used to the dark. There was a man standing at the foot of the bed. His head was rolled back toward the ceiling.

Don't wake up, she said.

She said, Do you believe in God?

My mouth was stuffed up with cotton.

Do you believe in the Devil?

COME MORNING, THE LIGHT WASN'T MORE THAN A TRICKLE THROUGH the boards. There were little motes of dust casting through the air. I rubbed the stiff out of my sides and looked around before I remembered where I was. The door was open and someone had taken out my tray, swapping it for a pair of cotton slippers.

Out in the kitchen, Stuckey was at the stove, turning over a pot of oatmeal. He looked at me and pointed over to the table with his chin.

You slept on the floor last night, he said.

I'm not used to beds, I said.

You'll learn.

He served up the oats in two bowls. They weren't boiled up all the way, and there were little mealworms floating in the milk. I picked them off and ate around it.

After this, all the meals, you cook. You know how to cook, don't you?

I told him I did.

Finish eating and I'll show you what needs doing.

After breakfast, he took me around to the back and showed me how to pump for water, how to split the firewood. He showed me the chicken coop all twisted up with wire and straw, not far from the cabin. Then he took me inside, showed what needed wiping down. The stove had to be swept out and the floors needed scrubbing. There was the laundry and the dusting and the mending. He showed me his socks that needed darning and the holes in his oilskin coat worn through at the elbows. He talked me through the piles and piles of junk. What to touch. What not to touch.

When he was done, he stooped down and put his face into mine. His eyes were lowered till there was barely any white showing. His face hung there, waiting on something. When nothing happened, he stood up and took his long coat off the hook.

Swamps are full of gators, he said.

He pulled on the sleeves, then checked the chamber of his pistol.

I'll be back by nightfall, he said.

IT WAS LITTLE THINGS. THINGS I FOUND CLEANING. A CUT OF CLOTH from the bedspread. A piece of shell out in front of the porch, who knows from where. I took little bits of hay and I tied them together with horsehair. There was a big black button I swept up from under the dresser. It had two little holes in it and was shaped like a little fish.

One time I found a bird skull, sweeping out the stove. It wasn't no bigger than a lump of coal, eyes filled up with soot. I dusted it off, then ran it out under the pump. The bone was gray and scorched, and the water made the ash muddy. It took a while to clean with me scrubbing it with just my fingers, blowing into the eyes and hearing my breath whistle back through its shell of a head. I kept that too, all tied up and neat, under the bureau.

They were mine. They were no one else's.

I WAS BEHIND THE HOUSE, CHOPPING WOOD. A CHILL HAD COME down on the swamp and tinted the grass blue. I had a hard time working the ax. The weight threw me instead of me throwing it. The swing would always come down crooked, and I didn't know how to score so that the cut'd go even and clean.

My hand was chafing so I rested awhile on the chopping block.

Then someone said, Black the mirrors.

I turned and there wasn't no one there.

Nan said, You have to black the mirrors and I will keep you safe.

HE NEVER SAID MUCH ABOUT WHERE HE WENT OR WHAT HE WAS doing. Come evening time, just before the dark got settled, he'd come up through the marsh, gunnysack over his shoulder, the fringe of his coat all draggled and muddy. The wood seemed to close behind him, what was left of the daylight shunted out by dogwood and blackgum and cypress. He'd pass beneath their branches, stooping just enough to clear his head.

He'd have me meet him at the porch, where he'd upturn his sack and the day's find would come clattering onto the floor. Most days there wouldn't be much in the haul—brass pots, teakettles, maybe a spoon or a knife. They'd be caked over with mud, and I'd have to take them out to the pump and scrub them clean. One time, he brought back a pair of boots.

The leather was worn and cracked, and a hole had been worn through the toe.

I looked at them like they were the first boots I'd ever seen. I held them up by their laces and let them hang in the air.

Try them on, he said.

The boots were a little big and the insides were damp and cold. He had me lace up and walk them around the yard. If I wasn't careful, the boots would ride low about to my ankles and slip off.

How do they wear? he asked.

I looked down and wiggled my toes. They'd do just fine.

Do you like them?

I said I did.

He stared at me. His bottom lip shook a little.

How much do you like them?

He took my face in his hand, like an apple, and bit my lip. Then there was a thing in my mouth that was his tongue except it tasted all like brass. He stood up and put on his hat. His eyes were all wet and he wouldn't look at anything except straight ahead.

Filthy, he said.

YOU LEARN WHERE TO STAND AND HOW. TEN PACES FROM THIS bush, an arm's length from that tree. You learn how to walk—swinging your legs saddle wide, then easing your weight across a width of earth. It goes up the calves, the fat of the leg, then across. All your weight is in your belly. Then the other leg. The ball of your foot. Back into the earth. The first time, I near sunk clean through. The ground was too soft, and the mud rose up into my boots. It drew in my feet, my ankles, up above the knee. I had to dig my way out with my hands, pressing into the cold yolky soil, pulling it back in clumps.

You learn to read the mud. Where the gators drag-belly downslope. The little trough of raised slime. You learn the stink. Where the swamp wants to fold you into itself.

HIS BOOTS WERE EASY. HE LEFT THEM BY THE DOOR FOR ME TO clean. I took a sharp piece of tin from a coffee lid and cut out a square from the heel. No one would notice if they weren't looking. At night I squeezed the rubber chunk in my palm. I liked to think of the small square of mud he'd track behind him when he went out. It gave me something to look for in the day.

～

I DID THE MIRRORS ONE AT A TIME, GOING IN A RING AWAY FROM THE house, spiraling out to where the swamp met the floodwaters. The bits of mirror were nailed up just high enough for my reach. I learned to do it in one stroke, my thumb and forefinger buttered with mud. You press down only a little so the mud'll stick after it dries. On a good day I could black the mirrors off eight or nine trees before having to head back to the house.

～

HE WHUPPED ME, OF COURSE. WHEN THE HOUSE WASN'T CLEANED right. If the porch wasn't swept. The first time I left my boots out by the door. He'd tripped on them and broke a clay vase. He had a piece of docking rope that he'd coil around his arm, and with the lank end, he'd set it on my back or my hands or my behind. He'd call me a lazy this and a no-good that, and the wax would break off and I could feel the rough of the rope. He'd holler and yell and spit, and then after, he'd go into his room. It was always then that I thought about leaving, taking my things and running out into the swamp—gators and spooks and snakes be damned. I'd steal his boat and row like he rowed and I wouldn't turn around till I made it all the way to Tallahassee or any-where else.

But later he'd come out and wash my cuts with a sponge. He'd hug me and say how sorry he was. He smelled kind of funny then, like burnt paper. Then he bandaged me, very careful so it wasn't too tight and the edges didn't stick. Then he'd ask me to pray with him, and he'd take me to the front porch where God could see us, and we'd go down on our knees seeking forgiveness.

Except I wasn't praying. I was looking out at the swamp. Waiting.

LATE INTO AUTUMN A FOG ROLLED IN FROM RIVERWARD, WELLING up through the trees. Stuckey stared out the open door, his coat still half on, one arm through, the other arm free. He watched the fog move, glancing sometimes at his watch and letting out a little sigh. Finally, he put the other arm through the sleeve and checked the chamber of his pistol.

Don't leave the house today, he said.

What about the chickens?

Not for any reason.

He slung his sack across his shoulder and closed the door behind him.

I did the darning and swept up real quick. When I figured it was time enough, I laced up my boots, threw on a cape, and set out toward the river. The trees stalked up through the gauzy air. I could taste the rot of sitting bog water in the fog—beading against my skin. Even without the path, I could feel my way through the swamp. I knew which tree was where, and how far it was to the next. I knew where the roots rose and the ground dipped then came up again or sloped down into a gator hatch.

There was hardly any sun overhead, just a boulder of bright cloud. Somewhere a squirrel scrambled up and went from branch to branch— the ice dusting down, some in my hair and some down my neck.

Pretty soon I found my tree. The mud was too packed for pasting, and already the bits of mirror looked near like jewels with the frost on them. I breathed against a piece and a shell of ice slid out into my hand. I put it in my mouth and it melted up cold and rusty.

Then Nan said, Go back.

But I tried to thaw another piece of mirror.

Go back.

And then I heard the crunch of grass that wasn't a gator or a croc or a coyote, but a boot meeting the brush.

Had he turned back? Maybe he got to the boat and figured the fog was too thick to row through. I pressed myself against the tree and tried to figure how far I was from the river line and the house. I hadn't been out more than twenty minutes. But then there it was again. It came in twos like the way a man walks. Crunch and crunch. The thump of heel. The toes finding the grass.

Then again, louder.

I stared out at the mist and I could see a figure take shape. The fog moved around his outline, darkening. I began to run.

I moved through the thickness back toward where I thought the cabin must've been. He'd heard me for sure because I heard a voice cry after me and the whipping of low vines and branches snapping. My lungs burned and the ground became uneven and strange. Trees appeared where they shouldn't have, and the roots caught me at my boots. My cape snagged and tore and I ripped the drawline from my throat and kept running. The white air was endless; I didn't know where I was going.

My boots got tangled up and when I fell, the ground wasn't where it was supposed to have been. I was tumbling, crashing into a curtain of high grass. Here, the ground was cold and wet. I tried to stand, but my ankle hurt like it'd been yanked too hard and I couldn't stay on my feet.

There was a snort and a grunt. Then I saw where I was—the trough of smooth mud, and the ebb of dirty green water. I could make out the dull gray hue of eggs behind the grass. Something dipped into the water, like a stone dropping. I scrambled up on my hands and knees, and the water burst and I could see the snap of jaws—its black rough hide racing through the churn and up the bank.

There was a crack and the burn of powder. The gator twisted. I stood myself up and pushed through the pain. I kept running.

He chased me to the cabin and I fell on the porch. I turned and saw the man coming through the mist—not Stuckey but shorter, younger. His face was all pinched and his cheeks puffed as he sucked in the air. He carried a gunnysack in one hand and my cape in the other. I could see the revolver swinging low from his belt.

I cried and I covered my face, pleading No no no no.

Dora, he said. My God.

And it wasn't till he pulled my hands from my face and said Dora, Dora, look at me just look at me—with his hands on my cheek, not rough but holding it—it was then that I saw his face, and except for the mustache and the way the skin had gone a little long under the eyes that I saw him and knew the voice. My God, he said. It's me. It's G.D.

scraped out the urn with a fork and he told me, Dora, no, please let me look at you, and I said, Coffee?, but he took my hands and said, Dora, don't you know who I am? Then I laughed and said, 'Course I know you, G.D. We used to go and play Sally Water. And his fingers were brittle so I pulled away and thought maybe he'd come apart like icicles. So I lit the stove and I made coffee and he stood with his Adam's apple going up and down.

He tried to talk but it ain't nice manners to talk when I'm making the coffee, what if I overburn it? So I didn't say nothing. I tended the flame and sniffed the spout every now and again. I poured two cups and spooned the sugar. One in mine, and one, two, three for G.D. on account of I like the sound, one two three for G.D.

He sat on the couch, fumbling with his hands, working one finger over the other. His gloves were set on his lap. G.D. looked like I remembered excepting those little hooked hairs on his lip and that he'd gone a little lean at the neck and cheek and eyes. He still had that big wide mouth, and that fleshy stub of a nose. I handed him his cup, and he couldn't stand to hold it. He put it down on the floor.

What are you doing here?, he asked me.

That's rude.

Stuckey know you're here?

'Course he does. Don't ask silly questions.

He stood up and tipped the cup over with his boot.

All that coffee went all over the floor and I scolded him.

Oh! Look what you did!

A pool of it was thinning out, going into the wood. I went to get a rag to soak it up. I pressed the rag deep, tried to draw it from the grain, but it wasn't any good. It wouldn't ever come out.

Look at me, Dora, he said, and he took me by my shoulders. I slapped him across the cheek. He stood there stunned. I'm sorry, he said. I ragged up the rest of the coffee, then went to refill his cup. G.D. looked at the window and touched his hands to his ribs, above the pearl inlay of his pistol. He stared for a moment, then turned back to me.

How long you been out here?

Then I asked him if he remembered that time him and Missy Baker went behind the church and Missy told the girls how he showed her his crawdaddy.

Dora, listen to me. How long you been here?

And I told him I didn't know, how it could've been weeks or months. The days all ran together.

Then I asked him if he remembered when the girls teased him and made little pinch claws at him. Then I showed him with my thumb and the pointy one going pinch pinch pinch, and remember how he got so fussed he went straight home and wouldn't play with us for two weeks.

Stop it!, he said. You shouldn't be here. It ain't safe.

Then I smiled and patted his arm. I'm only teasing, I said. I won't pinch you no more.

He took my hands gentle like, put them together, our four hands like they were waiting to catch something. We were squat down on the floor, me waiting for him to talk and him waiting for himself to say something. There was a click and we both turned to the front door.

Stuckey made a Stuckey shape in the doorway. His coat was wet and dripping, and his flannel was hung loose over his belt. He was very quiet, watching us, the air steaming around his lips. He stepped in and slid the bolt across the latch. He looked down at us.

You spilled coffee, he said.

I stood up.

G.D., he said. I see you've met Dora.

G.D. stood up slow. Been waiting on you.

I told you not to meet me here.

I got some things you're going to want to see.

Stuckey touched his lip, thoughtfully. Any more coffee?, Stuckey asked. Any not spilt on my floor?

I went into the kitchen to fetch another cup. When I came back in, both Stuckey and G.D. had their coats off and were sitting on the couch. G.D.'s sack was spread open between the two. G.D. started taking out the items: a brass candlestick holder, some forks and spoons and things, a little daguerreotype of a red-haired white woman. They haggled back and forth on prices.

I tended to the housework, dusting and sweeping, trying to be in the living room as near as I could. I refilled their cups, boiling up a new urn when we ran out. I looked at the coffee stain near where G.D. was sitting.

I got a fresh rag, then went on my hands and knees, my head bobbing. As I rubbed at the stain I could see G.D.'s gloves, lain flat across the couch arm. The cloth was frayed where the fingers ought to have been, with little flecks of dead leaves and bark caught in the gray wool. It looked like a pair of tiny chopped hands spread wide in waiting.

Stuckey picked up a rusted-up pocket watch and tossed it with the rest. You didn't come into my home to show me this.

What, you're not happy?

Don't play games, G.D.

I didn't look up, only at where the wood splintered, catching in the rag or my palms. My fingers pressed down hard, the pink under my nails going white. There was a long silence. Nobody moved.

Then finally G.D. took out a long silver pipe with etchings all on the body. Near the end was a little silver knob. He held it up with two hands. There were little gems, red and green and blue all over the body and when I looked closer, I could see they were eyes from some kind of snake. Stuckey took the pipe and rubbed the length on the sleeve of his flannel.

Where'd you get this?

Chinaman in the camps.

Stuckey brought the mouth end to his lips and blew through it. He plugged up the other end with a finger, then let the air punch through. Then he drew in. He tested the weight of it in his hands, turning it over and over, then moving a row of fingers down its etched scales.

How much?

Fifteen.

You're a thief, G.D.

I can always give it back.

Okay. Fifteen.

Stuckey got up and fished out the small key and went to his room. G.D. looked at me. I started to say something but he clapped his hand across his mouth. When Stuckey came back, there was fifteen dollars in his hand.

G.D. packed up the things Stuckey didn't want. They clanged together in the sack and he drew up the string tight, slinging it over his shoulder. Stuckey opened the front door. The cold air blew in and G.D. pulled his coat around him.

Always a pleasure, Pat.

Stuckey nodded, holding the door open.

Then Stuckey grabbed his arm. He pulled it down, forcing the hand beyond the grip on his holster. G.D. struggled a little but went limp when he looked into Stuckey's face.

I like you, boy. We do good work together, he said.

He let go and G.D. straightened.

If you come to my home again, I'll kill you.

G.D. smoothed out his sleeve. He looked at Stuckey then back at me, and he said, Good day, before he left.

I was still on the floor but I had already quit trying to clean. Stuckey picked up the pipe from the couch, walked past me and into his room. The door locked behind him.

G.D.'s gloves were still on the couch.

I swept them up with one hand and then they were in my pocket.

THEY WORE A LITTLE BIG, THE BOTTOMS SLIPPING OFF MY THIN wrists. The fingers were cut away and didn't cover near enough past the knuckle, so even when I was out in those woods, I was breathing into them, trying to keep the wool warm or rubbing the feeling back into my fingers. They itched and my hand would go sweaty and slick and the wool would start to stink. Still, even in the warm days, I'd wear at least one—the left usually since the right was for the mirrors. When Stuckey wasn't around, I'd wear them around the house, dusting and sweeping and cleaning. Bits of chicken feed caught in the little curls and hooks. At night, I'd light a candle and peck out the little grains and bits of dead leaf and wood. Then I'd put them on, and you can sleep like that, those gloves around your hands, like them and you was both kind of holding.

Stuckey did not leave his room. Not the next morning or the morning after—the space outside his door filling with sweet itchy air. Outside on the second day, the loblolly pines were starting to rust and bald, setting down their needles in a spiny carpet. It was a clear morning and I could see through to where the river purled behind blackgum and slash pine. I watched from the window, touching my knuckles through G.D.'s glove, thinking maybe that was his shadow cast across a far tree, melted into the bushes, and then gone.

I knocked on Stuckey's door and told him I was going to grain the chickens. There was a rustle and a cough, but he didn't answer. I put on a cape and I took the bag of feed from the hall closet. The morning nipped and chilled around my neck, and I followed the path down to the chicken coop. The dirt was pecked and feather-strewn, and there was the milky white at where they'd messed. I ducked under the wire and let it down careful so it didn't catch on my clothes.

The chicken coop was small, and even for me; I had to stoop. The hens were all set in their rows, their beaks stuck into their puffs, clucking on soft.

Here, here, I said, and I scattered the feed across the floor, and they wiggled their heads. Here, here.

But then my mouth caught and there was a hand over it.

And I shook and I clawed, but it would not let go.

And then G.D. said, Dora, quit it now, quit it. You'll have to be quiet. And he let go.

You have to run away with me, he said.

Oh go on, I said, because I remember when you took Lita Kelley's little hand and then made her cry afterward and played tricks like a bull-frog down her dress or throwing mean old clods of mud. So go on. Who you fooling?

He's going to hurt you, Dora. If he hasn't already.

Then he took my hand and he saw that it was his glove and let the hand drop.

I can protect you. He won't find us.

This is a chicken house and you ain't any kind of chicken, I said. I scattered the feed. The birds jumped off their warm little thatches, *put-put-put*ing on the wood. And then I looked at him, at how he still had his little-boy face, his hair all full of feathers and dust, the way the whites of his eyes looked near blue in the shade. He brought his hands up against his lips and touched the sides of his nose. He took a big sigh and stared up at me like he was doing a kind of measuring.

Be careful, he said, stooping under the opening.

He stood full up and dusted the feathers from his shoulders.

I have to salvage today. Will you feed the chickens tomorrow?

Then he was gone.

The next day, G.D. waited for me inside the chicken house, his shoulders rolled in, hunched under a low shelf of Rhode Island reds. He had cut a trap under one of the roosts that dropped him outside, under the coop so he could come and go without getting in sight of the cabin. He showed me how it worked, how easy it was. He showed me the foot-and-a-half step down onto the ground. We crawled under the floor, bits of feather drifting down, lighting on the grass blades and our hair and our clothes. When we got to the wire, he pointed at the grove of dogwoods, behind them, two days of hard travel, he said, then north toward Fitler, following the Yazoo up to Cary, Rolling Fork, then finally Anguilla.

Anguilla?

My older brother has a homestead there, he said.

I asked him to tell me about it and he said there was a creek out back, and a little pea patch behind the house, with the vines going all over, stretching across and across and across. His oldest brother cattled, and there were steaks and milk and honey on the bread. All of that in Anguilla. Across that wire.

There's room enough for us both, he said.

Stuckey's waiting for me, I said. He's wondering where I gone to.

G.D. sighed and wriggled out. He stood up and dusted the front of his coat. He lifted the strip of fencing over his head and pulled it over the other side.

That's all it takes, he said. Then he took off toward the woods.

Every day for two weeks, I saw G.D. Stuckey had stopped leaving his room except at night to leave his plate or a pile of his clothes in the hall. I spent longer and longer out in the chicken coop, an hour sometimes without anyone being the wiser. Sometimes I'd go out early and wait for the trapdoor to lift, G.D.'s round head pushing through on the other side. We'd get underneath the floorboards and stretch out on the grass— with those hens pecking around and pushing seed above us, the yellow dust coming down through the boards, on our hair and backs and clothes. We stayed down there, the two of us, like a couple of secrets.

G.D. talked on and on about Anguilla, and I showed him my little bird skull.

And he said there were all manner of birds in Anguilla.

Then in his pockets I found a little black rock and I said, What's this?

It's a piece of lodestone.

What's it for?

He put his arms behind his head and shut his eyes.

Reckon it can be for you.

He told me how him and Stuckey had started to partnering a week after the rains. Stuckey had stacked hay on G.D.'s cousin's farm, and on weekends, he'd take G.D. and his little cousins out hunting, the lot of them trekking back by sundown with a belt of squirrel skins or gopher or rabbit. They'd circled around to each other after the flood over in a camp out at Sunflower County. It was Stuckey's plan that they work salvage, with Stuckey working the waters and G.D. going by foot along the countryside, in the camps and flood towns. They'd go off on their own for weeks at a time and meet once a month to trade on news and supplies.

He told me how he'd go around with his trousers rolled and his boots tied around his shoulders. Buzzards set down along the roofs, tracking him as he pushed through the shin-deep water. G.D. picked carefully around the deadwood, feeling through the mud with his toes to keep from stepping on a nail or a piece of glass. He learned to figure by eye which houses would hold and which were about to give at any moment. There were jewelry boxes, silverware. Tins of money stuffed under mattresses. Things left behind in the rush.

People only take what they can carry, he said. What they leave, it must not mean that much to them in the first place.

And then there was a pain in my stomach and maybe some dust got into my eyes, but he turned over on his side and put his hand over mine. Then he looked at me for a long time and he said, I'd carry you with me. Then he put his hand on my face and set it there gentle like, his thumb moving along the ridge of my eyes. And he was looking and he was looking and he took so long that I just went ahead and kissed him.

The next day, he was waiting for me inside the chicken coop. He stood, stooping a little to keep from hitting the ceiling.

I started to go to him, but he put his hand up.

I know what you've been doing, he said.

What?

What were you thinking?

He reached into his coat and showed me. The little bits of mirror with the mud still on it.

You took them!

You don't think Stuckey is going to notice? For Christ's sake!

Then I cuffed him across his mouth.

Don't say that! You better put those back, I told him. Or else Nan is going to—and he—he—

What?

Put them back! Put them back, please please please . . .

Dora, you have to leave with me. He's going to notice what you done. Stuckey's going to notice. You don't know him. You don't know what he's like. I cleaned them near as I could, but—

He had cleaned them! I flew at him, beating at his chest with my fists. The chickens got all fussed up and started going every which way— flapping around, air full of feathers.

What did you do! What did you do!

Dora, calm down. Calm down.

No no no no no. You're supposed to black the mirrors. I need to black the mirrors. What did you do!

I started crying and I kept beating on him with my fists.

What! What's wrong?

You ruined it! You ruined it! Get out! Get out!

Dora, please. You have to come with me. It's not safe.

Get out! I started screaming.

He tried to quiet me down, but it wouldn't do no good so finally he left. He crawled out and went under the fence, then he was gone. There were little bits of mirror on the floor and I gathered it up and I kept crying and crying, and the chickens were all fussing around me and I had to knock them away and I didn't feel bad about it or nothing, I could've knocked every last one of them.

By the time I went back into the house, Stuckey was in the living room. His shirt was off and the sweat ran down in streaks. There were gashes all on his side and his back and his stomach, some of it already skinned over, but some of it pink and oozing a little. He looked at me sleepy eyed and I tried not to show anything.

You were feeding the chickens for a long time, he said.

Then he looked hard at me, turned around, then went back into his room. And I wasn't sure if I saw what I saw, with his eyes all droopy the way it was and me not really wanting to look into them anyway, but maybe his eyes flicked and maybe it was down and to the left, at the one wool gray glove still holding my hand.

That night he came into my room and said that he was hungry. It was full dark, and there was only his voice—Dora, I'm hungry, he said. I need to eat. I need to be fed.

And I told him that I'd make him something.

And he said, I'm hungry. I am starved body and soul.

And then he was on me and I could taste the bitter in his mouth. And Nan said, No, and I said, Don't, but then there was me and the sharp and the hot and he tore me. And I said, Please, and then it was, but then it was, and I said, Please please please, and my jaw would not make the no no and Nan would not say no no and then the mattress was gone and there was the wall and the slats through the boards, and out beyond it, the full dark, trees and swamp and river, and then Nan said, Look, and I would not Look, and Nan said, Look, but I could not would not, and it went through me, and there was not skin enough to hide my eyes and air enough to heavy my scream but there she was standing out in the blackgum, holding under the bits of mirrors that I did not black. Nan Peoria in the moonglow. And she would not could not look at me. And in my head I saw the trees and I saw the glass looking back at the not-looking, and she would not speak and I said I tried and please and please but she would not, held there in the blackgum, held under bits of glass, not speaking.

After that night, Stuckey put the Spirit in me. He knelt naked out in the open air, his breath steaming through his clapped hands. And he said Lord Lord, and the clouds doughed over in a purple roll, no moon no stars, only the Spirit spooling in my gut, the brass of it in my mouth. It hummed and cut. He pulled me down to my knees. He said, Pray for your forgiveness. But there was only my choking and the warm wet down my leg and the cold binding in my throat. And after his praying, he'd go back into his room, and I would wash under the pump, my jaw cinching and my stomach bucking under the cold water.

He came at me night after night. I closed my eyes and the hurt was in the meat of me. It slid and chafed and burned. And in the leavings there'd be blood and in the water there'd be blood, and the hurt would tight and slack and tight and slack; I thought it would snap and I would go with it, like chalk, in two: this a Dora and this a Dora. And times I would wake up in the night and feel the Spirit stitching through me, knitting up my guts so that it hurt to breathe and there was no honey on the bread, and no Good Words and Nan Peoria is down down down the Gulf of Mexico.

⌒

WINTER HAD COME AND THE WINDS HOWLED AND SMASHED AGAINST the walls. Leaves and twigs and sand blew in from the swamp, gathering along the side of the house. Stuckey had me run the stove through the night and come morning, the air was gray with ash. It stuck to the floors and chairs and table. It was in the salvage, rimming old pans and flower-pots, setting like a skin over stacks and stacks of books. It was in my mouth and my nose and it stung my eyes, and the only air was outside. I cleared the cull, chopped firewood. When I went to the chicken coop, there was G.D., waiting.

I had not seen him for weeks, not since we'd fought, and he was look-ing clean and good.

Dora, he said, and I knew that it was me, and he said it, my name, me, the sound *dor-a* and he held out his hand, reaching for Dora, but Dora did not move. The hens puffed into themselves, clucking, their eyes wet and clear and black in the light. He stood a long time looking at her. The winter light spangled at his shoulders, his breath going white and low.

Where's your glove?, he asked.

And my face came apart.

And when he tried to comfort me, his arms open like a cave, I shrunk. He looked at me, not speaking, the words all clumped in his mouth, pushing on his cheeks. He stepped past me and did not leave out the trap-door, but out the front, in full view of the cabin.

That night, it was hailing. Ice came down in a scatter, on the windows, the walls, the roof. It beat against the crossbeams, through the ceiling slats, pebbling and pebbling. They were like pearls slanting in the wind, crashing in the dark. Stuckey sat slumped in his chair, the stacks of salvage towering up behind him. He'd been smoking his pipe, and his mouth hung a little open, with his small breath rustling inside his chest. His eyes glassed looking out the window.

What's that?, he asked. What's out there?

There was flash and powder and the glass collapsed into nothing.

That was his finish. Poor Stuckey. I sat there and watched the life go out of him. G.D. came in through the door and he let the pistol go out of his hand. Bits of hail twinkled against his cheek. He went about the room and stuffed the pieces of salvage into his satchel bags. When it was time to go, G.D. picked me up by my arms and kissed me. We stepped out into the night and G.D. held an oilskin sheet over me to protect me from the stones. We moved very slowly together through the swamp, the sheet rippling around me, the air full of pearls and us, ghosts.

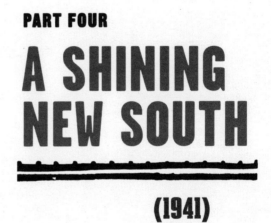

PART FOUR

A SHINING
NEW SOUTH

(1941)

I n Yazoo County sits Panther Swamp: thirty-eight thousand square acres of floodplain, bog grass, nuttail, water oak, black falaya loam. The Yazoo River courses down from an upridge of gray marl. At 32°47N 90°35W, the D.C. men chalk a line, 307.65 meters east, then south 683.03 meters, a square of map equaling to fifty-two acres of burrow pits, concrete walls, and a roadway running flank to the railroad line, wide enough to drive in the mixers, the CATs, the drill trucks. The men do math. Surface area by water volume. The wattage of the primary inflow into a catchment area of fifty-two thousand square kilometers. Rate of drainage against mean declivity downstream rejoining the Yazoo.

In a room, a projector clicks.

There are six million operating farms in the United States today. Less than 8 percent have electric lights. Less than 10 percent, running water. Runoff from outdoor toilet systems in conjunction with inadequate food storage has led to spoilage, typhoid, dysentery, undulant fever, ulcerative colitis, and a staggering rise in hookworm.

A projector clicks again. On the wall is a plan for a lock and dam reservoir system 115 feet wide and 580 feet long, with a vertical lift gate and a concrete spillway capable of generating over 162,000 kilowatts of power and transmitting nearly 6,900 volts to previously unelectrified districts.

Think. All the modern comforts of New York and Chicago. Light-bulbs. Frigidaires. Electric irons. Radios. Franklin Delano Roosevelt's voice in every hick son of a bitch living room from Podunk to Jerkwater. Imagine, at every dinner table an ice cold Coca-Cola, the Lone Ranger on the wireless, rich chocolaty Ovaltine chilling in a brand-new General Electric. Money changes hands. Businesses grow. There is solvency. Jobs. A shining new South.

Let's break for lunch.

In the cafeteria, they unwrap sheets of butcher paper from sand-wiches of corned beef, salami, sardines—grease on their fingers and lips and shirt cuffs. On a napkin, they write: cost of wages for engineers, surveyors, construction crews, dam tenders, local labor, housing; equip-ment by tonnage, cost of transport, upkeep, materials; permits, filing fees—against five years projected, start to finish. They talk out the numbers, checking them again and again, passing the frail napkin down the table.

Someone takes a dill pickle from between two slices of bread. He lays it on the napkin, brine and all, and the numbers start to bleed.

Say this pickle is the national budget.

He cuts it into eighths.

This is the Agricultural Adjustment Act. The WPA.

He portions it out. Eats a slice.

TVA. The REA.

He eats another. Then another and another until it's just a nub. Then he eats that too.

God bless this mess.

THEY WENT IN, EIGHT TEAMS OF FIVE, THROUGH CLAY SINKS, PEAT pools, chokevine—the low suck of their waders pulling from the mud bed. The swamp was airless, holding the sweat down against their skin, gnats ambering on their foreheads. They read from altimeters and leveling rods. They moved through gullies and berms, mapping a long silt wall along the gravel bar. They took plant samples, soil samples, water samples. At the perimeter line they tied yellow ribbons to low branches, marking the trees for demolition.

With their hatchets and their towlines, they went out—their bodies locked under the conifers, oilskin hoods drawn tight around their heads. They arced their axes into the base, snapping the wood away in clean white wounds. The trees gave and the towlines snapped taut. With each fall a column of rain would open in the forest ceiling.

There were signs of prior human encroachment. Symbols cut into bark, ash pits from old fires, the label off a can of Van Camp's Pork and Beans. One team found a set of jaw traps hidden in the weeds. A slab of meat sat spoiled on the weight plate. They photographed it, tripped it with a rock, and moved on.

In May they broke ground, and by June there were seventeen dig crews out in the back swamps. It was hurricane season and the Yazoo roiled and crunched. Under hard rain, the crews dug relief basins along the tributaries. The ground was too soft for the crane trucks so they worked by hand—shovels and spades and pickaxes—breaking the earth and carrying it off in thick slippery slabs.

It was George Burke's team off the main stem who put in the requisition for the slurry pump. Mr. Catkill held the yellow form up to his third-floor window, squinting through his bifocals. It'd been their third requisition since April, having destroyed their first and lost the other. The Panther Swamp project was already over budget, and the signs of incompetence made it harder to secure federal funding. He set the form down on his desk and folded his fingers together, knotting his hands into a praying shape.

At night, in his slippers, he would stir out of his bed, and he'd feel the thing in the room. It was vague, uncertain, and he would catch it only in glimpses. He'd shut his eyes and become still. It would pass above him, stretching like a sheet. Then one morning at the breakfast table, he sat buttering his toast. He watched the metal move against the stiff bread, the band of light that caught on the blade. Then all at once, there it was. Steel and glass and light. The beating pulse of a future.

Mr. Catkill looked out his third-story window and he sensed it just beyond the horizon—driving inexorably toward him. He had read the papers. He had seen the photographs. The crumpled suits. The sod caravans edging toward the coast, and in the cities, bread lines that stretched for blocks upon blocks. What he understood, better than his colleagues, was that this was a darkening world and he would have his place among the torchbearers.

He decided. He would sign the requisition form. He would meet with George Burke.

THE MORNING TRAIN PULLED INTO YAZOO AND THE CITY WAS SLATE gray with deep veins of light marbled into the sky. A porter wheeled the crate into the hired car and Mr. Catkill pressed a coin into the porter's glove.

The car carried him under the soft patter of rain toward the swamp. On the drive in, he sat stone-faced in the backseat, his pale hands folded across his lap, watching the mute and desolate country. The road was choked with stones and softening ground. Entering Panther Swamp, it was as if he were passing through a large organism. There were no clear roads, just lanes of stone and red mud, obscured by curtains of overhanging vine. They pressed through into forests of blackgum, dogwood, spruce, tracing a fence of cattails to a river crossing.

Burke's work site sat on a mud plain twenty yards from the tributary. Safety flags were posted along the perimeter of the dig, and behind it a network of craters and trenches five feet deep and over a hundred yards across. The crew was at work in the trenches, shoveling up the loose mud and reinforcing the walls with sandbags.

The driver pumped his horn and the crew turned toward the car. A man climbed up from the trenches. His body was slick and brown, and he wiped the mud from his goggles. Mr. Catkill recognized him from his file.

He rolled down his window.

You George Burke?, he asked.

Who are you?

Arthur Catkill, vice president of operations from the home office.

The foreman straightened and looked back at the site. His men had stopped work and were watching the exchange.

Let's go into my office, the foreman said.

They went inside a construction trailer where Burke kept a set of cabinets and an old oak-top desk. A kerosene lamp burned from a cross pipe as the rain sounded across the corrugated ceiling. The foreman stripped off his shirt and toweled down his large hairy body. His skin was pale and bloodless underneath the layers of mud. He motioned to a folding stool and Mr. Catkill sat down.

Nasty weather, he said.

Keeps the mosquitoes down, the man said. He offered Mr. Catkill a cigarette from his cigarette case. Mr. Catkill shook his head.

I've brought in your requisition. A model six slurry pump. Brand-new. I wanted to bring it in personally.

The man drew from his cigarette.

Much appreciated, he said.

Mr. Catkill could feel the beginnings of irritation prickling beneath his collar. He watched the man smoke, the cigarette pinched between two dirt-scaled fingers, the long deep pulls that dribbled out on his breath. Mr. Catkill cleared his throat.

I brought it in personally, Mr. Burke, he said. I take it it's an everyday occurrence for you that a vice president brings in your shipments?

The foreman arched his eyebrows.

No need for sarcasm, Mr. Catkill. I'm listening.

He eased forward in his chair.

Good, Mr. Catkill said.

Since May I've had over thirty-eight replacement orders put in for this capital project, Mr. Burke. Most of them coming from this crew. Orders for replacement drills, mixers, turbines, motor saws, and last week, a slurry pump. It seems like anything that can be lost, broken, or stolen has been eaten up in this godforsaken swamp—and before I release another piece of expensive machinery to your crew, I would like to know why.

The foreman Burke tapped his ash onto the floor.

Well, Mr. Catkill, these aren't everyday conditions here in Panther. There's a lot of moisture. A lot of heat.

Mr. Catkill screwed up his face. He hated being lied to, of having his intelligence insulted.

Oh, come on, Burke. Don't kid me. You think this is my first go-around? I've been to Black Canyon and I've seen what they use out there. Their equipment is practically ancient compared to what we buy. Doesn't that strike you as odd? Three model six slurry pumps in three months? You and I both know we're not talking about everyday wear and tear.

The foreman's eyes were two slate marbles. He crinkled them at the edges, taking a full long measure of the vice president of operations from the home office. After some time, the man stubbed out his cigarette on the edge of his desk and slid open one of his drawers. He brought out a set of metal jaws.

Found this not too far off-site.

Mr. Catkill lifted it by its chain.

It's a leg trap. A big one too. For hunting panther is my guess. We keep confiscating them, but they keep showing up. We'll pull one out of the bushes, and the next day there'll be another one.

I don't understand.

Some of my men have been saying they've been hearing things in the woods. Seeing things that aren't there. Frankly, I think they're a little spooked.

Of what? Ghosts? That's not what you're telling me, is it, Burke?

The man snickered. No, of course not.

Mr. Catkill touched his thumb to a steel tooth. It was still sharp.

Then what are you saying?

This is Panther Swamp and everybody from around these parts will know that you can clear a good haul on beaver skin if the season is right. Now, it may not say so on any map of yours, but this is hunter and trapper land and—

Mr. Catkill cut him off. This is government land.

Burke shook his head.

You don't know these people, Mr. Catkill. They're not like most trappers. They're worse than wild men. They got Injun blood mixed up with Scots and French and who knows what else. You see this place? Someone like you or me wouldn't come out to a place like this unless we were paid to. Mosquitoes alone will suck you dry if you aren't careful. Most days the heat is near unbearable. I got men on my crew who'll pass out where they stand if they're out in the sun too long. For us, it's a hell. But for trappers, this is their home. They live here because no one else can or no one else will. And with all due respect to the home office, Mr. Catkill, they don't give a damn about capital projects or budget sheets or requisition forms. They want us gone, and they'll keep doing what they're doing—setting traps and breaking equipment—until that happens.

Mr. Catkill's left eye twitched. His head had begun to ache and he felt the small stinging pulse behind his temple. He rubbed small slow circles along the bridge of his nose.

Well, have you tried the police?

The foreman laughed.

No. You reckon I should?

The heat rose into his cheeks.

Of course you should! What do you mean?

We're talking about livelihood, Mr. Catkill. Just like how I got to go out there and work my crew, that's my livelihood. And how you got to go into your nice cool office with all your papers and your books and things—well, that's your livelihood, and I'm not faulting you for that. But you take that away from a trapper, you're taking away his bread, his meat, his whole way of life. You're asking for trouble.

Mr. Catkill narrowed his eyes and looked the foreman up and down, at the trails of mud that'd dried across his belly. It wouldn't be hard to have Burke transferred to some garbage detail or even fired. Except for the problems at Panther, his work record was exemplary. But the dam needed men of singular vision. Burke did not understand. The story of any great country is a story of creating value from nothing. From dirt and dust and patience. From one man there can spring cities. This was the problem with his type. The lack of vision. The absence of will. The unwillingness to sacrifice.

• • •

There was a crack and they turned toward the door. Outside, voices were shouting over the rain. Mr. Catkill had started to speak but already Burke had rushed out to the site.

The men had massed and clustered all along the tributary edge. Get a rope!, someone called.

Stay back. Everyone stay back.

Mr. Catkill ignored the warning and pushed through. There had been a blowout in the basin and the river had swept up one of Burke's crew. Water flooded into the trenches, smashing down the weak retaining walls. Out toward the break, he could see the crewman. He was small and pale, spinning helplessly toward the river.

Don't move, someone shouted. It was the foreman. We'll get you out of there!

Burke lowered himself waist deep into water. He gathered the slack of rope around his hips and cinched it tight. He ordered three of his men to brace the other end, then he eased out into the basin. A ridge of silt rose up under his feet, darkening the water. Burke inched closer.

Mr. Catkill could see the crewman's small white hands grasping for the soft mud. He was slipping. It gave way in wet sloughs. Burke was almost upon him now. He had his hands up, trying to keep his balance. Burke swooped forward and snatched the man into his arms. The rope went taut and the men anchored tight against the weight.

There was a great whoop and the men cheered their foreman. Quickly, they hauled the rope back in. Mr. Catkill watched. One grown man cradling another. They pulled them up off the banks and wrapped the fallen man in a blanket before laying him out under the heat lamps. A hail of cheers went up as the foreman unknotted the rope from his waist. Burke looked almost defiant, coiling the rope around his arm.

Mr. Catkill averted his eyes. He looked into the basin.

Burke!, he cried.

Mr. Catkill pointed. His voice was high and clipped.

Look! The pump!

Somehow it had fallen in during the blowout. The crate rolled now on the current, making toward the break.

For God's sake, Burke. Don't let it get away.

No one would move. Catkill's teeth were chattering. The rain was smashing around him. He could still see the box gliding slowly downstream. Mocking him. For a moment Mr. Catkill could not understand what was happening. He was aware of the wall of bright gleaming eyes that were fixed upon him. The men's faces were dark and dirty, their hair set in wild cakey clumps. This was a mistake, he realized. He should not have come here.

There was a flash of movement. Something went up into the air, over their heads. Mr. Catkill looked up. It soared up, then plummeted back down to the earth. It lay muddy and inert at his feet. A work shirt.

Chatham!, someone cried.

Mr. Catkill turned. The men surged together, tightening around a single point. One of the crewmen, a Negro, burst his way through a wall of arms. The Negro raced toward him and Mr. Catkill put up his hands, tensing for the blow. But the Negro ran past him to the tributary edge. Burke reached out. It was too late. He grabbed at the empty air, and in one swift movement the Negro launched himself into the yellow water.

Last year on his twenty-first birthday Robert had fetched himself a shave and gone to a movie, a double feature. He shrank into the sticky velvet of his seat. The theater was full of people—dozens of staring eyes, silent as trees. He could feel their heat clouding the air, drawing over him. On the screen a white woman billowed out big and silky in her sun hat. Dust popped and crackled on her cheeks. It'd been eight years already since the fire in Bruce. It was a memory he kept tasting, faint like metal in blood.

He couldn't sit all the way through the first film. On the sidewalk, the afternoon was bright and hot. There were cinders in his eyes, and he mashed his palms into his sockets.

Around the corner, he found a bar with a COLOREDS WELCOME sign hanging from the door. The trash was piled to the windows, and a cloud of moths danced on the glass. Inside, the bar was empty and a stale smell like wet wool hung in the air. An electric fan was going, moving the dust around. He turned to leave when a man came in through a trapdoor from behind the counter. He was a white man, short and fat with swollen cheeks. His oily hair was parted in the middle. The man smiled and motioned with his smooth, fish-pale arms.

Sit at the counter?

He leaned over and wiped a stool with a rag.

Robert sat down and the seat was smooth with grease.

What can I get you?

I don't have but fifteen cents.

The man looked him over slowly. How 'bout a sandwich?, he asked. On the house.

The sandwich was stale and oversalted. Still he wolfed it down, chewing the hard rough bread. When he swallowed, he tasted blood and tongued the bright sting in his cheek.

New in town?

Robert looked at the man carefully.

It's just that I never seen you around here before.

I bale cotton on the Jones-Tennessy plantation.

That so?

That's so.

He turned back to his sandwich. The man rested his hands on his belt and the air shifted inside him. He cleared his throat and busied himself with filling up a glass with a pitcher of water.

What's your name, son?

Billy, he lied.

Those hands of yours are awful soft-looking for handling baling wire.

Robert stood up and pushed off from the counter.

Thanks for the sandwich, he said.

Now wait a minute. I was just talking.

Robert started for the door, but it opened inward in front of him. It would've smashed into him if he hadn't jumped out of the way. There was a girl on the other side. She looked up at him, startled.

That's my daughter, the man said from behind him. He was grinning.

Your daughter?

The girl was colored and there were wires in her teeth. Her eyes were big and staring, flecks of gold in the iris. She was smiling up at him.

You can call her Marie, he said.

Is that really your daughter?

Maybe, the man said. Are you interested?

The girl had already started to working. She was looking him up and down, dragging her smooth nail down the front of his shirt.

I haven't got but fifteen cents, he said. The man didn't say anything so Robert took her hand in his and said it again. Just fifteen cents.

She don't hear you. This one is deaf and dumb, the man said.

The girl slipped her hand from his and rested her arms on his shoulders, framing the sides of his neck. Her skin was cool and slippery smooth.

I think she likes you, the man said.

In the tiny back room, she moved expertly in the dark, first stripping off his belt, then his shirt. She went for the small flannel bag around his neck but he guided her hand away. No, he said. She tried again and he squeezed her fingers. No! He thought maybe she heard him because she didn't try again. Instead, they fell blindly onto the bed. She worked him through the zipper of his trousers and he wondered if her eyes were better on account of her being deaf. Could she see his face then, the lean and ashen hollow of his cheeks? She was warm at his tip. She slid down, soft, grasping. The breath went out of him. He felt his insides being drawn out. A weak queasy feeling flowed up his stomach, into his throat. The pressure built behind his eyes.

On the ceiling there were stripes of sunlight between the slats from where the afternoon was casting through. There was someone upstairs, their footfalls dislodging fine grains down over the bed. The girl was small and lithe, her body passing through the slashes of light. He leaned back and she shoveled down on him. He felt himself sinking first through the pillows, the sheets, into the mattress, then deeper still, to floor then stone then earth, down and down, into that cold low chamber. He opened his eyes and she was there still, her braces sharp and catching the sun.

When he came, she caught it in her palm and wiped it on his stomach. He didn't move, exhausted. The blood was thumping in his temples. He heard her moving in the dark, rifling through his clothes. He heard the dull thump of his shoes, the insole lifting, his last twenty dollars melting away.

The next day on the train out of town, he got hooked for freight-hopping. The railroad bulls came down with their fists and boots and clubs. He thought he heard his nose break. There was a crunch and his head filled with salt and iron. Not so beautiful, one of them said. His body was a rag doll, tumbling out of the car. The ground was hard and loveless. Behind his eyelids, there was the sun, warm and red. He spat strings of black into the dust. He listened to the bulls gather, the crackle of grit under their soles. They kicked him awhile, burying their toes into his ribs. He kept his eyes shut and tried not to yell. When they'd finished, they carried him into their car and drove.

He felt ashamed about the lie he told, the name he'd given to that girl. He wasn't sure why he'd done it, why it had been the name to come to him. He told himself it was a coincidence.

A bag went over his head and he could smell his own damp breath blowing back against him. It was sour and foul like something had rotted in his mouth.

The car ride seemed to go forever. The men were talking but he couldn't make out their words over the thumping of his pulse. His throat had tightened and he gagged on his own fluid. He thought in his confusion that they'd got the noose around him. Then he realized it was just the devil around his neck. He'd been pulling hard on the loop of twine.

When the car stopped, someone lifted him up by his arm and stood him on his feet.

This'll do.

They pulled the bag from his head. There was so much light, he thought his eyes might crack. His knees started to crumbling.

Please, he said.

Someone said something. A word of warning, maybe. Then a bright warm pain opened in the side of his head and he was gone.

In that deepening black, he dreamed again of the Dog. Not the Widow Percy's dog he'd seen in Bruce but a large black hound—lean and sleek—that looked out at him with deep piercing eyes from which no light could escape.

When he awoke, the grass was tattooed to his cheek. He sat up. His skull was crowded with pain. In the upper sky he could see the first splatter of starlight descending down. Then in the low violet bands, the sun set behind the western hills. He was in a field, unmarked save for a small creek a few yards down, burbling along the yellowed grasses. How long had he been unconscious? Hours? Days? Years? He touched the side of his head. The blood was still sticky. He pushed against the pain and stood himself up. Then he moved slowly toward the water. Grasshoppers grazed past him, their wings grinding through the air.

He sat down on a rock and listened to the blood click in his septum. The air was starting to cool. The pain eased into a dull humming ache. He leaned out over the water and washed the blood from his face. Then he angled his mouth into the stream and swallowed. It hurt going down but he drank again, sucking the inky cold water, drawing it in. His heart was beating. He was alive. He was still alive. Above him, there was the ancient sky, yoking back the heavens. Still holding. His eyes started to well.

...

The following day, he went on foot following two gleaming rails into the next town. In Hollandale, a boy was giving out leaflets written in a bad hand: *$2 a day. Strong backs wanted.* It gave the address of a small brick building a mile from the main stretch. He went upstairs and put his name on a piece of paper. The next morning, he climbed on the back of a truck and, with half a dozen other men, was driven out to Panther Swamp.

For a month he cleared the land, hacking through thorn and brush, laying down pounds of tree killer. There were fifteen-hour days crossing through the wet country, trailing the chalky white poison into the swamp. When the weather turned, he pierced the plates of hard earth to where the soil was warm and black and musky and he'd gouge out the brittle tangle of taproots with a spade. It was hard work and by day's end, his back would scream and his muscles would lie slack and dumb on his bones. On the truck ride back to the company apartments in Hollandale, he couldn't feel anything, just the warm throb where his legs had been. Out beyond the truck bed, the country darkened around him. There were lights in the far-off farmhouses and he'd try to count them before they'd pass or blink away.

He took an advance on his pay for an upstairs room in a boardinghouse on the edge of Hollandale. It was four walls and whatever light made it through the branches of the maple outside his window. He ate his dinners on the sill, looking out away from town. It was an empty country, big with sky and grass. On the weekends, he could see the small plots on the town's fringe, a gold-colored tractor chugging in the distance. A ribbon of smoke rose up from the distant chimneys, gray and curling and pretty, and his mind would set to wandering.

There were years now, marching fat and wide through the valley of his brain. He thought of Ellis and Etta, who were most probably dead now or at least good as dead. He thought of Hermalie. When they'd dug that limp small body out of the ash, he had barely recognized her. He stood at that windowsill, his food cooling, his head emptying. There were too many days for too much world, too much time to wrong and be wronged. And each day weighed on him heavier than the last—so much sun, so much sky and cloud—and he reached through those years, before Bruce and the Hotel Beau-Miel, to that miserable ramshackle cabin—his father, his mother, his brother, shaking beetles from their clothes, and part of him reasoned that somewhere still, they were there, the hearth fires going, the air heavy with sweet ash. He pictured his father's hand, forever big and warm on the back of his neck.

In three months he found his way to George Burke's crew, mucking out in the deep swamp. The crew worked seventeen-hour days, six days a week out in the mosquito nests, trying to slow the flow of the river. They dug trenches and piled mud and mixed concrete for the diverting walls. In the mornings, the men would watch their foreman wade out from the banks, clearing the rocks into the silver run. His shirt was off, showing his broad tan back. Burke would float a yellow rope into the channel, and the end would catch in the current, speeding forward, straightening out its slack. A man some meters downstream would call the time, signaling for Burke to halter the slack. Then he'd wade back, the rope coiled about his shoulders. Too fast, he'd call to the men. Still too fast.

The work was grueling, but Robert admired Burke. He never cheated him his pay or kept him from the machine work. In Burke's crew, he was allowed to drive plow trucks and graders and dig cranes. By day's end, climbing up to his apartment, he could still feel the hum of the engines in his body, the buzzing in his bones. His blood was toxic, the tang of diesel in his spit. He'd enter the dark room, sling off his boots, and lay his clothes out carefully on the chair back. But on his mattress, every nerve worked raw, he closed his eyes, and there on the other side of dreaming, the Dog waited.

Morning would come and the days would draw on. The order had come down for his crew to be reassigned to demolition duty. For months they turned chunks of green country into a fine burnt powder. Level this dam, bury that hill, fill that gully. They stopped their ears with cotton, and when the all clear was given, it was Robert who depressed the plunger. The ground quaked and an awful noise wracked the sky. They tucked their heads to their knees against the hail of mud and stone. His mouth was full of cordite. He brought his head up again and the ground was new, clear. The world hummed for hours after each detonation. He stepped from behind the bunker and walked across the halo of scorched earth. He stood at the center of the crater, measuring by sight its width and depth. He multiplied the poundage in his head. It was fortifying— the landscape blasting to pieces around him. Birds fled the trees. The blast traveled through his bones, rattled his teeth. The cascade of after-dust lashed his cheek. Slowly air and noise and birdsong returned again to the world. He was still there. Anchored. There was a freedom in that. He discovered the sphere of his reach, like a fighter, Death dancing just beyond his jabs.

He could not stop.

At every demolition, he'd pack more and more explosives into the charges and would ignore the safety protocols, often depressing the plunger before all the men could get to cover. He thrilled at every blast, standing exposed beyond the safety of the trench. He drew out the cotton from his ears and let the godly crack drive through his skull.

He grinned at the outraged earth.

Once there'd been a choke in the run and Burke took the crew upriver to investigate. By midafternoon, they found a beaver dam, eighty yards across, climbing six feet high from bed to pitch, stanching off one of the minor tributaries. A wall of mud and sticks and stone bowed into the stream. The surrounding marshland was soft with flooding. Protocol dictated that the crew was to shovel out the dam by hand and set out poison to keep the beavers from building again. To do it safely, it would be a month of backbreaking toil in mosquito country, cracking up the bits of stone and twig with shovels, little by little, and little by little widening the artery.

To do it recklessly, however, would take hardly any time at all.

Robert went on-site the next morning hours earlier than the rest of the crew. He went alone into the water, yoked on either side by a long yellow rope. He went in with cement putty and charges sealed in plastic and prepped along the dam, slathering the goo with the heel of his hand and fixing the charges in place.

From the banks Robert forced down the handle on the detonator. For a moment, there was nothing. Then immediately there was a series of three pops, sucking up the air. The river belched and gulped, and a rush of sediment shot across the channel. The air filled with smoke and mist and burning splinters. The earth groaned. The surviving pieces of wall shifted in the current and broke apart against the pressure of the stream.

Robert unstopped his ears. His skull was full of static. He could feel the blood returning to his face and looked out toward the bank where a large crater was now sitting.

When Robert returned to the camp, some of his crewmates were already waiting for him. Robert took in the stillness in their faces. There were four of them, each one carrying a piece of iron rebar, and he understood what it was they wanted.

The men spaced themselves out around him, enclosing him in a circle. One man approached and swung. Robert felt his breath explode.

He took a step back and looked up. A piece of iron came down and clipped the side of his head. One of the men was barking something, but already, he couldn't hear. His blood was pumping. The man was heavy-set, his dark eyebrows set into a scowl. Robert wrestled the man down onto the ground and began to beat him senseless before the other three set themselves upon him. It was George Burke who finally broke up the fight, spraying them down with the hose.

Later, Robert sat alone with Burke in his trailer. He was cold and still dripping and he could not get his mind to focus.

After a time, Robert broke the silence.

You going to fire me?

More than your job is at stake, Burke told him. You could be arrested. You could have been killed.

Robert looked at him. Burke seemed weary and tired. He reached across the desk and touched Robert's shoulder. The work whistle sounded and they both turned toward the window. The workday was over and the crew returned to camp, dragging their sorry bodies up the trail. They were more mud than men, their bodies streaked yellow and brown. Outside the trailer, someone had rigged up the hose and they took turns blasting the slog from their bodies.

We maim ourselves, Robert said quietly.

What?

Robert shook his head.

Nothing, he said and looked away.

And that day when he saw Burke lower himself into the river to res-cue his crewman, the chill closed around his own heart. He was wrong. The world was small. Far too small. Someone called his name. He was running. He saw Burke's face blanching, the eyes wide as he realized what was happening. Robert dodged his grasp and sped forward. He heard his name again, Chatham!, but already he was in the air, parallel to the surge of yellow. The water rose to meet him; icy, it took his chest and his legs and his face, then he was under. He felt the hard bottom against his stomach, the air blowing through his lungs, then a shock of warm spilling from his head, his name runneling out—Robertrobertrobert—like some prayer out into the dark. And then he was not Robert, but the meat of Robert, the bone of Robert, the throbbing clockwork of Robert's heart and blood. There was no ceiling, no bottom, just a velvet tongue of unending and deepening black.

When he opened his eyes, he was disappointed he was not dead.

You're all right, someone said.

I'm not, he said. Then it was black again.

He did not know where he was. There was the smell of earth. Sod. The bitter fetor of deep soil. Far in the distance, the horizon was on fire—a long curtain of sky unraveling at its fringe. He could feel its heat now, crushing down, and a cold sweat broke through his pores. He tried to will his eyes open. The lids would not part. His arms would not move. A voice murmured above him.

Look'ah' gon' com'rown.

The voice was deep. Husky. The groan of swollen wood. A second voice answered. Crimson streaked across the inner walls of his head. He tried again to move his arms. Something lifted from his brow. He touched the region above his eye gently. An undertow of pain rose to his skin. He saw a ceiling of thatched peat and amber light. A woman floated above him, the eyes pocketed in dark.

You alive?

Her hair was dark and matted, encircling her long face. Her ear was against his chest. She placed her hand over his brow.

Da-may.

He felt something force its way into his mouth. It was bitter and greasy. A finger.

Name?

It was a man's voice now. Thick. Harsh.

He worked his tongue around the taste and gave them the name. Robert Chatham.

Rowbear Shah'tome, the voice repeated. Why is you here, Rowbear Shah'tome?

The woman stood and wiped her hands on a leather apron. His throat hurt. He wanted water. She appeared again and laid a strong-smelling poultice across his forehead. A man materialized beside her. He was older, with steely blue eyes that peered out through the rough crags of his face. He knelt down close, their noses almost touching. Robert could see the flaxen beard moving under his breath.

Have I died?

The man and the woman looked at each other.

Give him sleep, the woman said. He could see she was seated in a chair now, wringing her hands. Her leg was bouncing on her heel. T'ain't no use how he a-fevered still. Give him sleep and sound him later.

Sa'rye. The man drew away, and for a moment, Robert was alone with the woman. She sat there, still bouncing her heel. Her eyes watched him. Cobalt. Unnatural. There was a split down the center of her bottom lip from where it'd been chewed near to black. There was something in her hand. A bowl. She stood up and crossed over to him with it, scooping gray and wispy slime with two fingers. She knelt down by his head. Ah, she said. She opened her mouth wide. He did as he was told and she pushed the paste onto his tongue. Then very gently, she closed his jaws with the heel of her palm.

She wiped her hands clean and drew a rug up to his chin.

Strong chains, she whispered. And strong arms to haul them.

Robert slept in fits. Time seemed to slow then stumble forward. He felt himself being jerked from one moment to the next. From dreaming to waking, then dreaming again. One moment he was hot, his brain a sun bursting out his eyes. The next moment his limbs were ice. He woke several times to find himself sobbing and not understanding why. Faces stood over him. They asked questions. He tried to answer but could not make sense of his words. They scowled. They threatened. Then they disappeared. There was a wasp in the room. It hung upside down from the ceiling. He watched its slow progress. Its swollen stinger throbbing. He saw it dislodge from its hold, fly down to his lips to drink the sweat on his upper lip. He blinked and saw that, no, it was on the ceiling still.

The woman came to him often. She would swathe his forehead in meal, then stretch out his limbs. First his arms, then his legs, then each finger, every toe. She'd rub them together in her palms, tease the blood back into the flesh. She carried bowls full of smells, and she'd smooth the pastes on his chest. He'd breathe deeply. When he shivered and howled, she forced down his left hand and cut his index finger with a knife and sucked out the blood till the fog cleared. Soon he could tell again where one day ended and another began. Then at last his fever broke.

The woman sat him up to change the rug, which had been fouled by his sweat and phlegm.

What's your name?, he asked.

It was the first thing he remembered saying for a long time. His voice was clear and strong. The house, he realized, was far smaller than he'd first thought. It was a small dugout that'd been made smaller by the animal pelts that hung from the ceiling, forming curtains. He had been laid up on a pallet of soft mulch. Shelves had been carved out of the earthen walls, and a small fire pit had been carved out of the wall behind him. Above it were a pair of rifles, crossed over a wood crest. The woman looked at him, startled.

Your name?, he said again.

She seemed caught off guard. She looked past the curtains then back at Robert.

I's Frankie.

He tried to stand. He balanced himself against the wall. His legs were stiff, new.

How long I been here?

Two, she said.

Two days?

Non, she said. Two weeks.

Her eyes were jumping from the rifles on the wall to the man who now stood in her path to them. He realized that she might be afraid of him. Her nostrils were slightly flared, and the sun had freckled her neck and arms. They stood facing each other, her shoulders hunched, as if she'd been cornered. Robert took his hand from the wall and held it out in front of him.

The woman called out to the other room, and two men hurried in. The older of the two was the man he'd seen earlier. The other was younger, and thinner, with a waxed mustache and an arrowhead of dark brown hair beneath his lip. They were in full trapper garb, draped in tanned leather, their rifles in their arms. The woman spoke hurriedly, too quick for Robert to understand. The two men kept their eyes fixed on him. He could see the younger one, his face impassive. His hand drifted down to his belt and found rest at the hilt of a buck knife. When the woman had finally finished speaking, the older of the two men stepped forward.

Rowbear Shah'tome, he said. You nah goin' nowhere.

The older man, the one the others called Bossjohn, took him out to the other room, where he sat Robert down on a small stone bench. He untied the belt around his leatherskin coat. His coat splayed open, revealing the large stomach beneath his shirt. He slung off the coat and hung it on the wall and took a seat behind the table. His hands were coarse and yellow. The fingers were hatched with nick marks. In the front passage, a crepe curtain fluttered with the draft. Morning brimmed on the other side, one end lifting and folding over. Out in the front there were troughs and a small wood rack where fox pelts had been stretched to dry. Bossjohn folded his knuckles into his palm. He cleared his throat and looked wearily at Robert.

We warn't sure you was goin' come through. You sooffee?

Bossjohn thumped his chest. Robert nodded. Yes.

Bossjohn mimicked him, moving his head up and down solemnly, as if he was pleased that he understood.

You work'n for there bugheways. Them in there swamp?

Bugheway?

Yeah. Like you. Bugheway.

The man patted Robert on the chest.

I did, Robert said. But if I've been here two weeks, it figures I don't no more. They'll have replaced me by now.

Bossjohn stroked his beard, nodding. Men were replaceable.

Two months now, they come. They fuss our lines. Break our traps. Why?

We're . . . they're building . . . they need to clear the land. Make space.

Space?

A dam, he said. They're building a dam.

Robert looked at the man and he could see he did not understand. He made a wall with his left hand and drove his knuckles into the heel. The project had been in the works for years. He tried to describe the immensity of what was happening, tried to repeat the words that had been repeated to him. A shining new South. He described what went on in the work sites. Trees were being felled. Waterways were being collapsed, expanded, redrawn.

The man had started to redden. He was breathing heavily now, the small hairs of his beard twitching. He turned back toward Robert.

How many?

How many what?

In Panther Swamp. How many bugheway?

I don't know, Robert said. Hundreds. More.

An angry voice called out from the other room. Bossjohn let out a huff of breath and he stood up.

Stay you here, he said and walked out.

Robert found himself suddenly alone. He went to the doorway and tried to place himself within the country. In the distance, the land was hemmed in by a wide swath of tupelos arching along the horizon. There was nothing for miles—no house, no fence, no sign of a road. A thick fog was breathing through the trees. Was he still in the swamp? The air was thinner somehow, faintly musty.

He heard a noise behind him.

The rifle was trained to his heart, and behind it, the woman. Her cheek leaned into the stock, her shoulder firm against the butt.

He paused in the passage for a moment. Then he stepped back inside.

Frankie made stew in an iron cauldron while Bossjohn and the younger man worked out front. In the heat, they'd stripped off their shirts, laying bare their reddening bodies. Robert watched them pass between them the limp body of a fox, consulting each other, drawing their fingers down along the fur to mark where the cuts were to be made. They hung the fox on a rack and bled its neck. It runneled down the rope, into the soil. Bossjohn tied its head to a brace as the other man separated the skin from the flesh.

Who is that?, he asked.

Frankie looked out to where Robert was pointing.

That Roan. He Bossjohn's brother.

The men wiped the sweat from their eyes and, in so doing, painted crimson tracks along their cheeks. Flies frenzied in a mean cloud around them, trying to suck the nectar from their temples. Robert looked out into the darkening evening—at two brothers—and he thought then of his own. Billy would've been twenty-seven now. The bones of their father's face set like struts on his manly cheeks. Their mother's nose broadening on his face. He would gray early like Ellis had, a bright lightning bolt of white striking the dark nap of his hair. There were the eyes, where when they were boys, Robert could already see the devilry twinkling in the corners. Almondine and mischievous. Where are you now? Under so many tons of earth, where in the vault that amalgam of meat and fat loosens from your inner walls. And those beautiful eyes of yours, burst to jellies.

He watched the brothers work. One fox, then another, then another. They moved mechanically, drawing the small blade along the milky throat. The nerves jumping in the legs. Frankie was humming behind him. She stirred the sludge in the cauldron. If he took her. If she screamed. They would paint the walls with his black guts. He could not stop thinking about his brother. Once, they fought—he forgot about what—and bloodied each other's faces. His mama pulled them apart and lashed them three times each across their legs with a hickory stick. Look at him, she'd said to Billy, who refused to cry. That's your brother, look at him. That's your nose you broke. That's your face you scratched up. You look at that.

Now, with this memory dislodged, they rushed up one after another, unconnected, memories that he'd forgotten, or only half remembered, each one vivid and new with the sharpness of a photograph: digging for worms in the woods behind Crookhand Farm, the blue light of morning around them; bolting up in a dark room and hearing the fury of his brother's hands moving under the covers. It was Billy who taught him how to climb. Not just trees but everything. The sides of barns. Tele-graph poles. Never know when you need to get away someplace quick, his brother had said. They did push-ups together every day for six months. They stood up on two toes on the edge of their father's mule cart till they were each individually shouted down. They put spoons be-tween their teeth, and on each bowl, an egg, as they scaled up and down the bur oak behind the house. And he remembered the day his brother was brought home. His lips were blue. The tongue lolled in his mouth. A dark blue crescent stained his neck. They wrapped him in white cotton and laid him out on the cooling board. His mama had not understood. It was because they shared this skin that they brutalized each other. They cut and bruised and bloodied and humiliated each other, to know them-selves. To see this range of themselves.

There was a cry. He looked up. The two brothers had stopped their working. They looked up toward the sky. Roan had his arm out and he was pointing. The sun was setting and bright plumes of orange lit up behind the trees, spindling into the yolky sky. Frankie came behind him. She let out a gasp. Then Robert saw. Swirling over them, riding along the draft, it climbed soundlessly to the upper reaches of sky. Then it snowed down. Robert held his hand out. He caught an ashy flake in mid-air and smudged it in his palm.

That evening Robert had to explain to them as best he could about the burn. When the crews cleared land, they left heaps of dead brush behind them. All the timber they could salvage was sent to the mills. Every-thing else went into the burn. Tree husks, taproots, brittle goitered knots of deadwood. The crews dragged it all to a yard beside the river. It was the excrement of the dam, laid high in a tinder waste pile, and at the end of each month a team would climb the mound and douse it through with gasoline. The smoke slithered through the gnarls, collecting into itself till it was thick and solid. Ribbons of crimson and ruby smacked through the whorls. And as it climbed the blaze sucked the air, commanding it down into its heart. The fire would last through the night and into the morning, eviscerating the tinder into white smoldering chalk.

You make them burns?, Frankie asked.

Around the table all eyes were on him. He was not the only thing that they had rescued. By his feet he recognized the steel casing of a model six slurry pump. Wooden boards had been laid across the top to make a table. At the center was the stew, simmering in a large clay pot. It was cooked thick and greasy, and islands of fat drifted across the surface.

Once or twice, he told her, though he knew it was over a dozen times. It was grueling work, and he was the only of Burke's men willing to do it. The fact was, he was drawn to it. The light and heat woke something inside him. He'd see figures in the blaze, open twisting mouths, faces without eyes whipping around each other. He'd hear voices. The wheeze of gas escaping. The suck and pop of air and wood. And in him a second flame burned steadily. A flurry of moths would cross the river and flutter at the edge of the heat, drawn toward that bright heart. He thought of making a pyre of his body. He watched the embers crash. He pressed the devil to his throat. He looked for direction.

The winds must have changed, he said, to scatter the ash out this way.

Bossjohn folded his arms and stroked his chin. His eyes had dimmed.

But why? How the reason?

Frankie balanced her head on her palm, pulling back the thick band of hair behind her ears.

Robert shrugged. For room to get the machines through. So they can start building.

Bossjohn nodded.

They did not know. They couldn't feel the future bearing down on them. There would be no Panther. No trapping grounds. No foxes. No furs. A pain like glass shot through his gut. He hadn't realized how hungry he was, how long it had been since he'd had anything to eat. The thick pungent soup on the table suddenly seemed so inviting. He would plunge his face into it, inhale every stinking drop.

Frankie rose to pour the stew into bowls. She stirred the foam with a flat stick and broke the top inch where the stew was clearer. She stirred up the bits of meat and filled Robert's bowl. When the meal was doled out between everyone at the table, Bossjohn announced it was time to pray.

They hung their heads down to their chests and clasped their hands together, resting them on the edge of the tabletop. Robert did as they did and Bossjohn began.

O Lord, fo' these grease 'n beans, and for hands and wits to kill them, and make of yor'n bounty, we frow up our thanks. Bless us with strong chains and strong arms to haul them, this day till judgment, amen.

Bossjohn had taken Frankie's hand and was massaging her palm. Robert looked away, pretending not to see. The younger man, Roan, he realized had been staring at him, his eyes still and alert. When Bossjohn had finished with their prayers, they all began to eat. He looked around him. There were no spoons. No forks. Bossjohn fished out a strip of pink glistening meat with his fingers. He dragged it along the thick yellow sauce and ate, craning his neck out to catch the drippings. Robert watched him. He brought the bowl to his lips, taking large steaming swallows.

Robert could glimpse the knob of a leg bone. He sucked it clean and used it to spoon up the thick paste. It was hot and heavily spiced in marjoram and pepper to hide the awful tang of rubber. The meat sang on his tongue. He didn't ask what it was. He didn't want to know. It went down into his gut, sending a hot rush of acid into his throat. Despite the taste, it was good to eat. To have something behind his ribs again. He took the bowl up with two hands and tilted it toward his mouth. He inhaled the mash, flooding his tongue with its bitter taste, the breath exploding from his nostrils. He forced it through the stiff muscles in his throat, drawing it down into the pit of his stomach. He'd never eaten before, really eaten. His jaws ached. His stomach cramped. He told himself to slow down, but his arms wouldn't listen.

When he'd finished, he set the bowl down.

They were watching him.

He was aware of the yellow splattered around his cheeks and the wad of hot mash in his mouth. He wiped his lips with the back of his arm.

Frankie grinned. You like?

He nodded, looking down at the edge of the table. It's very good, ma'am. Thank you.

Y'ought to slow on there supping. Gon' take ill et'ing so quick, she warned.

Roan muttered something low underneath his breath. Whatever it was, it'd caught Frankie's and Bossjohn's attention. They turned to him, their eyes wide and mouths agape as if they'd been struck. Roan stood up. He smoothed back the front strands of his hair with the heel of his hand, took his hat from off the wall, and disappeared outside.

They finished supper without Roan. When they ate their fill, Frankie and Bossjohn rose soundlessly from their seats. Robert stood, his back to the wall, watching them work. Frankie stacked the bowls and left them to soak in a pail outside while Bossjohn began striking apart the table. The planks were carried out and the engine casing was put away in the corner. Frankie went into the other room and returned carrying two bearskin rolls in her arms. She untied them and spread them into a pallet across the floor.

When he'd finished with the table, Bossjohn appeared in the passage. Rowbear, he said. He beckoned him outside with his large hand.

They walked out behind the earthen house to the back stoop where cords of firewood lay stacked together. Bossjohn sat down on the chopping block. Sit, he said pointing to a small bench beside the wood. Bossjohn smoothed his palms against his knees. He took a small pipe from inside his vest and fit it into his mouth. It stuck out from his beard like a stem as he tamped a wad of tobacco down with his thumb.

He pointed to a spot beneath the bench and to a box of matches.

Robert struck one and carried it carefully into the bowl. Bossjohn puckered, sending up spurts of soft blue smoke. He drew in deeply and sighed.

Robert shook the match dead and dropped it in the grass.

How long you plan on keeping me here?

He looked at Robert through the slits of his eyes. After a long moment, he reached into his vest pocket and held out a small yellow ribbon.

I find this in swampdeep, near a muskrat run. They was all over, hanging from there spruces. What they for?

Robert looked at the ribbon but refused to take it. He pulled on the joints of his hands.

They're markers, he said.

Bossjohn did not seem to understand.

They tell us where to clear next.

The man tapped the bit against his teeth.

How long till'n they clear here way?

Soon. A month or two I'd guess.

He moved the pipe from one side of his mouth to the other. A hum rumbled softly in his throat.

You work'm for there bugheway men, he said. You know how'n they think.

He touched the side of Robert's head with the crook of his pipe.

I told you everything I know, Robert said.

You be very Nice Jack and help us, Rowbear. You stay nice-so, then we loose you outta here. L'Etangs been trapping in Panther for seven and thirty years now. We not aimin' to pack tow and go.

Robert felt something on his ankle. A spider. It tickled at the short hairs of his leg. He scooped it up in his hand and let it run up the inside of his arm. He looked at Bossjohn and he saw him clearly for the first time. The man didn't understand. None of them did. It wasn't up to them. An undertow of sorrow eroded away at something inside him, and he struggled to keep it from showing.

L'Etang? That French?, he asked.

The spider trilled along his skin, upward, ever upward, toward his neck. What was in its brain, he wondered, that made it seek this height? When it reached his shoulder, he grabbed it, almost too roughly, and held it in his palm. He could kill it. And surely this spider, if it could pray, would be praying now. And who would deliver it?

Non. No French since mon Pierre L'Etang come down from Snakebite Creek to trap Yazoo. Pierre he go up'n down every hook 'n crook a this river. Thirteen year he work the beaver run. Wash the French clear out 'a him.

Bossjohn was grinning. Robert could almost admire this man, his insistence. The spider fought inside the walls of his fingers. He felt two sharp stings and he let it go on the grass. He squeezed his hand till four red dots pooled on the skin of his finger. He looked up. Bossjohn was staring at him now, his eyebrows forced together. The little devil had come free from under his shirt.

What's that?

Robert hooked his thumb under the twine and shoved it back under his shirt. He didn't answer him.

The Yazoo don't wash nothing, Robert said, waving him away. It's a dirty river like all the rivers in this place. It puts a slick on you that you ain't ever get clean of. All that waste and want and hurt just gums on.

The man looked at him, his eyebrows slanted together, the corners of his mouth tugged back in confusion.

A man can't wash out his own blood, Robert said.

Bossjohn shook his head. He looked up past the tree line, to where the sky was getting darker, coloring like a bruise. He took the pipe from his lips and sighed softly. The moon was white and faint over the rise.

Come, he said, standing. His voice was soft, almost rotten in his mouth. Tomorrow you gon' get to work.

~~~

THAT NIGHT ROBERT LAY ON HIS ROLL, NOT SLEEPING. OVER AND over, his mind bent toward the strange woman who was among his captors. When she had aimed her rifle at him earlier that day, it wasn't death that made him pause and cross back into the house. He knew his devil would not let him get run through with shot any more than it had let him drown in the Yazoo or burn in Bruce. He could not count the times he'd come so close to death only to be thrown violently again into life.

He saw her muscular arms train the barrel to his chest. Her eyes were tensed and full of white, the blood flushed into her ivory skin. She would've shot him dead. He thought this, alone in the dark room, atop the pallet she had prepared for him. *She would've shot me dead.* And so he stepped, not away but toward her, into the hot white cone of her blast. Her shoulders were squared. Her finger was taut on the trigger. She had no anger. No fear. And suddenly he felt the very real dimensions of his own body, the sheaths of muscle tugging along his bones. There were his arms, his heart beating in its cage, his tongue in his mouth. There were his feet, and the hard earth against his soles. He was here, made solid before her eyes, bright and full of blood. She could obliterate him.

This was why he stayed. The fluid redirected in his head. *I am staying.*

And had his brother said this too? I am staying. Did the same regions of his brain engorge with blood, did the nerves flame and blister in the same pattern? He could almost hear his life snap into place. For a moment, he wanted to be outside, looking up into that yawning maw above him, the blighted moons and bad stars, to face again that invisible judgment.

Through the night, he listened for her breathing, for their voices catching against each other. But for their part Bossjohn and Frankie were quiet in the other room. Their bodies shifted, their limbs reassembled around each other. Robert would drift in and out of sleep, waking with a start, his heart in his throat. But there was nothing. There was no one. His skull ached with dreaming. A terrible thought hummed behind his eyes. He touched the pouch, almost instinctively. He did not know how he knew, but he knew. The Dog was coming.

～⌒

BOSSJOHN TOOK HIM TO THE TANNING SHED BEHIND THE DUGOUT. The shed was small and drafty, with pins of light coming through the boards. Coon and muskrat pelts were stretched flat and nailed onto the wall. At the center was a chair and a beam to stretch the skins. He sat Robert down and stretched a bolt of possum hide along the shaft. Then he handed him a dull blade. For hours Robert grained fat and meat and vein from the underskin.

For weeks, he worked in the tanning shed—sometimes with Bossjohn, sometimes alone. There were jars of piss and dung, and he soaked the hides in them to make them soft, to give them give. The skulls he smashed against a rock to scoop up the spongy mounds. They were boiled into a soup and massaged into the pliant hides. The smell was unbearable, suffocating in the noontime sun. Out in the heat, flies would catch the scent and mob around his eyes and hands and the lobes of his ears. Sweat gathered in fat drops along his brow, his own skin blistering and welted.

He thought often about escaping, but where could he escape to? He was in a low sparse country at the outer ring of the swamp, what they called the Flats. They were hemmed on all sides by tupelos, and swamp oak and black willow, and at its edges lay broad miles of rough uneven earth. For those who weren't used to mucking, it made for hard travel. But a L'Etang could step through a thicket and disappear down a deer trail and follow the streams and arteries that fed in and out the Yazoo. Robert looked out into the dense rim of trees at the edge of the Flats. Beyond it were sinkholes. Bear traps. Deadfalls. During the summer floods, forests of bald cypress would become infested with mosquitoes, and whole sweeps of land would become uncrossable. He could see no escape.

And soon a month had passed into the peak of the hot season and Robert realized that no one had come looking for him, not even to drag his poor damned body from the river. He came outside the tanning shed after a long morning in the stifling heat. His hands were raw from tanning. He did not know what day it was, nor what month exactly. The thought occurred to him that he might've had his twenty-third birthday recently. That outside the swamp, he was a year older, but here, within, time had no meaning. Not the past, nor the future. He looked up at the clear cloudless sky and squinted at the bright burning center. He waited for a sign.

~

HE WAS SHAKEN AWAKE, AND HE OPENED HIS EYES AND SAW THE man, Roan, above him. It was early still, the light dim inside the dugout save for the two silver dollars of Roan's eyes bearing down upon him. Across his arms lay his rifle, the stock nuzzled into the crook of his elbow. How long had he been watching him? Rise up, he said. With the toe of his boot, the man pushed roughly against his ribs. Robert rolled over and the man hoisted him to his feet. He walked him out front, keeping the rifle trained on his back. It was morning, in the yolky red hour just after the dawn. The air was cool and sticky with dew, and he heard the noise of birds clamoring in the wild.

Are you going to shoot me?, he asked.

Roan stepped around him and then he saw the tin basin. It'd been drawn full of water.

Strip, the man said.

Robert passed his shirt over his head and stepped out of his trousers. He stood before him, naked, his chest rising and falling.

That'un too.

He gestured to Robert's neck.

Robert touched the stiff leather of the pouch. He paused for a moment, then let his hand fall.

No, he said. It stays on.

The man seemed to think for a moment, and then he shrugged.

Okay, Roan said. Bon. Now get you in.

With the rifle, he gestured into the tub.

Slowly, Robert climbed into the icy water. It was electric. A bolt of cold shot through him. He wanted to cry out, but he clenched down and shuddered weakly. The nerves jumped inside his legs, and he had to brace the sides of the basin to keep from falling over.

The man watched on, a smirk working across his face.

We gon' on a petit trip real nice-nice, muskie.

Roan crossed to a bucket and filled it from between Robert's legs. He raised it up and let it spill over Robert's head. A sun erupted behind Robert's eyes and he buckled. He heard his own haggard voice fighting in his throat.

But first we gon' get you nice clean, wash'm up good. Get'r that nigger stink off'a you.

The man took his time bathing him, filling the bucket then pouring it across Robert's shoulders or on his head. Sometimes he'd cluck his tongue like he was consoling a small child. He soaked a rag in muskrat oil, then he ordered Robert to stand and turn. Roan rubbed him down, working the dark brown cloth hard on Robert's neck, under his arms, and his groin. The smell was stomach turning. By the time the man had finished, Robert could no longer feel his own body. Only a cherrystone of nausea in the pit of his gut.

When Roan was satisfied, he ordered Robert out of the basin. Robert was shivering and his lips were blue, and the sun seemed to give no comfort. Roan dressed him in a canvas shirt and a pair of hide pants, and for his wrists, a pair of iron shackles. They were old and rusted and must've been part of an old animal trap. The thick links of chain were heavy and unfamiliar. It took all his effort to keep his hands up, to keep them from falling toward the earth.

Next came the rabbit box.

Roan held it up in front of him. The box was hickory and a foot deep in every direction. On the bottom was a folding panel that would lock around his neck. Roan was shorter so he had Robert kneel, and he set the box down over his head like a crown. The thing was heavy and uncomfortable, the rugged edges digging into his shoulders. It was a cage, he realized. Hot and moist and airless. Only the narrow slat inches from his nose threw any light, and all around in the invading periphery was a soft gray dark. Something cold and metal tightened around his neck, locking the box in place.

Bon, bon, he heard the man say.

From inside the box, it was hard to make out what was happening. At some point, Bossjohn and Frankie had come out from the dugout and had been arguing with Roan. Robert nursed the hope that they would force him to remove the box, but it did not happen. He felt a yanking on his chain, and so they began. For hours he followed the noise of their footsteps, of the grass passing across their shins—journeying through invisible country. He imagined them, the L'Etangs, passing through the pulsing wilderness.

Robert tired quickly. His head hurt, and it was almost impossible to breathe. Come the afternoon, the air had become warm and sticky and he could smell the tooth rotting in his own mouth. There were times he wanted to throw up, but he forced his mind clear. After what felt like days, they finally stopped. He felt the box raise from off his shoulders and the light hurt his eyes.

Frankie touched his arm.

Sa'sooffee?, she asked.

He didn't answer her. He looked and he realized they'd come to a kind of pond. He stumbled toward the bank and dunked his head into the cool water. He came back up, his eyes shut, his face throbbing. There was a smell, he realized. A stench. He looked out over the water. It was almost still. A cloud of mosquitoes pulsed above the shallows. Flecks of pollen crawled across the surface. For the first time in months, he saw his own reflection. He almost did not recognize himself. What fat there was in his face had dissolved, drawing the skin tight against his cheekbones. He thought, suddenly, that he looked not like Ellis but like his mother. The papery skin at the corners of his eyes, the square squat brow, the narrow bruised-looking lips. How strange family is, haunting your blood, with all those phantom faces lying in wait beneath your own. He felt ill.

Something flickered in the corner of his vision and he turned. There, in the tall reeds, was a mass of yellow and pink. It was an animal. Its belly was ripped open and its head was missing. Strips of moldy blackened skin lay in patches over the cave in the thing's chest. Flies struggled atop one another, pressing in and out of the yielding meat.

Robert dropped to his knees. His stomach unspooled and he heaved his sick onto the grass. Bossjohn made a clucking noise at the back of his throat.

He was allowed to rest while Roan and Bossjohn went on ahead to check their traplines. Frankie stayed with him. He lay down in the shade as Frankie gave him hunks of fry dough from her ration bag. There were spots in his vision still, blinking in and out, but the blood had calmed inside his chest. Frankie took off her hat and fanned warm slow waves of air against Robert's neck, shooing the flies from his face. Robert listened to her murmuring as she went in and out of her pack. Here and there he'd hear their name for him—Rowbear. He could cry. What he wouldn't give to be Rowbear! To be, like a L'Etang, baptized anew in the cold waters. But he was a Chatham and bad stayed stuck to Chathams.

When Roan and Bossjohn returned empty-handed, their faces a sheen of sweat, neither brother spoke. Roan kicked the soft carcass into the water, and they gathered up their things. Robert was placed again inside the rabbit box, and as the wall came down, he thought he could see a note of sorrow in Frankie's face.

THEY WENT THROUGH THE TRAPPING GROUNDS, AND INSIDE THE box, Robert did not see the stretches of blighted country—long waterways of dead water, blown-out hills, swaths of nuded grass and timberland. He did not know how in the summer seasons, they used to fat on rabbit and whitetail and shoot coyotes from the trees. For the L'Etangs, the traps themselves turned up little. A squirrel here. A mangy soreskinned rabbit with hardly the meat or fur to spend the effort. But all throughout, they came across kill like they'd seen by the pond—puddles of spongy viscera rotting in the hot wet sun.

These were signs of panthers. They kept territory in the palmetto to the north and west where they could feed on hog and raccoon, and it was rare to find them east, here, in the beaver grounds. Panther pelts fetched a high price at Fort Muskethead, but crossing a panther was bad luck. They drove away quarry, raided traps, and if they'd gotten this far, it meant that game was scarce all through the swamp.

But Robert saw the kill and he understood; the Dog had found him. He sucked the thick stale air inside the box. The links on his wrists chinked softly. Through the narrow slit in the rabbit box, he could see the wide fan of leaves, the sunlight filtering down through the gauzy canopy above him. There were birds. The machinelike whir of insects tearing through the invisible air around him. They came to a rocky narrow and they filed across in a single line, Bossjohn ahead, and then Roan tugging Robert by his chain. Frankie was behind him. He could hear her light step against the ground. Her hand touched the sweaty blade of his shoulder, navigating him through the forest. Even here, it'd found him.

They stopped that evening at a crumbling shelter in the middle of the swamp. It was a small wood lean-to put up by Pierre L'Etang nearly half a century ago. The walls were thin, pieced from cut timber and roofed with carpets of moss. There were shelves inside, and a small clearing in the dirt for where they'd lay their bedrolls. They refilled their canteens and stocked their pouches with jerky and tack. In the evening they bedded down next to each other, Robert against the wall and Roan wedged beside him.

Night came uneasy over Panther Swamp. A yellow moon moldered in the lower reaches of the sky. It was full and round and oozed like a pustule. Underneath, the air pulsed with cricket song. Heavy birds thrashed in the treetops, then winged soundlessly through the ink-blue air. Robert lay on his roll. He shut his eyes and he listened. He peeled back the night sounds, one by one, until finally he could hear it, clear as a whistle, the long lonesome call of some animal.

HE WOKE TO THE DRY VIOLENT SUCK OF HIS OWN BREATH DROPPING into his throat. He shot upright. His heart hammered in his chest. He was awake. He'd been dreaming—what about he could not remember, only knew that he could still feel the tightness in his chest. Robert touched his face, his lips. He fingered the cool links of his chain. He set his back against the wall and rested his head against the rough timber. He shut his eyes and tried to steady the jumping in his neck. He took a deep breath, letting it out between his teeth. He opened his eyes and let them adjust to the dark. There were his legs, the roll. There were the shelves against the wall, the sacks of grain, the jars of water. By the doorway, he saw Bossjohn, still asleep, the moonlight blanketed atop him.

The roll beside him was empty. Roan was gone, as was Frankie.

Now was his chance.

He sat up, gathered the slack of his chain into his palms, and very quietly worked his boots onto his feet.

Outside, the air was chill and damp and the ground was jeweled in dew. He was free, but he could not remember the way he had come. Every direction looked the same—thick impenetrable darkness that fed deeper into the swamp. Robert looked up. The moon was a cataract eye, white now and milky. He felt its gaze shoot through him. He was small suddenly, naked under its light. His hummingbird heart smashed itself against his ribs.

Robert flew deep into the swamp. The forest pressed in around him. He fumbled blindly through its walls of hooked and thorny foliage, which snagged his clothes and tore his skin. A fresh bright sting bloomed on his cheek and neck. He lifted up his hands to protect his face, pushing against the dense netting of weeds and vines. Something filtered down from above him. Dry and moldy. He pushed through, felt the ground slope down beneath him.

Here, the moon could not break through the trees. He could not see. He took a step and the ground was soft and yielding. His feet slid apart beneath him, and he stumbled forward trying to catch himself. On his way down something hit him hard across the chest. A rock. A tree root. He tried to stand but he couldn't. His right leg was deadweight under him. His mind flashed to the carcass at the water. He clasped the devil around his neck. His lungs were on fire. This last time, see me through.

He sat there, panting, the blood damming in his temples.

Without moonlight, he could not tell the foreground from the back. The night lay draped like a wet sheet around his face. Dark stretched for miles in every direction. His ankle was throbbing. He worked off his boot and pressed his fingers into the swollen tissue. He sniffled softly. Was this what it was like? To be under the earth. No sight. The dim *whoosh* of blood draining in his ears. A lozenge of light hummed inches from his eyes, flaring then dying away. Now another. And another, this time farther out. Slowly he rose, easing his weight onto his good leg.

Lightning bugs filled the space like stars. They pulsed in time, floating up on one side, and drifting down the other, churning slow through the air like a waterwheel. Carefully, he followed their yellow-green burn through the ether, feeling out the space in front of him. He came to where the path narrowed, hemming in against an earthen wall. He put his hand against its face. It was cool and soft, napped with roots. Here the air was ancient, yolky, rotted through with water. He'd been traveling along a dry bed gully.

He squeezed through the narrow and after a few yards, there was sky again. He found a place where the walls were shallow and climbed out. The swamp opened to a large uneven clearing. Ahead of him was a kettle pond, marked off in a square by yellow caution tape. Behind the tape, he saw something catch the light, an eye. He moved toward it. There it was, standing on its mount, a surveyor's transit. One of the crews had forgotten to take it back to the equipment depot. He reached for it, this alien thing, and touched the cool brass casing.

He looked again. It was not a pond at all, but a large crater. The edges had been dynamited out and support structures installed along the base. The beginnings of the Panther Reservoir.

Something crackled and all at once he felt himself being wrestled down. The ground came hard against his head and he became confused. The night crashed like a wave above him. He wriggled against the earth as blows rained down on his skull and spine and kidneys. His arms popped from their sockets. He cried out. He felt himself being turned over. Something thin and cold slid against his neck.

Voom'urie-eh-ci.

Robert looked up and found those cold hard eyes inches from his face. It was Roan.

You gon' be very still now.

The knife crawled thinly across his throat.

Is it now?, he asked himself. Here was as good as anywhere, just feet from the reservoir—their new shining South. Robert tried to ready himself. It had come. It had finally come. But he couldn't quiet the panic in his flesh. His eyes could not focus. The blood raged inside him. He could not keep his arms from jumping nor his teeth from chattering. That was the worst of it—to leave with that *clatter-clack* in his skull. The warmth was on his neck. The knife was gone. Roan too. The universe hurtled away from him. From the corner of his eye, he saw the Dog. Its hind legs lay tucked under its muscular body, foam gathered thick on its muzzle. Robert watched it, his heavy mind slow to turn. He saw it in the moonlight: the svelte sheen of its fur. Every furrow and wrinkle of its coal-black hide. A thick sappy filament unspooled from its chops.

It hurt to breathe, to sift the air through his still-raw throat. *I am soul and brain sick and there is no dog.* He shut his eyes, and it was true. He was not well. Had not been for a long time. There was too much time that'd passed, too many miles spent in lonesome country. I'm ready, he said. But then she was above him. Frankie. Her hands were crushed against his throat. Her mouth was moving, shaping words. He did not hear them.

The missing Negro had not slowed work at the swamp. When no family came forward, the Yazoo County Sheriff's Department filed Chatham, Robert Lee, among the other transients of the county. George Burke went every day for two weeks to see what, if anything, the police had found.

The deputy moved the piles of blue and pink forms across his desk. They stacked over three feet high. Too many to keep a count of, the deputy told him. The top button of his shirt was undone and his tie was set crooked. He assured Burke that they were doing everything they could. Burke thanked him and went out into the street, a cold wind threatening to blow off his hat.

He tried to put Chatham out of his mind. Within a week, a new man was hired to fill the vacancy on his crew. Late summer brought fair blue weather, and the crew worked long days, moving tons of yielding earth.

He'd seen men die before in blowouts and explosions. In his career, he'd personally pulled the mangled bodies of six of his crewmen from under fallen rubble. He remembered each and every one—the soft cast of their faces, still and chalky white save for the deep slow rose of blood incarcerated beneath the skin. There were sacrifices. Burke understood that. That at times, the world called for more than was fair or was right. But he'd never met a man who so vigorously sought out those sacrifices, who wanted to make that offering in his own blood and body.

The other members of the crew underestimated Robert Chatham. Chatham was quiet and didn't socialize with the other men. During lunch, he'd sit alone under a tree, outside the rough noise of cussing and dirty jokes at the chow tables. Every day it was the same meal—a ham sandwich with a single slice of cheese—and he'd chew slow and methodical, staring out from under the shade.

But Burke recalled when the crew was on demolition and after a blast how Chatham would walk across the craters. He remembered the beaver dam, the emptiness of his face as he stared back at him from across the desk. No shame or fear or surprise. And on the day of the blowout, he was inches away. Could almost touch him. His body broke through the river, his vulture form diving into the foam.

From the sheriff's department, Burke started walking. He was a large man and he made himself look small by stooping and shoving his hands into his pockets. He followed the trail of grit in the gutters, crossing one street then another. Cars churned dust in his direction as they drove past. He squinted and kept walking. He arrived at Chatham's boarding-house, unsure if it was an accident or if he'd been guided.

The landlady was an old colored woman. She let the door open just a few inches so that the space could frame her mouth.

Yes?

Ma'am. Good afternoon.

Afternoon, she said carefully.

I'm a friend of one of your boarders. Former boarder. Robert Chatham.

Robert didn't have no friends, she said.

We worked together. Don't mean to put you out but I'd like to see his room if you'd allow me.

The woman squinted hard at him and furrowed her lip.

Let me go talk to my husband, she said.

She closed the door. When it opened again later, she had a ring of keys in her hand.

This way, she said.

They went up a long narrow staircase and came to the door at the top of the stairs. Burke reached for the knob, but the landlady stopped him.

You know, he owes for the month, your friend. I'm out a whole month on account of him.

Burke reached into his wallet. He found some bills and pushed them into her hand.

Inside, the apartment was bare. The windows were open, letting in the cold. On the floor where the bed had been, there were marks where the posts used to stand. An empty footlocker sat pushed against the wall. The landlady flipped the lid down and sat on it like a bench.

This is it?, Burke said. This is where he lived?

If the landlady had heard him, she made no sign. Her leg was propped across her lap and she was massaging the veins of her ankles.

Burke walked to the window and rested his hands on the sill. He tried to imagine Chatham's hands there, looking out the same window. There was nothing out there. Flat, empty, nothing.

It true he took his own life?, the woman asked.

I don't know, Burke said. Where are his things?

Sold them. Didn't figure they'd do him any good now. Anything I couldn't get rid of is in that closet there.

Burke pulled back the closet door.

You can take anything you like, but you won't get nothing for it.

There were some clothes, worn through and moth-eaten. A hat that had lost its shape. On the high shelf he found a small box. He brought it down, the contents rustling within. He looked at the landlady and she shrugged. Burke blew the dust from the lid. Inside was a layer of fine white sand. He took some in his fist and let it run down his palms.

Is that . . . ?

He brought his nose to the lip of the box. It didn't smell of anything.

He brought the grains to his thumb and tasted it.

Well?, the landlady asked. What is it?

Burke worked his tongue against his cheek. He wiped his hands on the side of his pants and returned the box to the shelf.

Table salt, he said.

AS THE CREWS LEFT FOR HOME, BURKE STAYED IN HIS TRAILER AND decided to get drunk. The sun was sinking low and the sticky air seemed to sit in his lungs like a tar. He reached into his drawer and found the bottle of whiskey his brother-in-law had given him last Christmas. He wiped the dust from the neck and pulled the cork with his teeth. Outside, the last of the men were boarding the bus back into town. He went to the door and stood in its frame. The bottle hung at his side. He let its weight sway on the hook of his fingers, tapping against his leg. The sun always seemed at its most brilliant going down. To the west, he could see the start of towers rising from the swamp. Skeletons. He tugged from the bottle, saluting them. The plow trucks and drill cranes bowed their clawed heads.

The clamor of construction work faded, overtaken by the chorus of crickets and toads, the low pulse of swamp sounds. The sky surged bright gold, then pale, into a poisoned gloom. Soon it was full dark and Burke could no longer see in front of him.

They put us in a wilderness, he thought. But this was their job. To be in this wild and to force it back, to bury it under concrete and stone.

It was time to check that the equipment sheds were locked. He got to his feet and groped for his coat and boots. Then he tested a flashlight against the flat of his hand. Outside, the gate lamps were burning. He followed the fence line west, toward the supply depot, shining his light through the spokes. There was no wind, just his cold white breath dissolving in front of him.

Outside, the light threw a long arc on the floor. It was a cloudless, moonless night and above him spanned a deep and pervading black with no stars to relieve it. At the edge of the light, something moved swiftly away.

He swung the light to a narrow gap between two trailers.

It was a cat, sleek and black with yellow eyes.

He laughed at himself and knelt down in front of it.

Come here, he whispered. He reached into the gap, clucking his tongue, but the cat retreated. He felt in his coat and found his pipe and tobacco. His hands were trembling from the cold, and he spilled the leaves onto his lap. He lit and drew deeply from the bit. Well, he said to the cat. Her muscular rump was raised high. She rubbed against Burke awhile, flicking her tail at his chin. When she realized that he had no food, she stalked away to sulk beneath the floorboards of the trailer.

He stumbled on through a field of diggers, cranes, drill trucks whose forms stuck up from the ground like sepulchers. He thought he heard a noise. The crackle of frost. Clothes swishing. He brought the light over his head and steadied it. There was the noise again. The small hairs of his neck stood on end.

He panned the flashlight across the ground, the light sluicing along the short blades of shrub grass. It caught on some small piece of wire in the distance. It winked at him. He moved unsteadily toward it and came to a large gate. The lock had been broken and the gate swung open easily with his touch. He passed through the portal and walked on. As he went, he felt the earth climbing, the ground beneath him becoming steeper and steeper till at last he found himself on his hands and knees, forcing his weight upward. When he came to the top, he was atop a large earth embankment. Below him, the darkness plunged for miles. He shone the light into the pit, but it was no use. There was no bottom. Soon the bulb flickered, waned, and died and he threw it down into the pit. The future lay sprawled in front of him—no shape, no form—the low white drone of water in the distance.

rankie had reached her hand inside his neck and pinched off the gushing artery. She had saved his life and for this he hated her. He would no longer speak or eat or let Frankie near enough to change his bandage or lay to his neck any stinking paste. The gauze had turned stiff and black, and the wound beneath had started to draw flies. He was rotting and he did not care. In the corner of the room, he sat, his knees tucked up to his chest, staring hard at a knot of wood. She would speak his name and his eyes would drift up then fall away, uninterested.

Weeks passed in the swamp and the heat broke, calling down rain and wind. It whinnied through the trees and sent wood chips and twigs hurtling through the trails. When the storm had lifted, the sumac had begun to pink and yellowjackets menaced the air. The weather was turning and if they were going to live through the winter, they needed to go downland through the southern corridor where the waters were still warm enough to trap beaver and shoot wild boar. But Frankie worried that Rowbear would not survive the journey.

Mebbe it time t'leave Panther, she told Bossjohn. Go elsewhere.

Roan snickered.

You gon' put on a dress and go they bugheway churches? Spin yarn wit all they bugheway women?

We can go to Snakebite Creek, she said. We can start again.

Bossjohn rose suddenly. His face was red and he stood hunched and huffing.

Pierre L'Etang come down to Panther by he'self. One man he clear here timber. One man he drag chain and when go him North to Beaver, we lay they old bones down in there palmetto. Mon pere all laid under in this swamp. This we mud. This we home. You no fo'getting that.

Frankie became quiet.

Bossjohn stewed moodily in his thoughts for a moment until finally he spoke.

You's gon' take Rowbear back 'a Flats and wait fo' us.

You gon' leave her with that animal?, Roan muttered.

Bossjohn looked into his brother's eyes. Oui, he said.

Frankie cooked them a breakfast of fried cornmeal, and when they had finished, she watched them go, packs loaded, leaving Frankie her rifle, some shells, and enough food and water to last the week. The lantana closed up around them. They'd be gone a month. Longer if the game was scarce. Frankie kicked dirt over the fire and scrubbed the pan out with dust. She knew they were bound for a lean winter. She did not need Bossjohn telling her about L'Etangs. Her mother was Mathilde Haskins, and 'fore that, Mathilde L'Etang. Sweet Till, they called her. She was born of Horace and Therese L'Etang and was sister to Pierre, Maurice, Otum, and Tomas. She had flaming red hair and crooked teeth and arms like a bear—thick and strong. Back then, L'Etangs were still in the north woods and had never set foot in no swamp. Sweet Till was six years old when she had hired herself out to the lumber camps, carting hatchets and shovels and handsaws to the men and taking the dull heads to the whet wheel for sharpening. She'd hone them herself, her nose bent low as she rode the sharp against the stone, watching it spark. When she was old enough, she got a job with the camps and swung those selfsame hatchets. She drank and swore, and she'd wrestle the arm off any man fool enough to try her.

When she was seventeen, Sweet Till had broken the arm off a Choctaw shipping clerk from across the border. He was her opposite in every way. Sweet Till was a friendly heavyset girl, loud and exuberant. The clerk, Mr. Haskins, was small, thin boned, quiet. Never said more than three words to anybody. Those who'd met him said he had a dark temper to match his skin, but he had a pretty face, Sweet Till would tell Frankie later, near like a china doll.

Frankie was never clear on why the small brittle 108-pound Mr. Haskins would lock arms with Sweet Till L'Etang. Nor could she figure what was in her father's mind when he heard the pop deep in his meat, when his whole arm shuddered apart and folded back on itself. What she knew was that Sweet Till set his arm in plaster and took him home. She nursed him up on soup, sitting on the edge of the bed and spooning it into his mouth, though there weren't a thing wrong with his other arm. Mr. Haskins spent a month laid up with Sweet Till, and when that month was gone, he was gone with it. And when Sweet Till began to show, she quit timbering and her parents sent her down-country where her oldest brother, Pierre, had gone years before.

She rode the train alone across the border, a plum-sized thing inside of her. There were no windows in her cabin, so she'd steal out to the dining car where the views were huge and wide, and she'd watch the country roll around her, the mountains white as bone and the crisp evergreens in the distance. She felt herself being thrust like a bullet into this land. The sun was warm and bright, and she stood there, her palms against the cool glass, until someone from the waitstaff asked her would she please return to her car.

Her brother met her at the station and he was different from what she remembered. She was small when he left home and she had in her mind the image of a boy, thin, brown-eyed and fair-haired with large front teeth and ears that stuck out from the side of his head, like an ass. But now he was older, balding, his skin bronzed. He had a small paunch, and his back had taken on a deep stooping hunch. Pierre's front teeth were still large but there were less of them now, brown with chaw.

He came with his two boys, the older one almost a man, save for the fine down on his upper lip; the younger one hardly above his father's knee. The woman Pierre had taken for his wife died the past winter, and all that was left of her haunted those boys' faces. The dark hair. The dagger chin. Eyes so blue they made her shiver. Pierre pushed the boys forward to greet their aunt, and they each gave her a firm brave handshake. The little one, she would tell Frankie, would not stop crying.

She kept house for them in a small cabin on the outskirts of Panther Swamp. She dressed and cleaned their kills, fed them, swept out the cabin, and soon she found herself missing her days in the lumber camp. For Pierre, the world had opened inside the swamp. He killed beaver and nutria and wild boar, shot bears and panthers and swampdogs. He became renowned as a trapper in all the trading forts along the gulf. But for Till, the world had narrowed. Till who could singlehandedly fall a bristlecone in ten strokes and Till who drank fire and tore the arms off of men became Till the sweeper of floors, the darner of stockings. She hated this life, the swamp. She never told Frankie that outright, but Frankie could see it in her those months before she went North to Beaver, when the hate had marbled hard in her guts.

When her belly got big, Till got her hands on a stick of hickory and an old ax head and she made herself a hatchet. When the boys were out trapping, she'd go out to the back copse and get working. She'd hack away at the oaks, bringing it up across her shoulder, swinging down, the weight of the ax head swimming through the air. Piece by piece, she tore away at the oak, tore away at the swamp. And when a tree fell, she'd split its body into cords, bundle them up with twine, and carry them alone back behind the house.

She'd stocked that timber aiming to sell it and save the earnings for a little place in town for her and that bump inside her. She'd worked like that for six weeks, tirelessly, clearing away the land. Then one day, without telling her, Pierre traded the timber himself for corn whiskey, a new pair of fox jaws, and a hardly used Enfield rifle. They were on his land, he told her. They were his trees.

When Frankie was born, Sweet Till's hair was already brittle as straw. The color was gone from her cheeks, and there were deep blue veins in her hands and ankles. Her breasts had swole uncomfortably.

Often she'd look at her new baby and could not believe it had come from her. Its skin was white and milky, like hers, but already, it looked like her Choctaw father—serious, easily offended, beautiful with brown-black hair, narrow pinched lips. It was either by chance or by fortune, but two days after Frankie was born, Pierre was killed. Him and his older boy had gone panther hunting in the northern ridge when suddenly the winds changed. The cat had sniffed out the two hunters and circled behind them. The boy John fired on the animal, killing it, but not before it had taken his father.

Sweet Till buried her brother out in the mudflats, and she would've lit out from the swamp right then and there, but Pierre's boys, John and Roan, refused to leave. The older one had started to calling himself Bossjohn, and he took Pierre's place as the head of the L'Etangs. He took his brother under his charge and he learned him to hunt and trap. The new baby he also put under his care. When little Frankie would cry, it was only Bossjohn who could quiet her, holding the large dangling thing in his arms, bouncing her softly, and Sweet Till understood. She'd been beaten.

For years she said nothing. She became resigned to her place among her brother's children—sweeper, darner of stockings. Her cheeks turned wan, her eyes bloodshot. She fell sick often. She'd get dizzy and nauseated, and her mouth would fill with water. And one day, when Frankie was four, Till lay down under a bearskin rug and did not get up again.

Frankie remembered the night Sweet Till Haskins went North to Beaver. Her cousin Roan took her by the hand and led her out through the cabin doors. The moon was out, and Frankie felt the air move above her. There were owls winging silently through the dark canopy. She remembered what her mother had told her. One for good luck. Two for love. Black for life. White for death. She craned her neck up to see.

Roan took her to the dugout he and Bossjohn had built as a tanning house and they lay out on the smooth dirt floor. When she woke in the morning, their things from the cabin had been moved inside the dugout. She got up and ran toward the cabin, toward Till. But she paused in her tracks as she watched Bossjohn step out the front door. He looked at her, his eyes set hard under his thick brow. There was a cloth around his mouth and he pulled it down and took a big swallow of air. Then he took off his gloves and threw them in through the window. Smoke poured out and Frankie had the thought that that was her mother. All that was left of her, going up in gray black wisps, escaping through the slats, through the windows up into the air, toward the sun. Bossjohn knelt down and took her by her shoulders. She was tall, even then. He looked her square in the eyes.

You name L'Etang now, he said.

And so Frankie became who she was. She learned to trap and snare and shoot and muck and tell sign on the soft earth. She could tell muskrat from coon from possum. She could read the wind and pick them all by smell. When she was thirteen, she went panther hunting with Bossjohn. She remembered his command as he rose up from the blind. His breathing was smooth and easy. The barrel swung down and spat twice, one and two. And she remembered it was she who'd come to him. It was she who thought she loved him. He was older than Roan. Less wild in the blood. And even though he was rough and hardheaded, it was Bossjohn she'd clung to for warmth those nights they camped out in the leaf. He was the one who kept them fed, who bullied the meat and blood and hides from the wilderness.

But it galled Frankie every time Bossjohn wagged on 'bout Pierre L'Etang, never giving no mind to Sweet Till who was twenty-two when she died, younger than Frankie was now, and had given to this place more'n the rest of them. Frankie felt her mother inside her, a long time buried now, emerging in a noxious twisting inside her gut. She cast her gaze around the empty woods, the shelves of mushrooms growing on the bark, the sunlight breaking through the thick wet air. This was her home and she was sick of it. She knew nothing of the world that Till had come from except that it was not here. Here, nothing moved. The mud would catch you and hold you till it dried you up and snapped you like a reed.

A LOW MIST HAD SETTLED DOWN ON THE DUFF, AND THE MORNING sun made the air bright and ghostly. Grackles swooped down from their perches in iridescent mobs. Overhead the sun broke through cloud and tree cover. There was God in the morning, Frankie thought. The stock of the rifle was cantilevered against her shoulder, the barrel raised to a salute. She nudged the vines with the muzzle, clearing their path. Though he was still weak, Rowbear kept close to her, never falling more than a few feet behind. He seemed anxious and nervous, easily startled by the noises out in the deep swamp.

The gun was for his protection as much as hers, she'd assured him. There panther in here swamps, she reminded him. Above in the foliage, the branches riffled and Rowbear stiffened. Frankie laughed. Is okay, I protect you. They went for hours through the rough. The air had warmed and the rank of honeysuckle was thick around them. The ground had started to soften so they traveled upland where the soil would hold. By noon, they came to Mòskwas Run, a two-mile track of fast-flowing water where muskrat and nutria nested.

Frankie threw off her hat and knelt down by the run.

Hold my hair, she said.

She held the damp bun against her head and he took the mound in his fingers.

Tight now. Don't let her loose.

She dunked her head into the stream, taking the water in large swallows. She came back up and Rowbear was watching. His eyes followed her neck down to the dark wet of her shirt. She took his hand from her head and tried to hide her blush.

Go'head 'n slake you fill, she said. It's some time 'fore we get to the Flats.

Rowbear washed his face and his hands, and only after did he make a bowl of his palms and let a little into his lips. Frankie laid out her jacket beneath the dogwoods and they sat and lunched on knots of hard jerky. After they ate, he let her change his bandage. She wet a kerchief and cleaned out the dirt and blood from around the wound before packing on a thick green salve. She took his hand and showed him where to hold, pressing down against his Adam's apple. His skin was cold, clammy. He gaped up at her like a fish, his breath oozing from his throat, his eyes wide, his nostrils ringed with wet. She put a fresh cloth around the wound and he winced as she cinched it tight.

You breathe?

He nodded.

Bon, she said, Say bon. Don' itch it none.

She scraped a fleck of dry blood with her fingernail. It sting?

Just a little, he said.

His voice was rough and full of wind. They were Rowbear's first words to her in days.

You jes' lucky I seen you fo' Roan do you good.

Lucky, he said. Real lucky Robert.

When they'd finished, she tied the rest of the food in a canvas pouch and buried it by a sapling yew. When she returned, Rowbear was asleep. His eyes fluttered behind their lids. His breath rose and fell gently. It was still early in the afternoon, and she judged she could spare him the nap. She took up her rifle and went alone a quarter mile down the run to where she'd set a pair of ankle traps the week before. Above the water, dragonflies held the air, mincing the sunlight on their wings. Out across, she could see gnats churning the air, flashing amber like chaff.

Along the waterline were trails of animal prints. There were two sets—the first belonging to a mob of dog paws, and the second to a single animal, large and clumsy. By the impression of its hooves, she could tell it'd been driving hard through the mud. The prints traveled across the underbrush and disappeared at the bank. She bent and placed her hand inside the groove of its hoof and picked apart the flecks of dried grass and dung.

She woke Rowbear.

We go now, she said.

They washed the smell of meat from their mouths and hands and took off across the run. She held him tight by the loose of his shirt and Rowbear shuddered as the water coursed through his boots.

The prints began again almost immediately, taking up a mud slope. Frankie quickened their pace. She led him north, toward the grasslands, through thickets of brush and sedge and fall oaks. They came to a loess wall. Quick now, she said and up they went, pegging their boots into the footholds. They went on a few yards more before she clapped her hand over his mouth and pointed. Below them was a kettle pond of mud and peat, and in the shallows was a bull. Its fur was dark and clumped, its undersides dripping. Blood coursed from its nose. Along its flank, she could see where the flesh had been torn away.

No brand on him, she said. Feral. Must a wandered into the swamp here by heself.

She charged her rifle and steadied the stock against her shoulder.

Without a word, Rowbear rose and took off down the hill. Something caught his foot and he fell forward into the shallows. The bull snorted. Its eyes were large and bloodshot. They stared back at him through a rim of mucus. There was a crack and the bull knelt down. Rowbear fell backward. There was blood on his face and clothes. He felt himself. He was not hurt. He looked up the loess, at Frankie, at the ribbon of smoke. The bull tried to rise, but its legs would not hold. The beast trembled and fell again. Rowbear rose to his height and brought up his arms. There was another shot and the bull lay down on its side, shaking its flank. The beast heaved in the air, its tongue wagging against the mud. *Crack!* and something in its shoulder popped. It was done.

They lost hours as Frankie dressed the kill and cut the meat into steaks. She slit its throat and the blood drained out into the shallow wade-through. Her arms and clothes and hair were slick and red, and what she couldn't wash off in the brackish water was streaked crimson, her neck and cheek and face. Rowbear did not speak. He sat on a log and watched the bull carcass, silent, the chill of the water on his skin.

Come, she called out to him. Let me wash there blood off you.

He didn't move. His silence wounded her. It wasn't spiteful or angry. There was a care in it, a sadness. Some part of him seemed to have been closed away, a door slammed inexplicably shut. And this enraged Frankie.

The sun was going down, and to Frankie, he seemed to drink the light into himself, darkening into pitch. He did not look at her and she wondered if she could bear the gaze. They could not make it to the Flats in this darkness so Frankie pitched camp on the high ridge overlooking the kettle pond. She sent Rowbear to gather kindling. When he returned, she dug out a fire pit, laying down a bed of dry grass and rimming the pit with stones. By nightfall, she'd built two rolls out of moss and soft duff under the shelter of a fallen tree. They sat by the fire, eyes tearing from the smoke. She unpacked one of the steaks and cooked it over the flame. When it was ready, she recited the trapper's prayer and they ate.

She watched him, his eyes distant, taking slow measured bites of his supper. Supper she had tracked and killed and slaughtered. Supper that he hated her for. She wanted to spit in his face, to tear the food from his hands. He was dangerous and reckless. When he dove into the river. When he ran toward the bull. He wanted to die. She saw this now. His hand hung limp on his knee. His lips barely moved.

She fed the fire with the rest of the kindling, then pushed past Rowbear to her bedroll. The ground was cold and hard, and she turned her head from the firelight. She shut her eyes and didn't move and, though her mind couldn't settle, pretended to sleep.

Her anger was a small sharp blade and she honed it, waiting for sleep. It was some time before Rowbear tore himself from the fire to bed down beside her. Even near the flames, his teeth chattered. He coughed and sneezed and sniffled. It felt like hours, yawning deep into the black morning. She watched shadows dance on the bark, listened to a chorus of frogs pulsing in the pond below. She thought of owls. Tried to count them in the forest of her mind, sweeping the cold air above her. Eight for safe travel. Nine for illness. Black for life. White for death. Down she went through the hole, Rowbear's moaning in her ears whorling into that country of sleep and notsleep. Electric light flashed in the ether. Down and down. She was alone. The valley was flat and treeless, extending toward no horizon. She could see her breath in front of her. Her hands. A wave of loneliness washed over her. Above, the heavens stormed, rolling dust and sand and stone into their folds.

She awoke. Rowbear was crouched above her, his hand clamped over her mouth.

Shhh . . .

His face was pale, and his lips were chapped. It did not look like he had slept. She took his palm from her mouth.

What, what is it?, she asked.

Something. I heard something.

Rowbear took her to an outcrop of sandy ground. He pointed out into the darkness. She could hear it now too, down in the kettle. How many were there? Four? Five? Growling and yipping and snarling. Carolinas maybe. Or coydogs. They must've gotten buffed at the run and doubled back here when they could not find the bull. She leaned toward the drop and peered down. They were there with the carcass, blood mad and cheated of their prey. They fought for bone and cartilage and scraps. Carolinas were worthless but she could fetch eight dollars for coy hide at Fort Muskethead. She unscrewed her canteen and took a deep swallow. Then she took up her rifle and checked the chamber.

Stay here, she said.

Where you going?

Keep to the fire, you be safe, she said.

She walked the slow drop down into the kettle. The underduff crackled in her ears, but there was no helping that. She took up a clump of dung and smeared it on her coat. The trigger was slick now, and she wedged her finger hard against the guard. Her eyes started to adjust. She could see shapes, forms, edges. Down at the waterline, she spotted the bull carcass, its long brackets of bone emerging from the muck. The dogs leaped at each other, tugging at the thin strips of sinew.

She steadied her rifle.

They were four, the largest near eighty pounds by her reckoning. The lead dog pushed past the other three, the muscles of its stomach pulsing. Its ribs showed through its girth. It'd found a hole in the bull's side and pushed deep into it, pulling strings of gristle. The sky began to lighten. She sighted down the barrel and aimed at the soft hackles of the lead's neck. She levered the hammer back and drew in a breath.

The dogs stopped. The sun crowned up from the east, blazing copper through the shrub and grass. They turned toward it, noses against the breeze. She looked too. Rowbear stood atop the ridge, his shirt open, his cheeks still flecked with dried blood. There was a stillness in his face, his eyes half open. They'd smelled him.

For a moment nothing moved.

Then the pack took up the hill, toward Rowbear. Frankie found her hands again. Her finger had turned to stone on the trigger. She pulled and the shot disappeared.

They advanced quickly, their paws kicking up flecks of soft mud. Rowbear kicked one square in the head and sent it down the rise. He threw mud and thrashed the air, brandishing a rock in his hand. Frankie fired again, and again nothing. Just smoke and noise. She cursed and got to her feet and began to run across the kettle. Rowbear tried to keep the dogs at a distance, but they held their ground. Frankie fired once more, and one of the dogs fell down. Another two took off running, but one remained, too crazed to retreat. There was a blur of fur and noise. Then a dull sick sound.

She did not know what she was seeing. It was only after she'd come closer, after the blood and thrill had subsided, that she saw the two of them on the ground, the dog in Rowbear's lap. Its head was open, and the blood was black and sticky, and Rowbear brought the rock down over and over, chipping away bits of bone and brain. His eyes were wide and his mouth hung slightly open. He was in a trance. Frankie touched his arm. But he kept beating, slow now, hefting his arms like weights. It was morning and the sky was brightening, and on the ridge, the mist gathered and spilled, rolling down toward them. He brought his hand up. Tracks of blood runneled down his arm. And then as if his arms had turned to straw, the rock slipped from his hand.

It's not him, he said.

Not who?

Rowbear shook his head, his hands trembling.

Nothing. Never mind.

ometimes Robert wondered if this weren't all in his head—the light chipping through the high canopy, the *slush-slush-shlock* of his boots—if the rise and fall of the mud trails didn't sway in the same clay sloughs of his brain. Birds. Who would make so many birds? Fill the whole damn place with their lunatic cries? It was a sick mind made this swamp. That put crisp clean air so high above the bad. Here, everything crawled and curled and spidered, exploding from the ground in blades and fans and tendrils of poison green. The deeper he went, the more tangled the disease, twisting and knotting into itself, throwing up ropes of kudzu and creeper, and on that rope, bright purple flowers that burst open like sores.

And if this were all in his head, how did Frankie L'Etang fit inside it? She gained the ground, patiently drawing back the lashweed for him to pass. His thoughts pressed in like gnats around her, chasing heat, wheeling. Every few yards, she would glance back at him. Make sure he was okay. That he could follow. And those last few times. Was she grinning?

Eyes lie. Can't trust them. Things flashed in the edge of his vision then disappeared. Movement. A rush of color. A distortion of light. He told himself it was the heat on his nerves. This was not real. If only he could have air. If only this heat didn't squat down on him. He'd suck deep into his lungs and breathe through the poison. He could get his eyeballs to steady, and quiet that hum inside his skull. There were no voices. Not yet. Etta had the voices. She would speak into an empty room and smack her legs with the flat of her hand. Get! Get!

He looked at his hands. Frankie had undone the chains around them. He told his fingers, Flex, and they obeyed. He felt them meet his palms. Felt his own meat resist. This was real.

Was this living? Always having to decide between the two. This is real. This is not. He touched the devil through his shirt. And this? So many square inches of worsted yarn. Inside—rock salt, ash, an Indian head penny. He fingered the loops of twine, lifting it from the damp of his neck. He ran the underside of his finger across the coarse fibers. To mark the years, he had frayed X's on the twine—one hatch, then another, then another until there were over half a dozen. How many more could he fit around his neck? This is real. This is not.

It had protected him. He did not die. Not in Bruce, by fire. Or drowned in the river. Nor on the thousand night roads like arteries feeding into buckra towns, rope trees, torches, nor those stitches of railroad that fled into the furious cities. He'd been saved where others had not. Billy and Etta and Ellis. And poor Hermalie and all those girls who'd been sucked into the death that gloried around him. And now came the Dog. For what end, he could not be sure. To warn or threaten or to collect upon some soul debt? It did not matter.

He felt something sharp glide through his ribs. He had not felt afraid, truly afraid, in so long that it took a moment to recognize it. To feel his body come alive in riot against him. His heart. His muscles. His brain. His spleen. Every damned fiber of his existence burning for life. And yet, wasn't this what he wanted? To meet the sumbitch at his eye. To end.

Frankie was looking at him. She held something out between her forefinger and her thumb. Her face was furrowed in concern, and he realized he'd been looking hard at her. Sweat beaded on his face. She made a motion for him to take what was in her hand and he did. The brown greasy plug was in his palm. She gestured her hand to her mouth as if showing him how to eat it, then she turned away quickly so he could collect himself.

What is it?

Medicine. Eat.

They were in a cypress grove, the tall canopies above them holding down the heat. Frankie slung down her pack, then she took off her hat and combed her hair into a tail. Robert watched her fingers travel through the nest of dark hair, airing out its folds, her smooth white neck flushed in the humidity. This was not real. He felt the blood creep across his face and he turned away.

Hold we up a mo', she said.

Frankie undid her jacket and spread it out on the ground, her shirt soaked with sweat. He bit into the plug. It was hard and bitter, and when he swallowed, warm spread into his chest and face.

Why're we stopping?

Can't y'nose it?

Frankie closed her eyes and breathed, her full chest rising beneath her shirt. Robert shuddered. He bit down on his cheek, tried not to look. She was facing the sky, her arms splayed at her side.

It gon' pour.

They sheltered under a cypress hollow, Frankie's jacket draped across the knotted bark to make a lip. They lay side by side, their packs padded underneath them. The storm came sudden and full, hammering down in sheets of silver foam. Around them, the cypresses groaned from their roots. Frankie was asleep. She had laid herself lengthwise under the shelter, her legs crossed at the ankle, her felt hat set careful on her face. Robert gazed out into the frosted air. The earth was beat soft into a pudding. High above the heavens cracked. He saw fire lash down through the trees, strike the earth, and on that spot the ground cracked and hell bubbled forth. He shut his eyes. Opened them again. Rain. Just rain. He looked up. A flock of woodcocks were caught in the storm. They gave call, then broke through the trees, their large wings clumsily grabbing air. The rain had scared up worms and they took to the high boughs and waited.

You wake?

She had spoken through her hat. Didn't move, her rifle resting beside her. He told her he was.

Since you been here, I been careful watching you. And I sees you. I sees it.

Robert blinked. He could almost laugh.

What you see?

It ain't my business. All I's saying is I sees it, she said.

Outside this place, they would beat him, maybe kill him for the way he looked at her—his eyes traveling up the folds of her shirt. He shut his eyes. Swallowed. Tried to calm the tattooing in his brain. She shifted and her sleeve hiked a little. He saw the white band of her wrist, then the long slight fingers. He remembered those fingers in his mouth, pushing a taste across his tongue. Her body warmed the air around her. At the end of his life, he would hold to this image, her face obscured, her body at rest as the world tore itself apart around them. Already the world had turned and the heavens had locked into place, and that massive machinery of gears and weights and counterweights glided into motion. And it was funny, that they call it falling, because that was what it was. The ground giving up underneath you. The surge of air. He did not stand a chance.

ossjohn and Roan headed south into the corridor, neither brother speaking. Three days, stoving through the gnat swarms and the late-summer rains that came full and sudden and bone-cold. Half a mile out from the run they could smell its water. Warm and heavy and full of moss. They inhaled deeply through their nostrils, into their skulls, trying to draw the taste. When they came upon it, the run was big and beautiful and lash-tongued mean, the waters rollin' silver down the banks and dam flot ribboned across the surface.

They followed the trim, pitching their traps into the water and laying jaws and snares out in the dense clover. Where the water slowed, Roan built a blind to shoot whitetail or wild hog or anything thirsty for drink.

They made camp half a mile from the run, hanging their packs up in the trees and sleeping in the open air. In the morning they'd scout the country for sign of game. They came to a swath of dirt where the mud had dried. In the dirt was a long smooth groove, where a panther had banked her belly. They knelt above the imprint, clutching strands of dry grass, not talking. They knew that the bugheways were driving the panthers from their prowl lands, but they never expected them to come this way. The corridor wasn't good country for panther. The grasses were too low and the trees were neat and spread apart. Neither Roan nor Bossjohn could figure it. What they knew, however, was that the panther was

235

either brave or desperate, and by the ridge in the dirt, that she was in foal.

Roan hunted from the blinds, squatting in mud holes behind dense bramble. Chiggers crawled up his legs, on his back, his arms. They traveled up his neck, into his beard. They sucked greedy on his blood. He pinched one free, held it between his fingers. Its tiny jaws clamped the air. He did not share his brother's concern about the bugheway. Roan had been to Fort Muskethead. He'd seen the bugheway stock—soft and pink and full of milk. Can't trap. Can't shoot. Didn't have the sand to live here in the marsh country, and those fool enough to try would be sucked clean by skeeters. All that was wanted to shuck off the bugheways was strength. He looked down and grimaced at the red speck pinched between his thumb and forefinger, its legs struggling. He squeezed and wiped his hands across his leg.

For days, they hauled their chains and hunted the land, with little to show and few words between them. Roan watched his brother draw into himself. He was his opposite. Where Roan was small and slight, Bossjohn was heavy-built like a bear. Powerful and muscular under the sheaths of fat. In all things Bossjohn was slow and deliberate. His anger built in a slow burn across his body, pulling drifts of red across his skin.

Were he not the younger L'Etang, Roan could've led their clan, not hiding and sneaking like coons, but with salt and grit. Where Bossjohn was weak, Roan would have been forceful. He would not have brought that muskie home, would not have nursed that bugheway nigger on their food, on their kill, would not have left their cousin alone with him. First chance, he would've skinned him like a rabbit, do him easy and stretch that hide across a tree for all there bugheways to see. Bossjohn! His brother's weakness brought bile into his mouth. Slow up, he told himself. He tried to soothe the fire in his blood. He was a trapper. And if trappers understood anything, it was waiting.

FOR DAYS THEY'D SEEN THE SMOKE ABOVE THE TREES, THE SCARE of birds that fled into the sky. They rose hours before the dawn and made their way east through the corridor. First light broke and they went down on their bellies, Injun-crawling up the high scrub to where they could watch the bugheway, witness their great work. Below, in the gully, where there once had been a field of high grass to hunt rabbit, was a concrete pit and a large stone wall. The bugheway came in on their machines, beetling through pylons of dense forest. There was so much noise—the hornet whine of engines and metal groaning against metal. They watched for hours, Bossjohn turning cold and pale as whole walls of earth crumbled violently under the bugheway's command. There was a crack, and the air filled with red, rolling upward and through in a hot coppery breath.

They returned to camp to find their packs in tatters and their rolls shredded to bits. Their stores of food had been pulled from the trees and raided. What hadn't been eaten was dragged into the bushes and left to molder in the mud. There was sign all through camp—paw prints, scratch marks, a mound of dry hard scat.

Bossjohn and Roan salvaged what they could. They moved the camp north, flanking the river in hopes that the panther could not approach from behind. At night, they took shifts, gazing warily into the unbreaking darkness beyond the firelight.

Their fortunes turned when after a rain, they spied sign of stag near the run. They stalked it west, tracking a set of cloven prints that were fresh pressed in the rain-soft dirt. They gave it slack, let it gain ground, while they broke trail toward a hill, downwind from the stag. They spied it in a clearing through a fence of hedge cover. It bent its thick brown neck down to a patch of clover, whisking the flies from its ears. Roan set his rifle while Bossjohn sighted. He rocked the shaft slow on his knee, pivoting down—the nose aimed just above the neck.

Bossjohn rested his hand on his shoulder, squeezing lightly.

Easy. Easy.

Roan let the air slow through his nose. He threaded his finger around the trigger, drew back the hammer. It made no click.

Suddenly the stag raised its head. It looked off to the west, then took off into the bushes.

Roan looked from the rifle and down into the clearing.

Wha—!

Bossjohn hushed him. His hand clamped down hard on the shoulder.

Roan looked and he saw something move through the brush. It emerged into the clearing where the deer had been. A man. A bugheway. The man looked around the clearing, took a few steps back the way he came, then stopped again.

He lost, Bossjohn said.

Roan brought his cheek back down to the rifle. He pivoted again. Sighted.

What you doin'?

Roan gon' have he reward.

The man unhitched his pants and was now pissing against the base of a tree.

Roan tightened around the trigger. The gun jumped from his hand. A shot discharged, finding nothing. The man looked around, bewildered. Roan looked and saw Bossjohn's hand forced hard against the barrel.

What in hell you doin?, Bossjohn hissed.

Roan looked back down. The man had run off, his trousers drawn hastily over his lily-pale flesh. Roan's face burned with rage. He took his hand from the stock, let the rifle fall from his grip so he would not be tempted to use it. Bossjohn grabbed it up and stalked off down the hill.

Slow, Roan told himself. Slow, slow.

WHERE THE TREES BROKE, RED DUST AND SMOKE ROLLED IN FROM the east. It came like a locust cloud, falling earthward in headlong plumes. For days the run bled rust, and Bossjohn and Roan would pull drowned beavers from the rocks, their hides smelling, crawling with lice and maggots.

Then one night Bossjohn sat Roan down.

Mebbe Frankie be right, he said. Mebbe here ain't ground for L'Etangs no mo'.

Bossjohn heaved his body forward, let out a slow breath.

No mo' no mo', he sang.

Bossjohn measured his words carefully, flicking his eyes up to meet his brother's before casting them down again at his boots. Noises hitched and unhitched in his throat. He was tired, Roan saw. Old.

When here autumn come, gon' scrap we camp and head we down 'a Muskethead. Trade for what I's can, see'n if we can't set root out there a ways.

Roan nodded, saying nothing. Bossjohn looked at him for some sign and he gave him none.

Say bon? he said.

Oui, Roan answered softly. Casually. Say bon.

That night Roan lay on the grass while his brother kept watch. He did not sleep, but still he dreamed. In his dreams, he saw fire. Bright and red, choking the air in fullsmoke. It swept down like a rug on the country, then out, through the marshes, the forests, out into the bugheway camps, and it took in its breath the weak, the stupid, the dithering. Then it stood itself tall in a chimney from earth to sky and blazed on heaven high.

When his brother tapped him lightly to take his panther watch, Roan lifted his heavy body to the fire. The air was chill and sharp in his lungs. It did not take long. He heard his brother drop off, the deep sonorous snores sounding from his throat.

The hours passed and the cricket pulsed softly in his ears until all at once they became silent. Roan looked out into the darkness. He angled his ears and sniffed. He looked back at his brother's sleeping form, then back into the darkness. He grinned. The time had come. He took up his rifle, stood, and then he took up his brother's. Without a word, he walked off into the dark.

In the still-dark, Frankie would rise and make up their packs before setting out into the trapping grounds. As she and Robert hiked, she'd count the owls, swinging her arm through the inky air. They swooped invisibly from perch to perch, and she read their number with seriousness, prognosticating the fortune of the coming day's haul.

She would point and one would glide from its branch.

You see? Good luck.

They'd make their way west. The swamp, he learned, lay across a series of underground springs and aquifers, running in bands of salt and brack and potable water. He paid attention to the trees, how dogwood turned to willow turned to cypress turned to blackgum. They'd move through the rings, come to a pond of standing rainwater. Birds would gather in the shallows, puffing their breasts at one another. None of them big enough to eat.

She'd ask for his hands and he'd offer them to her, palms out. Then she'd slather on a cake of mud and when he looked at her bewildered, she laughed. Hide we smell, she said, and she did the same, smoothing the mud under her neck, in the pits of her arms.

They passed the days together, hiking through the dank country, trying to read the earth.

She'd slip her finger into his mouth and read the wind. Then they'd huddle under blinds of peat moss, breathing the same air, sweating through the same dank stink. Their muscles cramped and twitched and jumped, and they could feel the other's nerves sparking in the too small space.

Hours would pass. The sun would slide loose from its chamber, then down.

Most days, there was nothing.

They'd crawl from the blind, their limbs numb, crazed from hunger. In what little light they had left, they'd head back to the dugout. They'd start a fire and strip off their larrigans. Robert would lie under the warmth of his coat, the blood finding its way again to his limbs. They grubbed on beans and boiled hominy, swallowing it down before it had time to cool. They slept close to the fire, their backs huddled against each other for warmth.

On the trails, she showed him how to tie a sapling into a snare. Watch my hands, she said. They were smooth, white, bending down the stem, working it back, then around. She made a noose of a length of wire and strung it to a stake. She tripped the snare and the sapling unraveled. You try, she said, and he knelt beside her. He forced the tip down, hard so he thought it would snap from its roots. Slow, slow, she said. Take your time. He tucked his lip under his teeth, forced his thoughts to a single point. There were weights and pressures, angles of force. The sapling whipped away from him. Try again, she said.

He anchored the tip with the heel of his palm, the tension building in the still green bough. The sapling strained under the weight, and he threaded the wire back, around. Above him, the sky turned, the earth countering, each grinding to its place. He felt her at his shoulder, felt the space she took. There was a spreading quiet. It rippled outward, crawling, searching. The world bent to his hands. He rested his foot against the stake, pivoted, smoothing the bend. All at once, the trap sprang free. Something cracked beneath his eye. There was fire in his palms.

You bleeding, Frankie said.

Robert looked down at his hands, but it was his face she was staring at. She pressed her thumb to his cheek, forcing up the skin.

He swallowed, still in shock. The sapling stood upright.

She stitched him up, his head across her lap, him gazing into the sky of her face. From under her hat, strands of hair hung down, falling toward him like a rain. Her forehead smoothed and furrowed. Small noises gathered in her throat. He felt the thread passing through his flesh, tugging at his cheek. He tried not to wince, to keep his head still. Her hands padded across his face, angling and reangling, finding new purchase on his nose, his chin. When she finished, she swabbed his wounds and bandaged his hands.

Not so bad, she said.

He lifted his head from off her lap and sat himself up. She held the bloody cloth in her hand. I go bury these, she said. You stay here. She left him alone, and he felt along the raw terrain of his face. The gash wasn't large. No more than an inch. In time, it would heal but it would leave a scar—a smooth waxen grin beneath his left eye. His mama's baby boy. Uglied for life.

Night fell swiftly through the woods, driving through the ancient trees. There was no sound. No birdcall. His breath looked brittle and strange in the bruised light.

He was free. If he chose, he could've walked out of Panther. No one would have stopped him. The days would pass, and every day he would renew his promise to leave. He could start again, go into town, try to find work. But he didn't. He would wake in the middle of the night, trembling without understanding why. He'd bolt upright in his roll, cough out the thick black air in his lungs, and stare restlessly at the edge of camp. He would hear the wind through the boughs, piercing and wounded, and he would draw the rug around him and try to shake the howling in his brain.

THEY WERE TWO SHAPES RISING OVER THE WESTERN HILL, BLACK in the dusk. For a time, the clouds broke and they crossed under the star cover, the valley a bowl of silence around them. By dawn, a storm had gained and overtaken them. They moved against the gusting and slashing rain, their loads heavy, their stomachs light. By midday, they arrived back at the dugout.

Frankie took him by the arm and led him up the path to the house. They changed out of their clothes and she lit the stove and brewed coffee. He gazed moodily out the window, moving his hand from time to time to wipe the sheen from his nostrils.

He turned abruptly and found Frankie staring at him, her eyes red, the coffee in an urn in her hand.

This is a look of someone who has lost something, he told himself. That is all.

But her eyes were fixed to him, filling with wet. And when he spoke up in a weak voice—What's wrong?—she dropped the urn and burst into tears. She fell upon him, and in his shock, he found himself holding her. This white woman. The walls groaned, settling against the yielding mud. Against the dugout, water lapped against the boards, sluicing away the earth.

Her hands were wringing. He looked at her and she tried to force a smile. He knit his brow together. He took her hands and folded them into his own. They were so warm. A single sob broke from her throat. She tamped it down and shut her eyes. She stood up, leading him by his hand. They crossed into the other room, pulling the curtain aside. She laid him down on a pallet of soft hay and nestled herself into the crook of his arm. She put her mouth against his, the sharp bone of her nose digging into his cheek. Blood flooded her mouth. He heard his breath dam in his chest. She worked loose his trousers, slid down her pants, and guided him into her. The ground canted and heeled. She could feel him gripping her hips, his body rocking against her. She flexed against him. He was inside, pressing into her. He felt himself expanding inside her, and then at once, it was over. She climbed off and lay beside him, the both of them breathless and raw.

Robert woke to snow. Outside the tanning shed, it fell mutely, a faint crinkle like bolls of cotton pulled apart. He opened his eyes. Through the slats of the shed ceiling, he saw daylight. Frankie had let him sleep. He threw off the bearskin rug and went to light the smudge pot. He had not witnessed a snowfall before. The flakes were small and hard to see against the wool-white sky. Against the line of trees, they were clearer. Fine white grains gliding down in slow drifts, as if they had been shook loose, almost accidentally, from some far chamber above the world.

In the distance, Frankie approached from the woods. They saw each other and she hailed up one hand. Robert returned her wave. She raised the other arm, hoisting up a sack that she'd been carrying. Her face, he saw, was red and beaming. The snow fell around her, dusting her shoulders. Robert took a slow breath. The sky yawed wide above them, filling with soft white dander. It was warm still. It would not stick. But for the moment the Flats looked frozen under glass, cut off from the rest of the world. She neared, and his anticipation rose. A brassy twang inside his gut.

Sleep you good?

Say bon, he found himself saying.

She slung down her sack and warmed herself beside the smudge pot.

What'd you get?

She grinned at him.

Take'n you look.

Robert worked open the sack. At the bottom of the canvas, wrapped, was a set of three rabbits. He held one out by its scruff.

T'night, grease'n we on meat, she said.

They roasted her catch over hot stones. The meat was hot and greasy. He hadn't realized how hungry he was. He sucked the flesh off the bone and spooned the fat with his fingers. He could hear Frankie telling him to slow, but he couldn't. His hunger raged like flash powder. He burned his tongue and he scorched his throat and steam let from his open mouth. Still he ate, sucking his burned fingers, licking the bones. He gnashed them, sucked out the marrow. He ate the eyes and the head, spitting out the tiny skull.

They sat beside the fire. The snow had eased and above, a gray plain of sky smothered the dusk. The taste of meat was still in their mouths, and their clothes and skin and hair were perfumed with smoke. A western wind carried off their scents in a breath, toward the dark band above the horizon. He wondered what the smell of meat would call forward from those swamps.

Then, as if she'd heard his thought, Frankie turned toward the tupelos and stared hard into the dark. She narrowed her eyes, clenched her jaws.

Between the trees, a desperate form materialized. His clothes were in tatters. A long beard hung from his ghoulish face, black and matted with mud. But Robert could not mistake the knife that dangled from his belt.

⌇

ROAN STAGGERED TOWARD THE FIRE. HE PAID THEM NO MIND, falling to his knees and pawing the hot embers, peeling off the strips of ashen meat that had melted on the stones. He ate greedily, shivering from the heat, his eyes shut and rimmed with tears.

Roan, Frankie said. Her hand hovered above his stooped back.

What happen' a you?

Roan swallowed hard and sucked at the small keylike bones.

Where be Bossjohn?

Dead, he muttered.

Frankie gasped.

How y'mean dead?

Roan rose and grabbed Frankie's wrist and forced her toward him. He leaned his face into hers, their noses almost touching. He sniffed sharply. A look of confusion passed across his face as she backed away. Then he looked at Robert and grinned.

Tuk tuk tuk. You been much busy, muskie, oui? He cast his gaze around the camp. And you, ma' cousin?

Roan let her go, and Frankie looked away, her cheeks coloring.

Come, she said. Let's get we inside.

Roan sucked the grease from his thumb and nodded. They stood and headed into the dugout.

He followed Frankie into the other room while Robert stood by the door. He looked back out. The snow had turned to a heavy rain. Lightning cracked and crows took from their perches, filling the heavens with a sudden screaming night. He looked up and watched them crash above him. The horizon sparked and groaned.

Roan came out in fresh clothes. He faced Robert with a grin and sat himself down at the table. Frankie came out after him, shaken. She looked at Robert. Shook her head.

Rowbear, Roan rolled the name in his mouth. You like'n here, oui? Not every day big black muskie get to et' on white meat, non?

Roan rose. He was light and small, and he pinioned Frankie's arm behind her back. Robert stepped forward and Roan slipped his knife free.

Nuh nuh nuh. Sit you self down.

Robert looked to Frankie. Her face was white with shock. Robert put up his hands and sat down.

I's gon' put here house in order, y'hear?

Roan threw her down, and she smacked her head against the table ledge. Then he turned toward Robert. He took a quick step before Robert could rise; he plunged his foot into his chest. Robert fell backward through the door. All at once he was outside, the icy rain against his skin.

Roan kicked again, and Robert gasped, trying to suck down the lost wind. There was mud in his eyes and mouth and nostrils. He heard the door clap shut behind them. The skin on his back burned from the fall. He heard a choking noise gurgle from his own throat.

Roan was above him now. Robert could feel his thin lithe frame shielding him from the rain.

He tried to get up. A sky of white exploded against his temple.

How much time had passed? He could not be certain. He forced himself to his knees. He found the dugout wall before his insides lurched into his throat. His mouth filled with acid and he emptied it against the wall. He spit and wiped his lips. His head was burning.

He felt weak. The ground was soft, and it was an effort to lift his legs. He fell forward and his arms drove into the sucking earth.

This is it, he thought.

He let himself onto his belly. The mud was cool, soothing.

This is it.

He rested his cheek against the ground. He shut his eyes. If he could get his heart to quiet. His breath to slow. His lungs were raw and it hurt to breathe. He waited. For what, he wasn't sure. A light. A voice. He strained his ear upward, above the smashing rain, to the upper band of sky. But there was nothing. The universe seemed to pitch forward and fly into the void. He lifted his chin and opened his eyes. The night flashed and thundered.

At first he thought it was a trick of the light, but the sky flashed again and there it was. It sat on its haunches, its coat sabled with rain, the fur at its scruff raised to sharps. It gazed solemnly into his eyes. He felt a grief then, a rush of anguish.

Robert balanced himself on his knees and hoisted himself up.

He staggered into the dugout. In the other room, he heard them, Roan grunting and Frankie pleading. He walked as silently as he could. In the dimness of the room, it took him a moment to understand what he was seeing—Roan on top of Frankie, struggling at her clothes. His trousers were worked down to his ankles, along with his belt, the knife.

Robert moved slowly. He bent, took the cold weight in his hand.

Robert grabbed a fistful of hair. He forced it back and dragged a line across the neck. There was spray against the walls, a wet sick noise in his throat. Roan kicked and shook and finally went limp.

Robert dropped the steel. He propped himself against the wall, breathing hard. Then he collapsed.

THE NEXT MORNING, FRANKIE DRAGGED THE BODY OUT THROUGH the soft mud, fanning a Roan-shaped runnel out into the deep swamp. She buried him under clay and dirt and left the grave with no marker. When she returned to the dugout, Robert was still asleep. For the next few days, he would not speak and did not eat except for a little bread and water. He barely acknowledged her. At night, she'd sleep beside him in a crescent, nestling against his shivering form.

Then one night, he turned toward her. He cupped her hands in his and kissed her knuckles, softly.

I'm sorry, he said, though for what he never told her.

She woke the next morning to find that he'd left in the night, taking with him Roan's knife, a spare rifle, six rounds of ball, ten feet of rope, a rucksack, Roan's old coat, a pair of boots, a pound of raw oats, a half pound of jerky, a canteen, a stocking of salt, and three vials of dog urine. She felt something hidden underneath her roll. She took it out, held it up to the light. A small flannel pouch.

He wandered out of the swamp, half dead and all the way alive—every nerve singing. The nearest town sat under a clear blue sky, and he crossed the span of short grass to the borders. The streets were bitter bright and he felt like a stray among the houses. He was foul smelling and his coat was shredded to rags. A man had bumped into him and he could have murdered him, could have put his fingers through his soft neck. He walked for hours, the cold air on him, his memories a film with no lamp—just darkness and movement. He heard music and saw that he'd walked clear across town. He found himself before an old clapboard building with no signs, just rows of windows and music coming from the basement.

He went inside where it was warm. A colored woman sat behind a teak counter. She looked at him carefully. The music grew louder, and they both turned toward the door behind her from which it flowed. He could hear singing.

She opened a large leather-bound register.

You have to sign before you go in.

She held out the pen.

It's okay, she said.

He took it and drew an X and it seemed to satisfy her.

She smiled and opened the door.

Go on. Just don't disturb the others. They've already started.

He went down a flight of stairs, his hand on the wall to guide him. Above his head, there were pipes gathering dust in silken strands. At the bottom, he found himself in the back of a room, a dozen men and women out of their seats, holding hands, facing a low raised stage. They were singing. On the stage stood a man, his shirtsleeves rolled, his face dripping with sweat. Beside him, a coal furnace burned warm and red. The man lifted up his hands and a roar broke out. Then he brought his arms back down and the congregants silenced and fell into their seats.

Praise, brothers and sisters, praise!

They answered, Praise! Praise!

The man paced the length of the stage for a time, breathing loudly through his nose, his hands knotted behind his back. Through a small window near the ceiling, the brittle light streamed in. The man turned and caught the light against his frame so that when he drew his arms up, it was as if he were ablaze. Friends, he said, his hands lifting, life is not the highest good. Reverend, how will I save my soul? How will I enter through Heaven's gate? My clothes are shabby and there are holes in my shoes. My pockets are light and my Burden is Great, Reverend.

You say to me, Reverend, there is a meanness in this world, and I have fought and it has beaten me, and now I am so conscripted, let mean be laid upon mean, low upon the low! You wag your tongues but from that other mouth, you beg forgiveness, you plead for Spirit and Light. Reverend, direct me to Heaven's door, I am ready for my reward.

And the Poet says: Not so goddamn fast.

Because life is not the highest good.

Brothers, are we not made from the Divine? The same stuff that drowned the pharaoh, that cleaved the Sea. Are we not filled with that same breath that was breathed into Adam, made not of that same clay? I speak so answer! Praise that we may speak, and stand on two legs, and command the beasts and eat the fruit of this earth so then must we speak the Gospel, and bear your brother upon your back, and drive the Devil from the land. For it is him that I've come to talk about today. That low sniffling dog that now howls at our back door! Hear him, brothers, hear! He calls for blood!

Who then does it befall to turn him away? Who shall break his neck upon their boot heels? Mark! Mark! Oh you low, you dogs, you wretches, mark, where is that fine stuff now?

The man took a kerchief from his pocket and wiped his neck. Then he folded it again, keeping it in his hand—a square of white.

Now I've seen the elephant and I've heard the owl, and the mountain, brothers, climbs steep. The Devil is no fool. The Devil talks in pretty words and he takes from what he borrows you. He takes from our Greed and our Vanity and our Sinfulness.

The man locked his eyes on Robert. They were small and slitted.

The man brought his hand out and held it in front of him. The kerchief waved in his grip.

I quake, brothers and sisters. I quake. I can feel this world tearing itself apart. I can feel the air unraveling. Our families reduced to ash. Our homes being blown to dust. I tremble. Not for what I have lost but for what still may be taken from me. So let us take unto us the whole armor of God, that we may be able to withstand the evil day.

After the services, Robert waited for the congregants to leave. They filed out of the dusty basement, shaking hands with the man and dropping dollars in his basket. A few women came to him and they hugged him and patted his cheek. Soon it was only Robert and the man. The man filled a basin with water and began washing his face and hands.

Something I can do for you, brother?

I've seen you somewhere, Robert said.

In a vision, maybe. Perhaps you are called.

What's your name, Reverend?

Do you mean my earthly name or the name writ for me in heaven?

What do you call yourself here, in this basement.

Reverend. Just Reverend now.

What about before?

Brother, you ask many questions, but not for the answer you seek.

I have a gun in my pocket, Robert said. I'm going to use it to kill you.

The man smiled. He dried his hands on a towel. Then he seized Robert by the throat and tore open the front of his shirt. The buttons scattered and Robert struggled for air. The man let go and Robert fell backward. The man was still smiling, looking at the naked flesh where the pouch had been.

You didn't keep your promise, the man said.

Robert rubbed his throat, breathing shallowly.

The man looked at the back of his large hands, inspecting the nails.

Come on, he said. Let's go outside.

They crossed the street and circled to a small gated alley of pecan trees. Eli reached into his pocket and took from it a large iron ring. He unlocked the gate and they went inside. They sat down on a stone bench to rest. Out beyond the gate, they could see the gabled roofs of neighboring houses. A magpie was sitting on a line, watching them.

I wasn't sure I recognized you in the crowd. But then you came up to me and I knew it was you. That same stink-eyed boy from almost ten years ago.

What are you doing here?

My boy, I'm speaking the Gospel.

And fattening up on the way.

I admit this life has been kind to me, yes. My former employer, Mr. Duke, had a gift for recitation and it had an awful sway on me. I shaved my face and cut off my hair and answered the call.

Eli grinned. He stood up and brushed the pollen from his shirt.

What is it you want?

Robert looked at him. His heart was racing. He tried to steady himself.

There was a noise at the gate and they turned to see a woman behind it. She brightened when she saw Eli and waved toward him.

Excuse me, he said.

Robert watched him cross the alley to the gate. He said some words to the woman and stroked her hand. She didn't look more than fifteen. She put something into his hand and it disappeared into his pocket. Then she turned to leave.

One of my flock. The people of this town rely on me, he said. They look to me to unburden their souls.

Eli sat again on the bench.

Why don't you unburden your soul to me?

Robert grimaced. I don't have the money to spare, Reverend.

Eli laughed. You wound me. And rightly. Still, for you, it'll be on God's tab.

No thanks.

Robert turned to leave.

Eli called to him. And where will you go? How long you going to go sniffing and begging in the back rooms and alleys? Now you and I both know you haven't got a place in this whole cursed world to lay your head. Oh, maybe you got a place for tonight and maybe the night after. Some run-down ramshackle place to filter out the weather. Or maybe you got a nice warm bed somewhere, sharing it with some nice warm lady. But it's all on loan, brother. I'm sitting here and the Lord is sitting up there in his Kingdom above, and you got one chance to set the record, brother. We're both of us all ears.

Robert looked back at him. Eli had his arms outstretched, channeling in the air. Robert started back. Eli motioned to the bench, and Robert sat down and bent his head into his hands.

Put down your load, Eli said.

Robert let out a long breath and closed his eyes. There was a quiet for a time. He could not think how to start. He reached for the words and felt instead the dirty mop of Roan's hair brushing against him. He recoiled, shuddering.

Let me help you, he heard Eli say. Eli's hands were on his own now—those long still-soft fingers coiling around his wrists, pressing into his pulse.

You've done something. Something you regret.

This is a trick, Robert said. This is a game.

Something dangerous, Eli went on. Something bad, worse than has ever happened before. And you're scared. You don't know what to do. That's why you were in there tonight. Looking for answers.

I heard music, Robert said. I was curious. That's all.

No. Little man, you don't get curious. For you, music has no sound, food has no taste. And the days are endless.

You're wasting my time, Robert said. He went to take his hands away, but Eli held firm.

There's a woman, he said. A white woman.

Robert couldn't speak. He didn't move.

You did something with her. Something you shouldn't have.

Yes, Robert heard himself say. He started at his own voice—small and trapped in phlegm.

And something happened. Something you can't take back.

Yes.

Tell me, he said.

I . . . I've been seeing things. Sometimes I don't know if I'm awake or if I'm dreaming, if what I'm seeing is real. I can't feel my fingers, or my arms, or my body. Can't feel inside my own skin.

Tell me, he said again.

It follows me. I see it. It's always there. Just behind me, never letting me alone. No matter how far I get, where I go. It's there. It's always there. Like it's always been there. It watches me.

What's there? Say it.

The Dog, he said. He felt the word leave his mouth. It was the first time he had said it. Grief and fear surged through him. He could feel himself coming apart. The Dog, he said. Everywhere I go. It won't leave me alone. It wants something from me and I can't . . . I don't . . .

Robert began shaking. He realized he'd been holding his hand out, and it made a claw now. He gripped it shut and rested it on his lap. His eyes were closed and his lip was trembling. There was a pain now, dividing through the numbness, a hot knife. He drew in a breath and tried to collect himself.

I can't get clean of it.

Eli rested his hand on his shoulder. The touch felt like a wound. Tears stood in Robert's eyes.

Help me, he whispered.

Eli stood up. Robert began to weep. He lifted his head slowly. It was a man's face. Ordinary. The skin was rough and creased around the eyes and mouth. He looked into Eli's eyes and he was disgusted by the plainness of his face, how much like an egg it looked. Slowly, a grin crept across Eli's lips. His cheeks tensed. He was trying not to laugh, Robert realized.

Robert stood up and backed away. His face was burning. His heart was in his throat.

You-you told me, he managed to say. His voice was brittle and strange. Said we were tied to each other.

Who?

The Dog—that I was going to need it. That's what you told me.

Eli laughed and shrugged. You were a boy! It was just something to say to a boy. Something I made up. You say a dog is following you?

Robert felt his stomach drop. Something you made up?

I can't help you, he said. I'm sorry.

Go to hell, Robert said, starting toward the gate.

Eli glowed at him.

I have to admit, though, it was a pleasant surprise running into you. I didn't expect to see you again. Still, it is entirely reasonable, don't you think?

Go to hell, he said again.

Eli walked after him.

This is one thing I've learned. The one truth God has ever given to a man. And it's that the past keeps happening to us. No matter who we are or how far we get away, it keeps happening to us.

Robert kept walking. He was in the street now. He could hear Eli calling after him from the gate, laughing.

Robert spent that night at the bus station, turning over his choices. He paced the inside room, pocketing the pennies that'd fallen underneath the benches. He passed the station map again and again, pacing the length of the floor. He memorized the large swaths of unknown country, read out loud the Indian names, full of rolls and swallows—Pontotoc, Pascagoula, Natchez. He plotted the distance his money could take him. His eye found, again and again, the pale green thatch that is Issaquena

County—then the bold curl of river west of it. All night, the buses trucked in and out and he watched the people in them. They were tired, as tired as he was, their journeys buzzing through their bodies. It was late and he was hungry and they smelled so much like health. A family of Mexicans came down and one of them, a small boy, was holding his mother's hand, looking at him. Robert was sure he was disgusting to them—the filth of the swamp and sweat and dirt radiating off him. But the boy only stared, his eyes big and unreadable. He let go of his mother's hand and moved cautiously toward the bench.

The boy came closer and Robert saw there was something wrong with him. The boy's left eye stared away a little and had more black in it than the other one. The thought came over him that he looked kind of like a stick bug.

The boy stopped in front of him. Robert looked over at his parents, who were too busy arguing at the map wall.

Hello, Robert said.

The boy had something in his hand and he offered it up to him.

It was a wafer candy.

Cadejo, the boy said.

The candy hung there in the air for a second. Robert took it and it damn near broke him to pieces.

PART FIVE

ETTA

(1927)

When we were young, I called you My Etta and we went down to the cotton fields without our clothes, falling on each other and laughing and full of young breath. And you said what you loved was my arms, how big they were, how they could wrap you up and hold you in like a little pea inside its pod. So I'd hold you and we'd look up at the sky, almost like we was daring it to rain.

We had years together, don't forget, years when it was just you and me and we lived only for that warm thrumming inside each other—with no worry for what was coming or what had passed. We were outside of everything.

Then time finally came and we married. I moved us down to Issaquena where the soil was good for timber and Chathams both to set down roots.

Those early days, I'd come home bone tired from hauling timber and you'd be waiting with the dinner all hot, and the air inside our little cabin so goodly warm. But there was something, even then, I saw that wasn't right. Something in your eyes, in that faraway look that you got sometimes.

I remember the night we had Billy. You were in with the midwife, while I was outside, my gut in my throat. I was on the porch looking out into the dark evening. It was summer and there were fireflies all around, and crickets going, and everything singing out the great mystery of the world. And then there was me, my feet turned to iron and the rest of me just reed brittle and terrified. There was so much in this world and I did not know if I could measure up.

The midwife came and fetched me, and I saw you lying there, tired but glowing. And she gave me this bloody mewling thing. It was so small, I was afraid to take it, afraid that it might break somehow.

But you looked at me, my Etta, and you said, Ellis, hold your boy.

And the midwife put the thing in my arms and I knew then it was mine, that I could hold up its small weight and I would exhaust every last drop of my blood to keep us safe.

We named him William Cornelius for my father, but around us he was Billy.

We worried ourselves sick. Every cry and whimper and gibbering noise would steal away our attention and fray our nerves. We would stay up nights, made raw, listening to our little new thing kick and whine.

In time, our boy grew up. The hair came in full and black, and his face was strong and handsome. You doted on him, Etta, called him your brave boy. You'd see him jump into the bushes and wrangle king snakes and racers and you'd say my, how that boy just full of sand. But I knew my boy. How proud he was. You wouldn't believe me then, Etta, but when those snakes slithered out of their bushes, he was as afraid as we were. He just smothered it down, never letting on.

There were days I'd drive out with my partner, Skinny, on the mule cart, hauling our load over to the mill. And there'd be something in the air, maybe, some smell of magnolia or the look of a shadow on the road, and I would feel a change. Feel it right in my body. I knew I was no longer the person I was. What I mean is, so much of my life had been spent as one man—as one person—and now I was more than that.

And I could feel it, right then, actually feel myself stretching out. Feel my fingertips spanning outward until I was like a sail, flagged out against the wind, covering you, and me and our little boy, and I'd have no memory of who I was before. There weren't no fear in it, and no regret, but just a very real anxiousness to see our future.

And in that future came our Little Robert. Robert was so much like you—quiet, full of seriousness. He'd sit alone for long hours, his thoughts zippered up inside him. He never smiled or sought attention, except from his brother, who he'd shadow dutifully all around the house. And our oldest boy took his role as an older brother seriously. He would protect him, his small trembling blood kin, in a way that not me nor you ever could.

Where we would look at Robert and only see our little boy, Billy could see another person. Someone who could be his equal. Billy would take pains to coax his brother out of himself. He'd play with him roughly, teach him to cuss, include him in that gang of young toughs that romped around the country backwoods.

And maybe that was what I had begun to fear. That Robert would be too much like his brother. Too wild. Too smart. Too cunning.

God, it works up a sting to think this. To say this.

Some part of me knew how my son would die. I could feel it like a needle inside my heart, when first I saw my baby boy kick in his father's arms.

Do you remember years ago, when the boys had begged me to take them hunting?

You made us fatback and grits and we set out early—your three men, our bodies burning against the cold. We drove the mule out to Skinny's where I rousted him out of bed and bartered for the loan of his new Henry rifle.

That day we drove down a public road, rounding a thickness of woods, and came to a spot I knew. I hitched the mule to a fence post. Then we packed up and loaded the rifles, me toting my old Enfield and Billy carrying the new Henry. Little Robert I let carry the cartridges of rimfire just to give him something to do. I showed them both how to hold a gun, how to look down it, how to charge the ball.

We went in through a break in the woods. I recall it was rough travel for Little Robert—being gashed everywhere by weeds and vines and thorns, trying to keep up with Billy and me. Still, he didn't complain too much, just kept right on behind us.

When we got onto the trails, Little Robert and Billy kept quarreling over that rifle. Robert fussed and complained—Come on, let me hold it awhile. You held it enough—and Billy would growl back.

I told them roughly to hush. We went the whole morning, sullen and quiet, down the trails, pausing here and there to study over some dirt. I could see Robert watching that rifle in his brother's hands, the long dark hollow of the barrel. Billy cradled the stock, keeping the nose pointed to the dirt like I told him, but when he thought I wasn't looking, he'd mug with that Henry and tease his brother, smirking and stroking the hammer or petting the stock like it was some kind of pup. By the time we stopped for lunch, the injustice had brought Robert near to tears.

While we rested, I was trying to work myself down from an already mean and low mood. Do you remember? The night before, you'd told me how Billy had been fooling with some of the town girls, going with them off into the woods and getting into all kinds of trouble. You wanted me to set him straight and that's what I'd aimed to do with this whole trip. Problem was I had not worked out entirely how.

I told him what you'd told me and he swore up and down that he didn't do nothing with those girls.

I gathered my breath and looked down at my hands.

I told him, You almost eleven years old now, Billy. You coming to be a man and it's time you learned. Everything—every last thing—got to be paid for. You got to understand, boy, that you can't go around like you do. Because they'll take it out of you. Because they'll hate you for it, son. They'll shame you and they'll hate you for it.

The boy became moody and hang-dogged and I should've known then that those words didn't catch. I should've gone at him again; instead I sighed and got up and we kept on hunting.

Billy kept a grimace on his face, and we was all in a kind of bad weather. It was beginning to look like nobody was going to get to do any kind of hunting at all, our moods all being spoiled for it.

Then we came to it, right in the middle of the trail—a set of hoof tracks crossed into the bush, bothering the undergrowth. I brought up my gun, and Billy did the same, doing like I showed him, elbows tucked, cheek against the sight. We walked on quiet as we could, me keeping Robert safe behind me. We came to where the trail bent two ways in a fork and I motioned for Billy to go on the other way.

We crept on silently till I saw the buck. It lifted its head. Its eyes were dark and wet. Its ears twitched, shifting its antlers heavily in the air. I put my hand on Robert's back and inched him forward.

Take a look, I whispered. Don't make a sound.

I let him stand on my shoes, and from the height he could see the buck. Its throat was dirty white and there were almond spots across its rump. It did not move. I waited, trying to find sign of Billy, but he must've fallen behind somewhere.

Shoot'm Daddy, Robert said.

I shushed him and prayed that Billy was getting close. You don't know how I thrilled at the idea, Etta—our oldest boy, his first buck.

Come on, boy, I whispered. I trained my gun out. Come on.

There was a long silence. Then a shot. Just one shot. The buck fled. My first thought was that Billy had missed, but I heard a whoop from across the grass, and I saw Billy then, glowing back at me.

I waved to him. Run him!

We ran now. Even Robert. All at once, we were alive, all the tiredness tamped down into our bellies, all the mean feeling disappearing. The forest seemed to give way around us as I moved bent forward, tracks of sweat coming through my shirt, sticking to my back. We ran and ran, the air cold and harsh in our lungs.

Run him down, boys, run him down! I was laughing and shouting.

Then there was another shot and we all stopped.

All the air seemed to go out of me. I threw down my gun and gathered my boys around me, patting their bodies, their heads, their arms, their chests. We're okay, Daddy, Billy said. We ain't hurt.

Then Little Robert looked off into the distance.

I had heard it too. There was someone laughing.

We followed the noise down to two white hunters. They were kneeling beside the buck, lifting up its head, smirking at the hole in its neck.

The one holding up the buck said, Goddamn, goddamn, that sure was a shot.

The man took off his stalker hat and he was completely bald underneath, the top red and splotchy. The other one was unscrewing a canteen and drinking. He looked up and there we were. What we must've looked like just then—the three of us, dumb and terrified out of breath.

Wendell, he said. Then the bald one looked up too and they both stood up silently.

Well, afternoon, folks, the one of them said, the one the other called Wendell. What can I do you folks for?

Billy started to saying something—That's my—but I hushed him quick.

Just passing through, boss.

I could feel my boys looking at me, feel the shame in it.

Now wait a minute. Son, you was saying something?

And our boy said, That's my buck. I shot him.

The other man started to rear up real mean, but the one named Wendell touched his arm, smiling, his teeth all neat and bright.

Come here, he said.

He's just a young'un, boss, I said. He don't know what he's saying.

Little Robert grabbed his brother's arm, but Billy swung it free.

Let go, he hissed.

Wendell knelt down and looked him over and Billy leaned his chin forward, his eyes full of anger.

Son, we been sitting up in those bushes over there all morning. We killed this deer.

I shot him. I shot him and chased him out over here. And it was just your dumb cracker luck that he ended up over here.

Billy!, I cried.

Wendell chuckled.

Tell you what, son, we'll cut you a few steaks you can take home with you. Would that be all right?

I chimed in, That would be generous of you, mister.

Hell no! Daddy, these pikers are trying to steal my deer!

The one man stood straight up and his face darkened. I grabbed my boy by the shoulder and jerked him back.

Sir, your boy has got a tongue on him.

I know, boss. He strong-willed. I'm trying to correct him. Billy, say sorry to the man.

But Billy would not relent.

I won't say a damn thing! Everybody knows I shot that deer.

I clapped him hard across the mouth and for a second he was stunned, his eyes wide, full of water.

The man sucked his teeth with approval. He squatted down so that him and Billy were near eye to eye.

Matter of fact, everything in these woods is ours. You see, I don't blame you if you didn't read the signs but these are private lands, son, owned by my cousin Tommy over there. So if you ain't got his permission, you can't shoot at anything, or else it's like stealing, you understand, son? You can't even be here without his say-so, or else he could have you arrested. That sound about right, Tommy?

That's right, Wendell, the one named Tommy said.

Didn't see no signs, Billy muttered.

Wendell chuckled. Well, that's all right, son. We all make mistakes, don't we. And what do we do when we make a mistake?

Billy, I said sternly.

What do we do? What do we do when we make a mistake?

I pinched him hard on his neck and he glared at me.

Sorry, he mumbled.

The son of a bitch laughed and he reached out his hand and ruffled our son's hair.

That's a good boy, Wendell said. Say, that's a pretty-looking rifle you got there. What is that, the new Henry?

Billy clutched it close.

Wendell looked square at me.

Is that a Henry rifle?

I didn't say nothing.

Wendell laughed. Well, don't that beat all? Tommy, didn't you lose a Henry rifle in these woods just last week?

Tommy was grinning now.

That I did, he said.

Think of the coincidence! Don't that look just like the one you lost?

Well, Wendell, I do believe you're right. I do believe that that Henry rifle and mine are one and the same.

Our boy looked to me, his bottom lip quivering. Before I could say anything, Billy threw down that rifle, tried to smash it to pieces, but it lay there whole and solid on the grass. The one named Tommy hurried over to the gun, lifting it up, testing its weight in his paws. He couldn't contain himself, he was so happy. He looked across at Wendell and Wendell looked back at him, laughing.

Wendell turned back to us.

Now get the hell out of here, huh?

It was a cold, empty walk home. No one spoke. I don't recall how I squared it with Skinny that day, but somehow I squared it. When we came home, you asked us how we got on, but I didn't have no heart to tell you. That night, when I went to talk to our boy and salve him some, there was such disdain in his eyes and it wounded me through like an arrow. But as hurt as I was by that look, what I took to bed with me that night was fear. I knew then that Billy's tongue and hardheadedness would get him into worse trouble one day. That thought settled hard and cold in my lungs like a piece of iron.

From then on, Billy and me did not get on as we had before, and I was helpless against his growing recklessness—couldn't tamp it down with words nor whupping. And as the year passed, he became tall and manly with hair on his chin and heat in the blood. We argued often until, finally, one day he left us.

It tore me up same as you. Many a time, I'd catch you staring out the window or through the front passage out into the world while in the middle of some mending or sorting of peas. I would come behind you and put my arms around your smooth waist, hug you close, and such a terrible look would come across your face as if you were waking from some dream.

For a time, you hated me. We would lie apart from each other, the bed cold between us, not touching.

Which was fine, I suppose. I did not press you. Didn't force myself on you. At times, when the loneliness was raging inside me, I would climb from the bed and sit down in the front room and watch the night.

Then the day came that they brought our boy home. Me and you stood outside the house and watched that wagon come up the road. Before we'd even seen who they were toting, you sensed it, moaning deep and low. I took your hand and you squeezed into mine hard. Something went loose and stringy inside my gut. The cart slowed down out in front of the house and the driver, who was red faced and dust covered, took out a kerchief to wipe himself. He was a white man and looked a little embarrassed for his cargo. Riding in the back were two boys.

I told you to wait inside, but you came down with me to the road. The two boys in the back carried down the load. They had set him on the carry-cart, wrapped in two sheets and packed under with ice. You let out a horrible cry and threw yourself against the body, sobbing. I saw that bruised, purple-looking thing, couldn't match that bloated thing to our son. The tongue hung out of his mouth, the neck chafed and torn—the eyes not closed so they were dull and far away and looking at nothing. The same eyes that I would find you gazing out from in the coming days, as you followed our oldest son into the dark.

I pulled you to me, my pea, let you heave and sob against my chest. Your skin against me—it'd been so long. I had forgotten that warmth.

I walked you back into the house where you grabbed at Little Robert, who stared bewildered and afraid as his mama clutched and cried against him.

The boys offered their condolences. They said they knew Billy, that they were friends from Mayersville. One of them was a skinny, asthmatic boy. I'd learn later that he was the one who snuck over after the riders had left and cut the rope from Billy's sweet neck. Even the driver, who looked uncertain of himself around us, climbed down from his bench and offered up his hand to me before he took off down the road.

I invited Billy's friends to stay the night and they obliged me. You had fled to the other room and would not come out so I put the dinner together, the first I'd ever cooked—burnt rice and tasteless boiled greens. They waited, their faces bent over their steaming plates. I heard you in the other room, your painful sobbing. No one spoke. No one looked at each other.

In the hours before dawn, we worked fast to put the body under the ground. I suppose some part of me thought that if I could get him under, if I could hide him away, it would soften our grief somehow. We took him out to the edge of the back tract behind the house, where you and Robert couldn't see. We dug by lantern, and by first light we laid him under without coffin or blessing, in a dirt mound. When we had finished, we walked back to the house with our shovels, arms weary, backs spiked with pain. My head buzzed from want of sleep. I offered to let the boys stay another day but they refused.

I went inside and you were asleep. I lay down, my thoughts empty and useless, and found my way into sleep. When I woke up, Little Robert was looking down at me. He looked startled when he saw me. He jumped away and stopped himself in the doorway.

I sat up and looked at him burning with shame. Robert, I said. Then suddenly he took a step forward and I put my arms around him. I cupped his small head in my big hands and held him close, smelling of earth.

We each of us were rough and awkward in our grief. Little Robert I worried over the most. Outwardly he wasn't much changed, but inside, I saw storms. He didn't cry, but to everyone and everything, he cast a dark eye. To me, his solitude became frightening. When he scraped his knee or was startled by lightning, he no longer came to us for comfort and protection. I suppose he had figured that we were not much good for it.

In those early weeks, you would not let him from your sight. You held on to him, would sleep with him tucked hard against your chest. It seemed to soothe you some, but the smallest reminder of his brother would send you into violent spasms of grief and bring a black cloud over all of us.

You cried every day—cursing God and me and your damned life. You tore your hair and beat the walls with your fists. Your rage was something larger than you could handle. It wore you out—leached the black from your hair, pressed hard cruel lines about your eyes and cheeks.

Then one day, it was over. You stopped crying. Stopped talking. Stopped doing much of anything. We were just shades.

Wasn't long after that the Great Flood came. And though you saw those waters as judgment from on high, I could not find the same solace. Our family was broken, and I knew my part in its breaking.

Somehow, we survived, the high water and that bastard and his boat. On dry land they picked us up and trucked us from the flood ledge a half hour to Camp Mercy in Hollandale. Out the window were the stone-wracked road, the chain-linked gate, three and one-half acres of parkland, rowed with pup tents. The sky was a gray slate and the pines shimmered with wet. There were a dozen of us crowded together in the back of the truck, too spent to move. The rain was coming through the torn canvas, and we sat inch-deep in the water.

The truck took us to a brick house, where a line of refugees stretched out through the door. One by one, we climbed out and were given oil-skin ponchos and made to get in line. You wouldn't let me near you with the slicker. You turned away, protesting. In the end, I draped it around you as best I could, like a cape, and me, you, and Robert stood there in the rain.

When it came our turn, we put our names to a long list, and men came to separate us out. The boy was put with me, while two attendants tried to guide you into another room. They only wanted to help, Etta. But you saw they were coming and you seized up, let out a wail, and grabbed at our child. They tried to force down your arms but you wouldn't let go, clutching at him for dear life.

Finally the man in charge waved the attendants away and let Robert stay with you. I went into a separate room, where a man went through my hair with a comb and tweezers. They read my pulse and had me swallow a vitamin pill. I was led down into a basement, where I could change into a gusset shirt and pants. You and the boy came down soon after. We were given a ration card and a box of supplies and were shown on a map where to find our tent.

We hiked through the drizzle, across the parkland, going up and down the rows. The other survivors watched us from within their pup tents, their faces tense and silent. We found our shelter, at the edge of the camp, where the stink of the latrines was made worse from the rains. When we arrived, there was a man inside, asleep on the canvas flooring. His clothes were full of patches, and the tops of his shoes had been torn off.

The man startled when he heard us.

Sorry, he said. He stood up, excused himself, and walked out into the rain.

I unpacked the box: a change of clothes, three pairs of trousers and two shirts, not a one of them sized right. Underneath the clothes were two sleeping bags, a comb, two toothbrushes, and a pack of cigarettes.

We slept huddled, the rain pattering the canvas around us, the dead weight of our bodies on top of each other. I woke several times through the night, too empty to move, and I saw the raw morning spill through a tear in the canvas, the sky mud yellow, clanking with rain, like the first dawn on the ancient Earth. We woke rested but hungry, and when the ration truck came down our row, I fought my way through the mob for a parcel of powdered milk, rock hominy, two pounds of hash, and a bar of soap.

The days turned to weeks, and those ragged half-drowned souls would pour into Mercy stinking of mold and rot and dysentery, their bodies rain-beat and shiftless. Mosquitoes ranged the camp, hunting blood as we fought and clamored for the short supply of netting. At all hours, men who could no longer stand were carted in wagons to the medical tents. They were pale and feverous, their skin spotted with carbuncles.

Rumors spread that the deathly sick were doped with morphine, then trucked out to the river and thrown in. And still every day more refugees were trucked in, each more desperate than the last. When they ran out of housing, the refugees were placed in cots inside offices. Soon they cut our rations to a parcel every two weeks and men were driven to thieving. At night I slept with an iron spike under my shirt.

It didn't take long for the troubles in Mercy to call down the greedy and opportunistic. Pimps, pitchmen, and Bible-thumpers beset Mercy's borders. At dusk you could see the painted women slip into the pup tents, and at dawn the snake-oil men would square their territories on the avenues and yodel into the crowds. They were a circus for the sick and desperate, filching what little we had managed to salvage of our former lives.

Because I was among the able-bodied, I joined one of the labor crews.

The work took me away from the camp, away from you and Robert, but it earned us an extra parcel come delivery day. Five days a week, I'd take the work truck out of Mercy through Hollandale to the flood shelf. There, with a few dozen men, I'd sift through the wrecked towns. Homes that hadn't been destroyed in the flood had been gutted and looted. In the streets, the smell was unbearable. Waterlogged bodies floated in the knee-deep water, the flesh coming apart like rotten fruit. We worked for hours with no protection from the biting flies that trailed the corpses.

It was a hell but still I went. I told myself we needed food. Supplies. My travel pass let me come and go out of Camp Mercy, into Hollandale, where I could try to barter for better food, blankets, medicine. But truth was—forgive me—a part of me was glad to get out every morning, away from you. You got worse as the days went on, and I would not let on how bad it got. You muttered to yourself and barked like a dog. Didn't dress nor bathe no more, and there were times I felt so frail that I could not carry another burden.

It fell to Robert to tend to his mama, and he did so without complaint. He bathed you, changed and washed your clothes. Little Robert helped in a way no child should ever have to.

Then one day, when I had come home early, and I found you inside the tent, my Etta, a strange look across your face. I came closer and the smell overtook me. You were not embarrassed or angry or sad. Just frowned a little. Robert wasted no time. He held your arms straight up. Before I understood what was happening, he'd lifted the dress over his mama's head. A hard sour grief overtook me. I saw my Etta, my sweet Etta—body, mind, and soul lay in ruins. A woman older than her years. Her body covered in sores, folds of skin hanging from her belly from where she'd wasted. Little Robert kept his eyes to the floor, tried not to look at his mama, her large sagging breasts. I could tell he had done this many times before. He fetched a wet rag and wiped you clean. Then he rubbed salve on the insect bites that covered your thighs.

God forgive me.

In the next three days, I managed to scrounge up fifty dollars. I made arrangements with a woman named Lucinda Quinn, the owner of a cathouse who had been scouting for promising girls out of Mercy and into her employ. She looked at me queer when I offered our boy up for an apprenticeship. He was well behaved, I told her, and good at house duties. He cleaned and swept and did the wash in the camp and did not eat much. She had no call for boys in her trade, she told me, but after she'd seen the sorry state of the boy's parents, she relented and took my money. I woke Little Robert at midnight, prying him from your sleeping hold. I dressed him quick and took him out across the camp where the wagon would be waiting. He was still groggy, eyes half shut, moaning.

That night I worried over what I would tell him. What words were there to see him through the coming years without his mother or his father? When we got to the wagons, there weren't none I could muster. I prayed that when he was older, he would understand and that if my one blood child left would hate me, let him hate me for my weakness and not for my love.

Our boy looked at the horses, bewildered. Their breaths were steaming. I spun him 'round to face me, too hard, that there was a look of shock on his face.

I opened my mouth, but there wasn't nothing coming out.

I stood up quick, shame and tears galling my throat. I sought out Lucinda Quinn, caught her look so that she understood that the boy was here, and then very quickly I turned away and left our one living son in a cold dark field.

~

THERE IS ONE MAN, A PREACHER, THAT SNIFFS AROUND THESE parts, skimming up the poor souls. After days of trying, he'd managed to hunt me down. He come to me with his little black book and said that I was aggrieved, with my son lost and my wife ill, that if any soul needed comfort, it would be mine. Said the Lord was here to lighten my load if I was willing to let him. Then he opened up that little book, read some of I don't know what, then he said that God made man for living and dying both, that all that happens is part of the Lord's plan for me, and that we may all be rejoined in the kingdom of heaven, and on and on and on.

I told him that I surely wished that were true. But I am not a man for tall tales. My life is over. It begins and ends in the same place, where the past will keep happening.

And now it's you and me again, Etta. And there are days when I am here beside you, holding your hand, that a great lonesomeness falls upon me. But then there are those brief, stolen moments where you look on me with such kindness. Not love, but kindness. And in my mind's eye I can still see that cotton field, our bodies across each other, the scent of sweet clover in our lungs. And the grief becomes too much.

I look on you and I'm the one who has been left behind. Sometimes I can glimpse the world in which you live. It's a place better than this one—where our sons still live, and we are young, and your husband is a better man, strong, assured of himself, and not this damned fool beside you, holding out his nigger heart.

PART SIX

HOME

(1941)

obert fled through bristlegrass and acacia, along the hogback into a deep blue strath below the dell. There was no moon, only thatches of starlight through the cloudbreak. That morning he'd cut his beard with his knife, clearing the lice from his face and blooding the air. For days the Dog ignored the traps he'd laid—snuffling at the poisoned meat then loping into the bushes. No matter where he went, it was always ahead of him. He'd double back, change directions, but at every turn, he'd find evidence of its passing. A broken trail, paw prints in the soft black earth.

He had seen it only once. The third day out it rained, and the gulch he'd fled across had engorged. He pulled himself up to a weeded ridge—the powder of his rifle wet and clotted. He began to strip away his clothes, and as his shirt passed over his head, he saw two yellow eyes sheltered under the lantana. He did not move. They watched each other, the rain passing between them. His knife was on his belt, new and strange. He did not move.

The Dog yawned and flicked its tongue. After a while, it drew away. Robert drank his canteen empty then refilled it in the stream. Then he drank again, hungrily, his throat throbbing. When the rain stopped hours later, he continued, trying to avoid the fresh tracks in the mud.

Now the wind heeled through the grasses, his hair, his clothes. He shivered and his eyes began to water. The clouds broke and a lobe of moon cast down across a meadow. A hundred yards away, the forest began again, and he strained his eyes toward the darkness. Somewhere the Dog howled. It was ahead of him, how far he did not know. It howled again, lonesome and cold, sliding up through the gusts. The wind changed. It was on his back now and at once, the howling stopped.

He wiped the wet from his eyes and got to his feet. There, in the dark, he saw a shape. They regarded each other. He brought his rifle up slowly and leaned into the sight. It stepped toward him, then circled. His fingers were stiff in the cold and when the shot discharged, the barrel swung into the wind. He recharged the rifle, but the shape was gone.

There was a low whistle. He turned. Across the dell, a train ran along the blue hills—two lights racing behind skirts of dogwood and mayhaw. It threw up a steam plume above the forest, then disappeared around the bend.

He headed back into the forest and built a bivvy and a fire beside a fallen tree. He let himself sleep into the late morning before picking up the trail again. He headed north, northeast, toward the hills where the train came through. The Dog kept a pace ahead of him, a few miles at a time, resting in places, before continuing on again. It was mocking him. Soon the forest fell away, leading out to a grass valley and a dirt road along the train tracks. At the crossing, he found a mound of scat, jeweled with horseflies. It'd been left in the square of rails like an offering. A car came down the road and Robert stepped to the side. He waved it down.

It must've been a Sunday. Inside the car, a white family was in their church clothes. The woman was holding down her straw hat. The man had his blond hair standing on end from the wind blowing through it. There were two boys in the back, all stockinged and blue-eyed. They looked at Robert, disgusted.

You know where this road goes past these hills?

Town of Anguilla, the man said. He looked Robert up and down. It's got an ordinance.

Then the car sped off again.

Robert started walking.

Up the hill there was an old grain silo that hadn't seen use in some time. He pried his way in with a metal pipe and had a look around. The grain stores were eaten through and rotten with rats. The roof was falling apart so the ceiling was freckled with sky. He found a lamp with a little oil in it, and he broke it down to make a tiny fire pit there in the dirt. Then he slept with his back against a wall, the fire burning to keep the rats away. His sleep was dreamless and when he woke, it was already dusk. His throat was sandpaper, and coils of heat were searing his lungs. He stood himself up. His body felt like concrete. He picked up his gun, his pack—the whole weight of the world on a strap against his shoulder. He trudged on.

Three miles out, he could see where the town began—a cluster of clapboard buildings, run-down and slaughtered by the weather. There was music coming from one of the houses, something bright and full of longing. He followed it down the road and came to a juke house off the main road. Buckets of ice sat on the porch. Inside a Negro minstrel was sitting on a stool, working a cigar box in his lap. The front of it had been hollowed out and three steel cables stretched down from the top of a broom handle. The minstrel slid the back of a knife along the cables, making them sound. There were chairs arranged around him, a drunk splayed out on one of them, and on the side wall, the barman was chipping a block of ice into a tub. His shirtsleeves were rolled, and he looked up at Robert, wiped his mouth, and went back to his business.

Robert sat down at the counter and listened to the minstrel play. The man fretted the knife against the strings, rang the cables low and rusty, then glided into a high hum. Robert felt his soul rising out of him, leaving him empty.

When the music had finished, there came a loud snore. A man had passed out at one of the tables. The barman reached into a bucket for a piece of ice, then tossed it at him.

Jesus Christ, rise up, you son of a bitch.

He threw another.

The man jolted awake and squinted over at the counter.

It's near end of the month and you still haven't cleaned out that shithouse!

The man picked his head up. There was a deep bruise below his eye.

Hey, I'm talking to you, G.D.!

The man stood himself up and smoothed down the front of his shirt. He passed his fingers through his greasy hair. Robert watched him. The swing of his arm, the square of his jaw. The man crossed the room to a small cabinet, and he took a shovel and a kerchief. He tied the kerchief around his face so it was only two eyes then, two brown centers, the rest full of white, the dark angry slashes of his eyebrows.

Robert followed him out behind the jakes. He watched him get down on his knees and work open the pit door. The smell hit the man and he turned to suck clean wind. Then he cinched the kerchief tight over his nose and mouth and leaned into the pit, hacking down with the shovel head.

It'll be a while. You can go across the way, the man said.

You don't remember me, Robert said.

The man struck the shovel down hard so that it stuck and stood himself up. G.D. pulled down his kerchief and balanced himself against the frame. His face was bright with sweat. He was looking into Robert's face, squinting, his brow beetling. Flies buzzed drunkenly on the rim of the pail. It took minutes but when G.D. recognized him, he let out a loud laugh and threw up his arms.

THE BARMAN SCOWLED WHEN HE SAW G.D. COME IN AGAIN. HE shifted a wash rag back and forth between his hands. Then he smacked it hard against the counter.

You do like I tell you with those jakes?

G.D. ignored him. He went up on his toes and reached for a bottle of shelf whiskey on the wall. The barman grabbed his hand.

Drink's for those who can pay. Not drag-ass layabouts, G.D.

G.D. squinted into his face. He smiled broadly.

I said I'd clear them, so I'll clear them. I got a friend come see me just now.

He pointed with his chin and the barman looked at Robert, the rifle slung around his shoulder. The barman eased off his grip and G.D. wriggled his arm free. He gathered up the bottle and two glasses, and he and Robert set themselves down at an empty table. G.D. poured and they clinked their glasses, though they never said to what. The whiskey was hot and sharp, and it bit hard against Robert's throat. Tears rose to his eyes. G.D. looked at him and laughed.

So what? You some kind of bad man on the run from the law?

Robert shook his head. Just passing through.

Like the rest of us. G.D. nodded solemnly at his joke. He shifted in his seat, leaning forward.

Look at you. All growed up.

He smacked his hand hard against the table, then lifted it up slowly. He grinned at the squashed fly in his palm.

Well, you can see I'm doing well for myself, he said. He wiped his hand across his trousers. There was a long pause. His mood seemed to darken. He refilled their glasses and they drank again.

He leaned back on his chair so that it rested on two legs. He was talking, but Robert could not make out all the words. G.D. couldn't stop his mouth running. His talking circled on itself, never touching on anything straight. His long muscular arms gestured widely, described the room, punched the table, stabbed his finger at the air.

He talked quickly, heatedly. Robert could feel the eyes in the room bend toward them.

The barman told him to quiet down.

G.D. scowled. He threw the empty bottle toward the bar, smashing it against the wall. Suddenly everyone was rushed outside.

It was night then. Warm. Clear. There were so many stars.

A circle had formed around G.D. and the barman. Robert stood at the edge. *Just like when we were kids,* he thought. For a time the two men danced around each other, the crowd goading them on. G.D. jabbed wildly before the barman plugged him once across the jaw.

G.D. straightened, dazed. The man hit him again. G.D. took a hesitant step back and sat himself down.

The barman wiped his face and spit. He looked at Robert. Take him home, he said.

As the crowd made their way back inside, Robert lifted G.D. to his feet, holding him under his arm. He jammed a kerchief against G.D.'s battered nose. G.D. muttered something, then pointed down the road with a limp finger. Robert looped his arm around G.D.'s back, his shirt sticky with another man's sweat, and walked him toward his home.

G.D. lived out on a shotgun to the north of Anguilla about a mile from any of his neighbors. Robert could see it in the distance, sitting under all that sky, the land choked with creepers. The grass was hard-packed, gritty, dead. There was a light on in the window, and by the way it blinked he could tell there was someone inside, waiting on him.

They got to the porch and G.D. said, You'd better stay the night.

The blood had backed up into his nose, and when he spoke, his voice was soft and cottony.

Robert took him inside where a woman was waiting to collect him.

He's had too much, Robert said. The woman made no answer.

She was small, slender, beautiful. There was a streak of silver in her hair. G.D. grabbed her and kissed her roughly on the mouth. Then he stumbled over to the couch and laid himself out, boots and all. She snuffed the candle and climbed in beside him, paying no mind to Robert.

Robert did not recognize her right then. There was the vague tug inside of him, a sense that something important was happening. He ignored it, put it off on being still a little drunk. He thought about leaving, trying to get ahead of the Dog. Instead he went into the kitchen, where he set down his things and spread out his coat. He could hear them moving in the other room, the wood creaking under their shifting weight, G.D.'s night sounds. Robert lay down on the stiff fabric; the ceiling was turning. It dawned on him that this was where the Dog had been leading him. All the miles and roads and wearied passways had been laid for him in advance. He put his arm over his eyes and felt the blood in his face.

<hr/>

IT WAS MORNING AND ROBERT LAY THERE, AWAKE BUT NOT MOVING. He heard the woman talking to herself, softly. He roused up his head and peered down into the next room. She was squatting on the balls of her feet, working a soapy rag across the floor. He saw her from behind, the morning light streaming in through the door. He watched her work, her round bottom bobbing, the blades of her shoulder flexing. She laughed lightly, chided herself, and then started to whisper.

Robert sat up and cleared his throat.

She turned toward him, startled.

Her mouth hung open. She looked down at the rag, folded the corners into its center, and then looked back up. Her hands were thin and slender, passing a slip of hair behind her ear. She looked like she was about to say something, but instead, she wiped her forehead and gathered the rag again and started polishing the wood.

Robert stood up, his erection painful. He stepped around her and walked barefoot out of the house and around the side. He closed his eyes against the sun and let loose into the grass. The pressure eased in his kidneys.

He finished and went inside. The rag was still on the floor, and for a second he was afraid that he'd dreamed her up. But then he saw movement in the other room. She'd found his rifle and was holding up the stock.

Don't, he said.

It seemed too heavy for her, the barrel bending to the ground, her finger feeling around the guard.

He stepped slowly toward her and she wheeled it on him.

Dora, he said. He realized it was true as he said it. His voice was a dry clack. If she heard him, she made no sign. She stared, not at him, but past him, somewhere far away.

Dora, he said again. Don't.

She took her hand from the barrel and the thing dropped and discharged into the floor. She jumped and started laughing. Her hands were up in the air shaking. She looked at Robert, covering her cheeks. Her laugh was throaty, stupid. He felt the warm trickle between his toes. Robert looked down. There were splinters in his shins. Blood dribbled down slowly. Dora saw it too and gasped. She grabbed the rag and started soaking the blood from the floor.

It was her. He was almost sure of it. The span of her brow, her lips. He recognized these first, then the eyes, the deep taper at the edges that called out from some place dark and deep and ancient. From there the rest rushed into place. Dora. Dora who had kissed him under the old Bone Tree, who'd slipped her hand into his and put in his palm a question. The name had flown out of him like a dragnet through the dark. It was her. But she was different somehow. In his memory, the girl was sharp and bright as a knife edge. Now she knelt before him, seeing him but also not seeing, her dumb attention on the rag she crushed to the floor.

Robert picked up the rifle and hurried off to the field behind the house. The land was a stretch of dead earth, marked with crows. Along the furrows, where the ground was still soft, he dug himself a shallow. Then he dismantled the rifle and buried the pieces. Blood was pumping through his heart. He could not catch his breath. Seeing her, he felt a claw dredge a fresh stinging trench through his life. He had not thought of her in so long.

In the distance sat what was left of an old plantation house, its walls choked with ivy so that when the wind blew through, it would lift its scales and shudder. It was a grave-head grimacing over the surrounding flats. He walked across what must've once been a cotton field. There were faint lines in the dust marking where the earth had been plowed. He came around the back, found the servant's entrance, and pulled a sheet of vines away from the door.

He passed through the doorway, into the dark and mildewed air. He was inside the kitchen. The walls had rotted and the ceiling sagged down above him. The drawers had been ripped out. Looted. He passed through a swinging door. A shaft of light touched down in the center of the room. He looked up at the ceiling and saw a wound of sky passing through two floors, through the roof.

In the parlor, he could see on the wallpaper where the furniture once was—a full-size mirror on the wall, a bureau, a settee. There were boot prints of ash tracking around the carpet that marched to where a sideboard used to sit and then disappeared altogether, like someone had walked straight through the wall.

He came to a set of stairs and climbed a flight up before the wood started to strain. Something buckled underneath him. He stood still, not moving. If he fell through and hurt himself, no one would ever find him. He looked up the staircase. Just one more landing. He gripped the railing and decided to chance it. He took up the steps, testing the wood with his foot first. When he got upstairs, he saw that the floor was completely rotted, the boards warped, the nails thrusting from their holes. He stepped carefully along the edge of the wall. The hall was long, the walls scorched black. He entered a room on his right and saw the holes in the floor and ceiling.

This had been someone's bedroom. There was a rocking chair in the corner. Between the ceiling and the roof, he could see where a bird had built its nest, learned itself better, and moved on. In his dizzy and agitated state, the room felt like a puzzle piece that somehow fit with Dora's reappearance in his life. Robert sat down. He stared up through the space in the ceiling, a cone of dust and sun, waiting for someone to answer.

By nightfall, he headed back to the house. From the field he could see a man approaching from the road. It was G.D., staggering and weaving, barely able to keep on his feet. Robert ran to him and helped walk him inside. G.D. stumbled into the main room, huffing, gripping hard to Robert to keep his balance. Dora watched as Robert carried him to the couch. G.D. stretched out across the cushions, coat and all, his eyes full of shine.

G.D. looked up at the two of them and smiled wide. Tonight we gonna feast like kings, he said.

From his left coat pocket, he drew out hunks of bread and cheese, and from the right, three potatoes. He offered them up to Dora.

Go ahead and make these up. That's a good girl.

Without a word, Dora gathered the food into her arms and went into the kitchen.

You all right? Robert asked. Let me get your coat off.

G.D. waved him away. His collar was soaked with sweat, and there was blood rimming his nostrils.

Go help her with the supper. I need a sec. Need to catch my breath.

His head lolled back and he shut his eyes.

Robert went into the kitchen, but Dora made no notice of him. She'd drawn a pail of water and was busying herself dunking the potatoes one by one, trying to wash the soil from the skin.

Dora, he said. You remember me? My name is Robert.

She paid him no mind.

He went beside her and tried to take her hand. She jerked it away back to her work. Robert sighed, took a potato. They were still gritty with dirt. No doubt stolen. He clutched the bulb in his palm and started cleaning.

After dinner, they cleared away the table and made some space on the floor. G.D. dug out the wireless and switched it on. Bob Wills and the Texas Playboys were performing live from the DeVoy Hotel at WMPS Memphis. Dora seemed to brighten at its sound. The band struck up. Then the horns. G.D. clapped his hands together and she took them in hers. He danced her there on the floor, both of them out of time and sync. Robert was seated in his chair, watching them. G.D. tugged at her hard and she laughed and spun into his arms. He was so much bigger than her. She buried her face into his chest and put her arms around his hips and they swayed a little for a while. When G.D. was danced out, he rubbed his head and sat down.

Okay. No more dancing.

She whined and tugged his arms.

No more. I can't. Why don't you dance with our guest?

They both looked at Robert.

I can't dance, Robert said.

G.D. grinned. Hell, you done worse than dance, I'm sure.

G.D. stood up and steadied himself on the wall. He shook his head and smiled to himself. I need a bath, he said. Then he turned up the dial on the wireless and went into the other room. Robert cleared his throat. He stood up out of his chair, and he walked over to the radio. The music was something different now. The shimmer of fiddles. The slow roll of a horn. He leaned toward her and held out his arm.

Just one, he said.

She looked at his arm, her chin down, trying not to meet his eyes. She took it and they started to dancing, not close but close enough. She kept her head down, watching her feet while Robert stared out past her shoulders. Her hands were clammy. His own were rough. He could hear her dress crinkling, the alien swing of her body off time from his own.

When the song had finished, they both stepped away from each other.

She still would not look at him. Her hands rose protectively to her neck, and she kept looking at the floor. Robert sighed and switched off the music.

Thanks for the dance, he said.

It's nothing, she said.

He looked at her, startled. A small smile flitted across her face. For the briefest of moments, she looked back at him. Her eyes were brown, large, wounding. Then immediately the moment was gone. She broke away, brushing past him, into the other room, to help G.D. with his bath.

ROBERT PASSED THE NIGHT IN THE SMALL ROOM NEXT TO THE kitchen, a heap of quilts and blankets to pass for a bed. He tossed and turned, unable to sleep. Finally he roused himself and went out into the morning air. Outside, the sky started to blush, rose suffusing into the deep high ink. He perched himself on the back stoop and rolled his hands to fight the chill.

His head buzzed. His lungs burned.

The plantation house sat in the distance, dark against the rising sun. Even from here, he could feel its size. Its presence. Its long shadow threw a cape over the dust fields. He needed to leave. Now. Before they woke up. Before the Dog could catch up to him.

Behind him, he heard the back door open. G.D. stepped from behind him, turned to the side, and aimed a hot stream of piss into the weeds.

You sleep okay?

Robert nodded.

G.D. shook himself dry, then hawked a wad of phlegm into the dust. Then he sat down beside Robert.

Tell you the truth, I'm glad to see you're still here, he said. Didn't know if you'd stay when you saw her. The way she is, I mean.

What happened to her?, he asked.

G.D. scowled. Well, what happened to you?

Robert saw G.D. was looking at the scar beneath his chin. The sparse beard that was growing could not hide the long purple streak along his neck. Robert touched it. It was smooth and rubbery.

Something that couldn't be helped, Robert said.

G.D. sucked his teeth. Uh-huh. Well, Dora's a good girl. It'd surprise you how kindhearted she is. Like she's got all of her right on top, right where the skin is. All her sweetness, all her kindness.

Robert didn't say anything. He had suddenly become very tired, like the muscle had become dead and slack on his bones.

And she's smart, too. Don't go thinking she's not.

I never said a word otherwise, Robert said.

Good. 'Cause that's something I won't stand for. She's all my family now, you understand?

The flesh had become puffy on G.D.'s face. Around his eyes the skin was still swollen, and it made him squint through those bloodshot and mucousy globes. Robert was surprised by how upset G.D. looked. His jaw tensed. His eyelids fluttered.

Robert held his gaze.

You take care of her, don't you?

G.D. softened. He worked his lips back and forth.

We take care of each other, he said finally. I'm sorry if I came on a little hot. I hate mornings.

G.D. let out a sigh and rubbed his face.

I just didn't want you to leave here with the wrong idea about things. That's what you're doing, isn't it? Leaving?

G.D. grinned at him.

Don't look so surprised. I know when a fella is gonna cut out. And you, my friend, look like someone who's done his share of cutting out.

He pinched Robert lightly on the cheek.

G.D. laughed and Robert laughed along with him. Robert liked G.D. He remembered this from when they were boys, the way G.D. would move quickly from one thing into the next—one game into another, from anger to tenderness to laughter. G.D.'s was a rattling infectious giggle. Now the two of them cackled, tears oozing from their eyes.

He clapped an arm to Robert's shoulder. When they'd stopped laughing, G.D. hugged Robert to him.

You're safe here, you know, he said.

Robert looked at him, stunned.

Whatever it is you're running from, I mean. I know how it is. You don't got to stay if you don't want to, but all I'm saying is you don't got to leave, neither.

Robert shook his head.

You don't want any of what's coming to me.

Here you got Dora and you got me, and that's two more than if you were on your own. I don't know. I don't know what it is exactly you're mixed up in. But near as I'm concerned, you got a place here with us.

G.D. stood up.

Come on in when you want your breakfast, he said.

G.D.?, Robert said.

G.D. paused at the door.

What happened to her?

G.D. smiled, his mouth going soft and sad.

What happened is I didn't look out for my family, he said. Not enough and too late.

Then he went inside.

⤙

HE DECIDED TO STAY ONE MORE DAY, AND SOON THE DAYS PASSED into weeks, and the weeks into months. He could live here, Robert told himself, the three of them in this ramshackle shotgun shack. In the mornings Dora would cook their breakfasts, and Robert would keep the house, clearing away the rubbish and chasing the dust from the walls and floor. And at night, G.D. would come home, drunk and happy, and he would take the bottle out from under his shirt and they would laugh and drink and eat and dance, while the lunatic world spun on without them.

G.D. was madly in love with Dora. That was plain to see. And though that brought some bitterness to Robert's throat, he ignored it for an echo, a faint whisper of a long gone past. He was happy for G.D., happy for Dora, and, when he could admit it, happy for himself. They made him smile—G.D.'s clownish personality, their childish bickering, like full-grown adults playing house.

He became settled in Anguilla. He managed to find a job killing rats at a bakery in town. The owner was a fat ruddy man, offering a nickel a head. They're eating me out of my trade, he told him. He showed him into the kitchen, to the flour sacks where the stitches were chewed through. Robert spent his four afternoons a week in the warm kitchen, rolling strychnine into balls of dough. There were prints in the flour that tracked across the floor, the counters. Ten or twelve of them at least. A family. They were in the floors. He could almost hear them breathe. He picked the dough from the web of his fingers, worked it into pellets. He laid the poison down by the cracks, carefully, like an offering.

He thought, *If Frankie could see me now.*

For days, they didn't touch the pellets. Must've smelled him on them. But then he noticed a small pile of droppings, greasy and toxic smelling. He opened one of the cabinets and saw one of them lying on a butter dish, its tongue hanging out. It was no bigger than his smallest finger, its small almost-human hands tucked to its body.

It wasn't dead. It opened and closed its eyes slowly. He held it in his palm. It was already cold, its fur matted in bile and urine. He stroked his thumb against its stomach, hoping it was of some comfort to the thing, then up the neck. Then, with a flick, he felt a pop and it was done.

But then he'd come home and there were his friends, glowing with joy enough to bleach out these small miseries. And times would come he'd catch himself mulling too long on Frankie, feel the strange rough quake in his soul, and G.D. would materialize in his doorway, a full glass in his hand, a grin already cracked across his face.

His friend loved him. They acted like fool boys, boxing and wrestling and cussing while Dora watched on, shaking and giggling at their antics.

This could be a life. A good end.

Then one Sunday came and Robert finished work early at the bakery. It had rained in the morning and now the air was cool and easy. The smell of bread was on his clothes, his hair, his skin. Warm. Sweet. His boss had given Robert a loaf to take home with him, and he carried it now tucked under his arm. Soft. Still hot. He made his way through the main square. There was a leather Stetson in a window display and it reminded him of Frankie. He went inside and bought it. It was large, the crown dented low, the brim drooping.

The stretch of road from Anguilla to the house was a flat treeless few miles that gave full view of the sky, with tufts of switchgrass to break the horizon. On either side lay long ranges of buffalograss and grama. The breeze was fresh and bracing. His free hand swung limply at his side.

There was no way around it. He missed her.

His time in Panther, just four months ago now, felt like a dream that, in the waking world, he could not configure together again. There were only snatches. Impressions. Dull flares of memory. He would pass along the river on his way to and from town and watch the water run around the rocks. A pang of guilt would strike from some unknown depth inside him. And as the days drew on, he could feel the dream turn solid inside him, each day a little more vivid, a little bit firmer, till there were hard edges, a weight, a shape to his loneliness.

When he got back to the house, the front door was open. He found Dora slumped on the couch smiling stupidly at the ceiling. Robert stood over her and she blinked lazily. She didn't seem to see him. In the kitchen, G.D. was pacing the floor, pressing a kerchief to his temples. It had turned dark and rose-colored with blood.

G.D. fixed his eyes on Robert as he came in and then as if he was coming out of a dream, he said, Nice hat.

Robert set the bread on the counter and G.D. looked at it mournfully.

I brought back some bread, Robert said.

G.D. nodded and walked past him out of the room.

⌒

AT NIGHT, THERE WERE VOICES IN THE WALLS. SHOUTING AND cussing. Robert would hear the furniture crash the boards behind his head. He'd lie on the blankets, staring up at the ceiling unable to sleep. He'd wake up, his bowels in knots, his mouth raw with acid. And in the morning, G.D. too would emerge from the room, his face ravaged from drink, his lips chapped and scored with blood.

Every day Dora seemed to get worse and worse, and neither Robert nor G.D. could find any pattern in it. Any small thing could set her off. One supper, she rose abruptly in the kitchen and poured hot cinders on G.D.'s lap, laughing deep and throaty as he jumped and hollered.

The sight of a bird at the window could start her crying. And not a low weeping, but a mad frenzied yowl that would last for hours. And when she had done all the crying she'd aimed to do, she would all at once fall silent and go about the house as if nothing had happened.

Sometimes she looked like she was lost in a thought. Her lips would press tight together and her eyes would become large and staring and all the color would leave her face. G.D. and Robert would call her name or clap their hands but it wasn't any good. She would not respond. They had to wait it out. Then at once, she would stand up or get out of the chair and walk into the kitchen and smash the plates on the table edge.

At night she sweated through her sheets. Soon she was too weak to get up from the bed. In time the house fell into disrepair. Robert found himself taking on more of the house duties, brooming the floors, doing the wash, cooking up charred unpalatable meals for the three of them. He worked only half days at the bakery. Dora would throw up constantly. Her clothes were in tatters, crusted with vomit, her eyes were bloodshot, her skin gone all gray. Once she came in on him while he was in the kitchen. She stood there, holding the door frame to keep herself up. She put her arm out like she was reaching for something, then she fell down and started shivering on the floor. Robert picked her up, her skin sticking to his hand. He held her from her hips. Her muscles convulsed. It coursed out of her. Hot was dribbling down his hands. He looked at her mess. Her blood.

Robert had wanted to send for a doctor but G.D. said, No.

This is our family, he said. We do this on our own.

So they kept on and every day as Dora weakened, G.D. seemed to diminish with her. He became thin and wan. Robert asked again about the doctor, but again G.D. refused.

You're dying, Robert said.

His own voice startled him. It was small and reedy, like there wasn't breath enough to get the words out. G.D. wasn't sure who Robert was talking to but he turned his head and squared his eyes on him, and there was no anger in it, nor remorse nor pity.

You're dying and she's killing you.

G.D. said nothing. He walked into Dora's room and shut the door behind him.

Robert awoke one night to his name thundering from behind the bedroom wall. It was G.D. He bolted upright and struggled through the dark to their room. The door was splintered off its hinges. Inside, a small lamp glowed. They were both on the floor, naked, G.D. straddling Dora's torso, trying to force down her arms. Blood was streaming from his forehead. Dora was screaming. She jerked forward and back, her face twisted in pain.

Get the pan! In the kitchen! Hurry!

Robert ran into the kitchen. He took a frying pan from off the shelf and stood in the doorway, unsure of himself.

Dora sank her teeth into G.D.'s arms, and he roared and fell off her. She sprang to her feet, nearly knocking Robert over. Robert shut his eyes and brought the metal down hard. He felt the dull clap deep in his arm. He opened his eyes. Dora slumped over. His hand went dead.

It's okay. It's okay now, G.D. said.

G.D. picked her up gently and laid her down on the mattress, pulling a sheet over her naked body.

Robert sat down on the edge. He looked at the mess around him, but his eyes couldn't focus.

You had to, G.D. said. I made you do it.

Robert nodded absently.

G.D. smoothed the hair away from her face. Then he bent down and kissed her forehead and let out a sigh. He put on a robe and gestured Robert out of the room. They took the lamp out to the back porch. G.D. went to the barrel and washed his face with a damp rag. They sat down on the stoop.

She'll be all right now, he said. She'll sleep through the night.

G.D. took out a pouch of tobacco and tried to roll a cigarette. His hands were shaking.

You all right?

Get that light up and have a see.

Robert stood up and held the lamp up to the cut at G.D.'s hairline.

Looks pretty bad, Robert said. Ought to stitch it.

You know how?

I can try.

G.D. got up and brought him some whiskey, a rag, a spool of catgut, and a needle. Robert hung the lamp on a hook and touched the wound. Blood oozed out. He dabbed it dry, then soaked the rag with whiskey. He laid it across the wound and G.D. winced.

Try not to fidget, Robert said.

G.D. grumbled something.

This happen a lot?

Not a lot. Sometimes, he said. She's a sweetie—God, I get tired sometimes though, don't I?

Robert didn't say anything after that and took up the needle. G.D. managed to get the cigarette rolled. He set it to his lips and sucked deeply. Christ, he said. It's a nice night, isn't it though? Didn't think God turned out nights like this anymore. Not too hot. Not too wet. Just . . . right.

He started to chuckle.

I told you don't fidget, Robert said.

Sorry. Sorry. It was just . . . it's funny because I was thinking, the last time there was a night like this, we were kids. You know the time I'm talking about?

Robert thought for a moment. No, not really, he said.

He laughed. It was just like this . . . just like . . . like something is about to happen. I used to feel that way all the time. I used to just wake up in the middle of the night, and I could feel it right in my gut. Something is going to happen. God, how it used to work me up. Like there was something in me, trying to get out.

G.D. reached for the whiskey and let himself have a little.

I'd tear off my shirt and run outside and want to be wild.

Robert finished with the wound. Done, he said, but G.D. didn't seem to hear him. He was sitting there, blinking and smiling, looking at something far off.

God, it was something though, he said.

I'm finished, Robert said again.

He turned his eyes to Robert, then he took his hand and squeezed it. Thank you, he said.

<hr />

BY MORNING, IT LOOKED LIKE THE WORST HAD PASSED. ROBERT WOKE to the crackle of fat sizzling. He looked out into the kitchen. Dora was by the stove, making breakfast. The color had come back to her cheeks, her left foot tucked behind her right as she bounced her heel on the floor. G.D. was at the table, smiling, his hair pushed down from where it lay on the pillow. He look tired but happy. He lifted up a finger in greeting.

But Robert was looking at Dora. The glow on her face, fresh like the earth after a rain. He could not stop staring at her. She smacked the pan down hard on the stove.

Stop it, she said. You'll make me blush.

And for a time, there was no more screaming, no more crying. They slept deep and easy in the house. One night, G.D. called them in from the other room. He showed them the bottles he'd stole from work.

We need to celebrate, he said.

Dora squealed and Robert examined the bottle. What are we celebrating?, he asked.

G.D. clapped him on the arm, his lips spread into a grin.

Life! He laughed and hugged them close. Strange and unexpected and wonderful life!

So they drank, them three, whipping their necks back, laughing and swallowing whiskey, catching the runoff on their fingers, holding the wet at the first and second knuckles, then sliding their fingers into each other's mouths. They were low-flying birds, inches from the ground, beating the dust, trying to keep level against the rising floor. They sang and swore. They moved the furniture and they danced each other, beat their feet against the aching wood. They were bodies, twirling, leaping, launching across the room. They turned the music so loud sometimes you couldn't hear it at all except for the flare of horns, the cymbals crashing.

Then come dark they fled the house and took off to the hills to pick strange nameless blue flowers, twining them into chains, pulling the petals from the hearts. Loves me, loves me not. They brought them home and made them into capes and garlands and crowns. Kiss me, G.D. had said. And she did. Now kiss him. Kiss him like a mother, our little boy. And she laughed and took Robert by the face and put a tongue in his mouth. And she reached where he wished she would, and then let him do the same, and they all had a laugh, G.D. louder than them both put together. It was a game, just another game, with G.D. again leading them on. She was their Sally Water again. They watched her part her hair, run her hand along the line of her neck, feeling the deep invisible currents of her body. Shake it to the east. Shake it to the west. And the thought came to them, separately, in that moment, that no one has to suffer.

Robert woke, his head full of lead and aching. For a long time, he was not sure what it was he was seeing. A long black cape swept and danced like a flame, drumming the air, stretching out like a net. He watched it, not moving. There was fire in his chest. At the last moment, it pulled away. He felt wet on his face. It was drizzling, the droplets cool against his brow. With some effort, he sat himself up. They were crows, he realized, and he had fallen asleep in the field behind the house.

He touched his throbbing forehead and groaned. He could not remember how he had gotten here.

There was a noise. The sound of a girl laughing. The hair prickled on his arm. Robert sat up. He could see Dora in the distance. She was naked, her lithe brown body launching back and forth at the edge of the field. Her clothes were scattered around her. Lightning flashed. She let out a loud whoop and danced naked through the mud, her arms up, shouting in bright frightening joy.

Robert took off after her and led her back into the house. She was wet and shivering, her hair hanging in front of her face in dirty clumps. He tore the sheet from her mattress, toppling the mess on top, and wrapped her tight to get her dry. Then he lit the stove and sat her in front of it. Don't move, he said. Just stay right here. She followed him with her eyes but said nothing. He set on the kettle and then he withdrew from the kitchen to hunt up some dry clothes. When he returned, he paused at the door frame, and from there he watched her, his arms resting against the jamb.

Dora?, he said.

She turned and looked at him.

He showed her the clothes and helped her into them. She did not resist. Then she sat back down near the glow of the flame.

He waited for G.D. to come home. He'd give him that at least. They'd shake hands and Robert would go again on his way. There was no use his being here, raking through these spent ashes. He stared at the trembling hull, the sheet cinched tight around her, her head weaving for want of sleep. What happened to you?, he wanted to ask. But he knew she couldn't tell him, couldn't reach into that black and unknown depth inside her. Her head drooped, and slowly she fell away into sleep.

When the kettle began to whistle, he took it off the stove and poured the water into a cracked mug. She was still asleep so he drank it himself. He did not realize how cold he'd become.

Hours passed and the day went to night—the silver sky sucked down into the horizon. Still no G.D. He patted Dora gently on the hand and woke her up. Let's go, he said, as he helped her to her bed. He laid her down and put his hand against her burning brow.

Dora looked up at him from underneath the blankets, sweat beading her forehead, her expression soft.

She whispered something. Robert couldn't hear what. He leaned in closer and she slipped her tongue into his mouth.

He pulled away in shock. The taste was sour and rank. She started to laugh, then broke into a fit of coughing. Then she turned over and fell again to sleep.

ROBERT SEARCHED UP AND DOWN THE ROAD FOR HIM, NORTH TO the old field where the plantation house sat squalid and decaying in the distance, then south again, out past the grove of yellow poplars, into Anguilla. It was dusk, and the last of the day's light stretched itself out in a band before the horizon. By the time he made his way to the juke house, the crowd had already packed themselves in. Chairs and tables were stacked up against the walls. There was a band in the house and they roared their music, stamped their feet. Folks were dancing, scraping their shoes against the floorboards, swinging their arms. Robert sat down at the counter and tried to get the barman's attention.

The man tore himself away from a young woman at the other end of the bar. He walked over slowly, slapping his towel in his hand.

You seen G.D.?

You Robert?, the barman said.

Yes.

Just a second.

The barman stepped away to the other end of the bar.

The band finished their number and the dancers made their way back to their seats. The air was thick with smoke and Robert was finding it hard to breathe. Robert's arms were shaking and his heart was beating and his thoughts tattooed images in his brain—of G.D., of men with horses. The barman came back with a glass of something brown and dark in one hand and a slip of paper in the other. The paper was folded neatly into a square. In an uneven hand, his name had been written across it.

G.D. told me if I saw you, I was to give you this note and this here drink.

The barman set them down in front of him.

Cheers, the barman said. He rapped the counter with his knuckles and moved back to the corner.

Robert grabbed the drink and took in a mouthful. It was worse than piss but he swallowed it down. The acid bubbled in his gut. For the longest time he stared at his own name, not touching the note. He did not need to, he decided. He knew already what it said. Outside, moths were crashing around the windows. He drank down the rest of the glass, this time slower. There was hardly any sting left and he let it dam in his mouth, then all down his throat. He breathed deeply, felt the air tear on his teeth. It was full dark now and there were owls somewhere, their calls multiplying endlessly. Through the window, he could see the moon wasn't but a sliver, like the sky was torn and behind it stretched some brighter canvas.

Frankie did not stop to sleep, kept moving, through dusk and dark and again the breaking light, head buzzing, hungry. She clutched the satchel to her chest, did not risk a fire for fear that the smoke would give her away. By now, they would have found the house. She imagined them pawing through her things, her family's things. Bugheway bastards. She had heard the explosions. Then the crackle of gunfire. The bugheway were clumsy, drunk—firing blindly into the leaf. They came with a parade of dogs, howling, foaming, down the western corridor, then north. She backtracked, stayed off the trails, waded through the brack and peat to mask her scent, till at last, three days later, she made it out the other side. The air was different here. Thin. Sweet with grass. It made her sick to breathe it.

She came to an unmarked road and started down it, trembling, her heart pressing against her teeth. She found an abandoned grain silo and saw in the dirt, boot prints. Robert's. They were old but she knew right away, the deep etch of the inside heel, the lip where the toe had lifted. She took it as a sign and went inside.

The first night she slept under the pelts and woke up to pigeons fluttering above her, dust and feathers falling from the rafters. She winged one with a rock, stepped on its neck, and cooked it on a spit. The meat was hot and tough. She crunched through the bones, delirious, burning her tongue and mouth; she didn't care. She lifted a sleeve of dead skin from the roof of her mouth. A week passed. No one came for her. Not Robert. Not the bugheway. She wept alone, exhausted, burning with sorrow and relief.

She resolved then to go into town. She'd sell the skins and, with the money, start again up in the north woods. Saskatchewan.

On her last night at the silo, she awoke to the noise of hoofbeats. They thumped dully through the earth, an old Injun trick. She climbed out from under the skins and saw riders across the valley, a least a dozen strong. They held torches and were whooping brightly, dragging something ragged through the dust.

Come nightfall, the wind tore into the paneling at Fort Muskethead. The trappers helped nail rugskins to the windows to damp the cold. The electric lights flickered then went. They could see the outline of the cage, the trader's silhouette against starlight, busying himself with the hurricane lamps—his hump riding to his shoulder. They shoved against the caging, rattled it from its hinges. Hurry up, you old hunchback. The glass caught the glow, and the trader passed the lamps through the slide window.

They set them on the sills, the floors, the tables, then lined up again in front of the opening. One man muscled through in front of the others and he passed his license through the window. The lamps haloed just enough glow for the trader to make out the bull mark. He looked up at the trapper.

His beard was caked in parts, his cheeks scabbed and dirty. The skin had started to peel on the round of his nose, so it looked thatched with frost. The trader passed the license back through the slide window and watched him gather it into his hands, two fingers stumped above the knuckle of his left hand. The trapper took the paw from his rucksack.

The trader held it above the lamp. The paw had been chopped below the knee. The bone had splintered and cracked. He felt along the toes and the padding, then slid the money through the slot.

Frankie watched the light move across the old man's face. She clutched her trapsack to her chest and joined the line. They could smell her, she knew, like they could smell a kill. The tealike odor of frenzy and panic. She looked around the room. Their eyes glittered.

She came to the front.

License?

None, she said.

The trader blew out through his lips. Next.

I's a L'Etang.

I know a John L'Etang. You of those L'Etangs?

She nodded impatiently.

Well, where are they then?

Gone North to Beaver, she said.

The trader looked into her face. Her eyes were full of wet.

Sorry to hear that, he said.

He moved the lamp closer and brought a slice of soft light against her cheek.

Let me see what you have.

She went through the furs one by one and splayed them out for him to see. He brought out a small comb and combed out the kinks, spreading the skin out with his hands, bringing it to the lamp. There was a pop, and the electric lights flared then fizzled out again.

Sable's been on the fall lately. Won't fetch more than fifteen.

Fifteen? Need more 'n that.

The trader closed his eyes and rubbed the bridge of his nose.

It's not a world for trappers. Not anymore.

Twenty-five. Give a' twenty-five and I's go.

Someone behind her snickered. The blood rushed into her face, and she had to keep herself from starting a fight.

You're welcome to try in three weeks. When the new numbers come in.

Can't wait three weeks. Need to leave quick jack. Twenty. Please. I go on twenty.

The trader looked again at the skins. They were old. Probably infested with moths.

Eighteen, he said.

Okay, bon. Eighteen.

The trader counted out the money and she stuck it into her coat and walked out. Out on the road, she touched the soft damp bills in her pocket. The hills were full of wind, and moving downridge, it lashed the dust around her. She'd planned to bed down again at the silo, but she'd misjudged how long it'd take her to get to the trading post. It was too dark to head back. There was a glimmer of light in the distance— Anguilla maybe, or one of the small hamlets outside town. She moved toward it. Eighteen dollars. A few days of food. A box of shells if she could get it. A knife and something to whet it on. Eighteen dollars. It'd have to last at least to Snakebite Creek.

The wind was cold. She kept moving, chanting the trapper's prayer. Strong chains. Strong arms. She made her way closer.

She came to a fork in the road and, deep in its wedge, a barn. The wide doors were thrown open, and a warm orange light bled into the darkness. There were people coming and going, their long shadows sweeping across the brittle grasses. She moved closer, her face gone of feeling. There was laughter. Music. A Negro man brushed past her, mumbled something, and threw up in the bushes.

She went inside and the room went quiet. A dozen black faces turned to face her, their eyes wide and full of white. There was an old Negro at the raised plank stage, his beard full and gray. He'd been playing his guitar and had stopped when she came in, his crepe hand flat against the strings. In front of him was a footstool with a glass of beer on it, golden and full of foam. She could hear it crackling.

Frankie moved slowly to the bar. A man got off his seat and offered it to her.

The barman came and she asked for something to warm her.

He took her money silently and poured a glass of gin.

She sipped and winced.

Bon, she said. Mercy.

Then at once, the music started up again.

She sat and listened to the old Negro play. In front of him, a space had been cleared and men and women were dancing, clicking their heels and shaking their hips. He stomped his feet and bashed the strings. In his beard, a bright red mouth opened and flared his voice through the din. He hollered at the crowd and the crowd hollered back, and the man laughed and roared again. They danced and danced, faster now, dizzied and fevered, hands clapping, shoulders shucking.

Frankie finished her drink and the barman poured another. Now she could hardly taste it.

The barman said something, but she couldn't make out the words.

She felt someone's hand on her shoulder. She turned. It was him. Robert. He seemed thinner and gaunt in the face. She almost didn't recognize him. He put his hand lightly on her elbow.

This way, he muttered.

They sat down on a small workbench outside of the barn. There was a small oil lantern going and a bed of warm coals to boil the coffee. Robert poured a little for himself and for Frankie.

Drink this, he said.

She took the cup in her hands and moved to kiss him. He pushed her away.

No, he said. Not here.

The cup was warm against her hands. She wanted to tell him about the swamp, and the spreading bugheway and all that had happened to her, but the words welled up inside her. Through the walls, the music sounded far away.

Is very good seeing you, Rowbear, she let herself say.

Let's just sit here awhile, he said.

He sat with her while she sobered. Once he held her hand and squeezed it, but then soon after let go. From time to time, he would be called away inside to wipe down some mess or to break up a fight. Still he'd return shortly to his place on the bench beside her. They didn't speak. Frankie stared at the embers, felt the warm return to her face. She fell asleep with her head against the barn wall and when she awoke, he was still next to her, asleep as well. His eyes were closed and she looked at his long womanly lashes. She stroked his hand and he awoke with a start. Robert looked around him, slightly dazed.

Good morning, he said thinly.

She put her hand to his cheek and he jumped.

Please.

The embers were dead and he took the kettle off its stand.

I have to go, he said.

Can I see you again?

Robert gazed at something in the distance. Frankie couldn't see what it was.

This afternoon. Four o'clock. Right here.

He returned the kettle inside the barn. Frankie wondered if she should stay here and wait for him to come back, but she decided against it. She stood up and made her way to the road.

• • •

In town, she met a rancher who was driving his herd north to his graze lands. For two dollars, he'd truck her as far as Coahoma along the Arkansas border. From there she'd have to find her own way. When?, she asked him. Tomorrow morning, he said. They shook hands and arranged to meet outside the market at dawn. Frankie spent the rest of the day wandering the nearby countryside. In the morning sun, the wind was cool and swift. She loved the crackle of dry grass, the sweeping blue of the sky above her. She winged a rabbit with a rock and roasted it on a spit. The meat was tender and hot and sweet.

She napped on a hillock and thought about her mother's country, Snakebite Creek, where the first L'Etang had crossed into the knee-deep cold and washed the French from their blood. It was a place she'd heard about only in story—a trapper country where the waters were swole with trout and beaver, and where the L'Etangs fatted and thrived. She wondered why Pierre had laid root so far south, away from kin. She watched the clouds roll in from the west, wide and plowed and full of country. She knew.

She found a pond where she could wash her face and hands. A skein of geese circled overhead then taxied across the water.

There was a rustle in the bushes. Frankie turned to find a large black dog making its way toward the pond edge. It was mangy and hobbled, its hind leg scabbed purple. It did not seem to notice her. It bent its head to the water and lapped at it. She felt a swell of pity. Its gray tongue darted back and forth. She reached into her pouch for a piece of rabbit. She called out to it, but it did not hear her. She moved toward it and knelt beside it. The animal swung its head around and looked at her dully. She showed it the meat. It would not take it.

She left the meat in the dust and walked away.

• • •

By four, Robert was where he said he'd be. There were chairs stacked against the barn wall, and Robert busied himself with them. The wood had been stripped to the white and he was working the seats with a wash-rag. His shirt was dark with linseed oil and as Frankie made her way from down the road, he dropped the rag and rinsed his hands in the wash bucket. She watched him straighten, hands dripping. He wiped them on his trousers and left two large prints. She tried not to smile.

I'm glad to see you, she said.

Robert looked at her. He was moving something in his mouth. There was a cut above his eye that was still fresh. It made him squint.

What happen 'a you face?

He shook his head and waved it away.

I's a goin' north. Not coming back.

I see, he said.

Come with me.

I can't, he said.

Something inside her snapped free and plummeted. The color rose to her face. She wanted to ask why, but the question was small and stupid. She was small and stupid. She looked at him and his face softened. He walked to her and put his arms around her. She could smell the linseed, strong and chemical. He combed his fingers through her hair. His body was warm. She felt some muscle buckle inside of him. She thought he might break.

Okay, she said. Bon.

She pulled away and his head drooped from her shoulder. He wiped something from his face and stared at the grass. She wanted him to look at her and meet her eyes. He wouldn't. She tried to think of something to say, something pretty or lasting, but there weren't any words.

• • •

The next morning, she waited outside the market in the full dark. The rancher rode in on an old-fashioned horse-drawn and they set out north on the road to Coahoma. He wrangled thirty head of piebald cattle, and they drove through the indigo light.

There, he said to her.

She turned to where he was pointing, his gloved hand stretching east. There was the sun, burning behind the hills, brittle and beautiful.

Robert watched the man at the bar pitch forward, then slump. The man cradled his glass and muttered to the barman and the barman nodded and said, Yes, yes, I know. Who doesn't know? I know. The rest of the juke had cleared and they were anxious to close. The chairs had been stacked, the barrelheads wiped clean. The other glasses were sitting in a tub of soapy water, and Robert propped himself on the table edge and fought against sleep. The man shouted something, then tried to stand.

Easy, Joe, easy, the barman said.

The man took his squashed hat from the stool next to him and placed it on his head.

You're right. When you're right, you're right, he said.

He shook the barman's hand.

Goddamn it when you're right, he said.

He smoothed out the wrinkles in his suit and made his way out.

When he'd left, the barman let out a sigh and grinned at Robert.

What was he saying to you?

The barman laughed.

Who knows? Who even listens anymore?

Robert cleaned the last glass and swept up behind the bar. The barman counted the money in the till and portioned out Robert's wages, stacking the soft bills on the counter. Robert reached for it and the barman laid down his big fat hand.

I want to say I really like the work you're doing here, he said.

Robert put the money in his jacket.

You've got spirit, you know? Not like that friend of yours. That layabout, G.D.

Go to hell, Robert said.

The barman laughed again. Don't forget to shovel out that shithouse tomorrow. It's been backed up for ages.

Four in the morning, they closed out the juke and chained the doors. Robert took a small oil lantern home to light his way. He looked over his left shoulder and saw the moon there, big and scarred and ugly. He climbed up onto the porch, set the lantern by the door, and went inside. Dora was already asleep. He could hear her snoring softly on the mattress. He undressed and lay beside her. She let out a soft moan.

What time is it?

Almost morning. You want to sit up and watch the dawn?

She mumbled something, then started snoring again.

Robert lay on his side and looked out the window. The night was solid black and there was nothing to see. He wondered how many more hours till first light would break through the pane. *Forget it,* he thought. He turned over and shut his eyes and felt the heat of the small warm thing beside him. Little by little, he felt himself slipping, sinking beneath his own body, through the mattress, the floor, into the cold earth, and deeper still in the yawning dark, to that place of lost and losing.

EPILOGUE

I hear my black name ringing.

Here, through these lowlands, a basin full of sky and aching. Here, through the towns I've worked and bled and danced and loved. Here, I hear my black name ringing. In the fields and levee camps and steel mills, in the out-turned churches and shotgun shacks, my black name rings. Bright and searing as the day.

Outside, the grasslands plunge. I see where my mama was born, an earth cabin where the ground comes up to the walls. There's clothing on the line and the jumpers catch the wind, dancing, personless. And down the way is the creek where they baptized me, where I killed my first fish and I told a lie to feel a girl beneath her skirt.

They razed the town and we built again. For months the trees were full of ash.

Here are the notches on the boughs.

Here is where I stole. Here is where they stole from me. Here, my mama closed her eyes and rested her head on a pillow of hair. Here is a coin in my hand.

And still the country rages on, sad full—a cape of blue raised high over spruce and elm and hillocks, the villages and shantytowns. I danced in every hall, I beat my hands against the walls—the country rages, I rage.

The sun rises. I pass Leland, Indianola, and Moorhead, where the Southern cross the Dog. She roils and laps and foams. And through the air are the long slack ropes that carry spark and light. And I will follow her down, past the watering station, the grain elevator, a grove of Warren pears, at last into town, down a road to a high building made of brick and mortar. They'll put me in a suit and pomade my hair and I'll make my bracelets shine. And there I will stand and meet that man in a long black robe. And for you I will sing and dance and stomp my feet to beat the Devil.

Acknowledgments

This book would not have been possible without the generous support and confidence of a great many people. To these people I am forever indebted. Thank you to my parents, Betty and Peter, and my brother, Ben, and the great sea of Chengs and Paks behind them; to my editor, Dawn, her confidante, Shanna, and all the hardworking supporters at HarperCollins; to my agent Nicole and her crack team, Christie Hauser and Duvall Osteen, for pulling up a seat for me at the grown-ups' table; to fellow travelers Jeanne Thornton, Anton Solomonik, Kevin Carter, Miracle Jones, and Tim Miles, with whom I would proudly march toward Bedlam; and of course, to my wife Olga.

To the great giants of Hunter College and my brothers-in-arms—Scott Cheshire, Kaitlyn Greenidge, Sunil Yapa, Carmiel Banasky, Brianne Kennedy, Tennessee Jones, Phil Klay, Katie Vane, Sarah Goffman, Lauren Holmes, Vernon Wilson, Victoria Brown, Alex Gilvarry, Liz Moore, Jess Soffer, Noa Jones—thank you for the hours, for the blood and sweat and tears.

Thank you to Jonathan Landsman and Elyse Orecchio, who were there before the beginning, and thank you to Erin Propersi, who will one day finish this book and find her name here.

Thank you to Dina and Alex Pester and Zina Shturman, and thank you to Roz Bernstein of Baruch College, who has guided millions of lost lemmings away from the cliffs.

Most of all, a heartfelt thank you to P and N and C, whose names, while not cited here, have already been written large and in full upon this book and life.

And to the ghosts of Big Bill Broonzy, R. L. Burnside, Reverend Gary Davis, Honeyboy Edwards, Son House, John Lee Hooker, Lightnin' Hopkins, Mississippi John Hurt, Skip James, Blind Lemon Jefferson, Robert Johnson, Robert Junior Lockwood, Blind Willie McTell, Charley Patton, Pinetop Perkins, Muddy Waters, Howlin' Wolf, Bukka White, and all the late great bluesmen who have given me so much and whom I shall never have the privilege to meet except by way of your music and your words and your stories—this book is for you.